W9-AOW-061

BETRAYED HEARTS

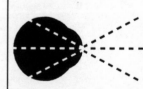

This Large Print Book carries the
Seal of Approval of N.A.V.H.

RAINBOW FALLS

BETRAYED HEARTS

SUSAN ANNE MASON

THORNDIKE PRESS
A part of Gale, Cengage Learning

GALE
CENGAGE Learning·

Farmington Hills, Mich • San Francisco • New York • Waterville, Maine
Meriden, Conn • Mason, Ohio • Chicago

GALE
CENGAGE Learning®

Copyright © 2014 by Susan Anne Mason.
Rainbow Falls #1.
All scripture quotations, unless otherwise indicated, are taken from the Holy Bible, New International Version®, NIV®, Copyright 1973, 1978, 1984 by Biblica, Inc.™ Used by permission of Zondervan. All rights reserved worldwide. www.zondervan.com
Thorndike Press, a part of Gale, Cengage Learning.

Thorndike Press® Large Print Christian Romance.
The text of this Large Print edition is unabridged.
Other aspects of the book may vary from the original edition.
Set in 16 pt. Plantin.

LIBRARY OF CONGRESS CATALOGING-IN-PUBLICATION DATA

Names: Mason, Susan Anne, author.
Title: Betrayed hearts / by Susan Anne Mason.
Description: Waterville, Maine : Thorndike Press, 2016. | Series: Rainbow falls ; #1 | Series: Thorndike Press large print Christian romance
Identifiers: LCCN 2016042432| ISBN 9781410496331 (hardcover) | ISBN 1410496333 (hardcover)
Subjects: LCSH: Large type books. | GSAFD: Love stories. | Christian fiction.
Classification: LCC PR9199.4.M3725 B48 2016 | DDC 813/.6—dc23
LC record available at https://lccn.loc.gov/2016042432

Published in 2017 by arrangement with Pelican Ventures Book Group, LLC

Printed in Mexico
1 2 3 4 5 6 7 21 20 19 18 17

To my husband, Bud,
and my kids, Leanne and Eric,
for their constant love and support.

PROLOGUE

The click of the door echoed as loud as a gunshot through the silent house. Lily Draper's heart battled to escape her chest. She pressed her back against the cool wall of her father's office and made a valiant effort to calm the roar of blood in her ears.

No time for fear. Focus on what you're here for.

The familiar scent of cedar and moth balls threatened to swamp her with nostalgia, causing memories of her beloved mother to spring forth with a ferocity that spiked an ache of longing through her.

Mama, how I wish you hadn't died. If you were here now, my life wouldn't be such a disaster.

She pushed away from the wall, grim determination stiffening her resolve. She refused to dwell on thoughts of her mother, knowing how disappointed Mama would be with the drastic action Lily was about to take.

She felt her way in the dark to the desk where she snapped on the brass lamp. Dust motes danced under the short beam of light aimed at the open Bible. With a pang, Lily ran her fingers over the worn pages. She used to love when Mama read her stories from the Bible. But that was before God took her mother away and left her with Tobias. With each punishment Tobias doled out, he cited a judgmental, angry God who waited to punish Lily for the least transgression. Lily wanted no part of a God like that. She shook her head to clear her thoughts and focus on her mission.

Dirty coffee mugs and stacks of newspapers littered the surface as well as much of the floor. Obviously, her father needed a housekeeper, though she doubted Tobias would ever find someone willing to put up with his clutter or his surly personality.

Not her problem. Hadn't been for years.

She pulled open each desk drawer, rifled through the contents, but didn't find what she sought. Where did Tobias keep his emergency money? She fought to recall his routine when she'd lived here. A mysterious, metal box came to mind.

The clock on the bookshelf ticked out its

ominous threat. *Hurry, Lily,* it seemed to chant. Beads of perspiration slid down her back, gluing her T-shirt to her skin. According to the church website, Tobias' weekly Bible study lasted two hours. Still, she needed to *borrow* the money and get out as soon as possible. If she were lucky, he would never even realize the money was missing until she could return it.

Lily scanned the cluttered room, where long shadows danced over the piles of papers and books. The box could be anywhere. Her gaze swept past the long window shuttered by wooden blinds to the closet in the corner. She crept to the other side of the room and opened the door. A puff of stale air wafted out. Lily pulled the cord and a single light bulb flared, revealing an equally messy storage space. She moved the clothes aside, peered on the floor, and found nothing but shoes. She straightened, pushed up on her tiptoes, and brushed her hand over the shelf above. When her fingers met cool metal, her pulse jumped.

She reached up to pluck the box from its resting place and carried it over to the desk. The lock wouldn't be a problem. She had her penknife. One useful thing she'd learned from Curtis before he put a hole in her living room wall.

She jimmied the lock with the thin blade and flipped the lid. The sight of a large stack of cash made her knees weaken in relief. Thumbing through the bills, she estimated over eight hundred dollars. If she were careful and found somewhere modest to live, this money could tide her over for a month or two — until she could put her wreck of a life back together.

Lily didn't know what made her look at the papers underneath. The documents seemed harmless enough, yet as she pulled out the first tattered page, nerves fluttered in her stomach.

Could her self-righteous father have something to hide? Secrets that might prove he wasn't so holy after all? Lily wet her dry lips. After all the torment he'd put her through, she had to find out.

She opened the first page, a newspaper article from more than seventeen years earlier, describing a murder-suicide. A well-known doctor, David Strickland, had shot and killed his wife and two sons before taking his own life. Police found six-month-old Chloe Strickland unharmed in her crib but did not expect five-year-old Addie Strickland to survive.

Lily frowned. What did this have to do with Tobias? She removed the remaining documents from the box. The first, a set of adoption papers, was of little interest. Her adoption was not news to her. The second piece, however, caught her attention. It took a moment to register that she was looking at her own birth certificate. Lily Adelaide Strickland. Mother: Margaret Ann Sullivan. Father: David Allen Strickland.

The blood in Lily's fingers turned to ice water. The man from the article — the man who had murdered his family — was her biological father?

She snatched the article and re-read it. The older daughter . . . Addie Strickland . . . critical condition. They'd been talking about her. She was the girl not expected to live. But obviously, she had. Another more important detail burned into her brain — a baby girl had survived as well.

Somewhere out there, she had a sister.

A slow burn rose up Lily's spine and settled into a tight band across her chest. Tobias had lied to her about so many things. About her birth family, about her real name, about how they'd come to adopt her. Her family hadn't died in a tragic fire as he'd claimed — they'd been murdered. Worst of all, he'd never told her she had a sister.

The papers floated to the floor as Lily grappled with the enormity of the discovery.

11

Had Tobias kept this information from her mother as well? Or had Mama planned to tell her when Lily was older?

Older . . .

Lily scrambled to the floor to retrieve the papers. Hunched over her knees, she read the article again. The date . . . seventeen years ago. Her sister would be almost eighteen by now.

Where? Rainbow Falls, North Dakota. What were the odds that her sister would still be living in the same town all these years later?

The sound of gravel crunching in the driveway seeped through the fog in Lily's brain. A car door slammed.

Lily jerked up from the floor. Tobias was home early.

Panic clogged her throat and threatened to choke her. She jammed the papers and the cash into her purse, yanked the chain to turn off the lamp, and forced herself to think logically. There was no way to reach the back door without passing the front entrance. The only way out was the window.

She wrenched up the blind, flipped the lock, and pushed open the window. With one leg over the sill, she glanced back at the darkened interior and then froze. The metal box sat open on the desk, the closet door ajar. Tobias would realize right away the money was gone.

No time to worry about that now.

She dropped onto the damp grass below the window, thankful for the high row of hedges surrounding the yard — even more thankful she knew a shortcut through the back alley to the street where she'd left her car.

Ignoring the cold fear in her belly, she sprinted through a gap in the shrubbery and ran.

Lily's steps faltered the moment she pushed through the door into Hank's Tavern. How was she going to do this? Say good-bye to the one person who treated her as though she mattered?

The familiar smell of stale beer and barbecue sauce teased Lily's nose as she crossed the floor. The loud hum of voices competed with the overhead TVs. Lily scanned the room, noting Tracy, the other full-time waitress, lugging a large tray of drinks over to one of the corner tables. For a Wednesday night, Hank's place was uncommonly busy — probably due to the hockey playoffs. Lily walked farther into the bar, clutching her shoulder bag to her body, as if the unusual amount of cash inside would jump out and proclaim her a thief.

"Hey, kid. You OK?" Hank set a foaming glass on the counter in front of a beefy customer and peered at her. "You look a bit seasick."

"I'm fine." Lily attempted a smile to reassure her boss. She didn't want him asking a bunch of questions she couldn't answer.

"That low-life ex of yours isn't bothering you, is he?" Behind the bar, Hank set down the towel he was holding.

"No. Curtis won't be back." Now that he'd bled her bank account dry and gotten her evicted. Her gaze bounced around the room not knowing where to land.

"Something you want to tell me?"

Two customers seated on stools at the bar did nothing to disguise their interest in the conversation.

Lily swallowed before meeting Hank's gaze. "I'm leaving, Hank. First thing tomorrow." The heaviness of her lie weighed on her conscience like the leaden wad of cash in her purse. She'd be gone long before tomorrow.

He scowled. "What did you do now?"

It was scary the way Hank could read her. "Nothing you need to worry about."

Hank picked up a wet rag to scrub the countertop. "You able to work your shift

14

tonight?"

Lily sneaked a glance at the clock over the bar. Had Tobias gone into his office or straight to bed? Lily couldn't take the chance that he'd alerted the authorities. "If you can manage without me, I think I'll call it a night."

Hank squinted at her. "You sure you're not sick?"

"I'll be fine by tomorrow."

Hank studied her for a moment longer and then nodded. "Go on. Tracy can handle this crowd."

"Thanks." Lily headed toward Hank's small office in the back of the tavern, but her feet stalled. Ever since her landlord had evicted her two weeks ago, Hank had set up a cot for her there. Never once pressured her to get out or grumbled about the food she had eaten. Never even took a penny out of her pay. Hank was a good man — the only man she trusted — and she owed him everything.

Lily changed directions and moved behind the bar to lay a hand on his arm. The tension in his jaw told her how much the news of her departure worried him. And it wasn't about her job. He could replace her with a new waitress in minutes. Hank was like a father to her — the one Tobias should have been.

"Thank you, Hank. For everything."

He turned abruptly to the cash register. "No need for thanks."

"Yes, there is. I don't know where I'd be if you hadn't hired me two years ago. I'm going to miss you."

He cleared his throat just as he always did when getting emotional. "I'll miss you too, kid. Keep in touch . . . when you can."

She reached up and kissed his cheek. "I will."

He shot her a sidelong glance. "If you need money, you only have to ask."

"It's more than the money. There's something I have to do." Lily fingered the strap of her purse, picturing the papers inside. "Turns out I might have a sister. I have to find out for sure."

His eyes widened. Knowing of her estrangement from the only family she had, Hank would understand the significance for her.

He gave a sage nod. "Good luck with that."

"Thanks. I'm not going to tell you where I'm going. Better that you don't know."

Hank closed the till with a sharp bang and ran a hand over his close-cropped salt and pepper hair. "Try to stay out of trouble for once, will you? I got enough gray hair without you adding more."

She managed a sad smile. "I love you, too, Hank."

1

Parked across the street from the two-story red brick house, Lily loosened her death grip on the steering wheel of her beat-up Toyota. "At least this one's not a dump."

In a small town like Rainbow Falls, North Dakota, decent lodging appeared to be a scarce commodity, unless you liked rats for roommates. This house would make the third rental property she'd seen since yesterday, and so far from the outside, it seemed the most promising. Maybe the third time would be a charm.

It had to be. She was running out of options — and money.

With unsteady hands, she adjusted the rearview mirror, reapplied a layer of strawberry-flavored lip gloss and patted her dark hair into submission.

"That's as good as it's going to get." She scowled at the smudges shadowing her brown eyes. What she wouldn't give for one decent night's sleep.

Taking a deep breath for courage, she stepped out of the car and crossed the street to the flagstone walkway leading up to the house. A wide porch, complete with a wicker rocking chair, gave the building a homey feel. A pang of longing shuddered through her, but she shook it off. No time for regrets. She was here on a mission and needed to keep that at the forefront.

Shoulders squared, Lily climbed the stairs to the front door and jabbed the bell, taking in the pot of pink geraniums in the corner while she waited. A cool spring breeze rustled her hair and lifted the collar of her thin jacket. Seconds later, the door flew open in front of her.

"I can't believe you're on time for once —" The pixie-like woman in the doorway sported spiky red hair — definitely not her natural color — and large, silver hoop earrings. "Oh, you're not Jason." Wide hazel eyes held Lily in a curious gaze.

Doubts wreaked havoc with Lily's composure. Could she have the wrong address? "I'm looking for a Mr. Logan."

"Of course you are." The girl grinned, scanning Lily from the toes of her pointed shoes to the top of her windblown curls.

Lily tried to shake the feeling she'd missed

the punch line to some unknown joke.

Still grinning, the girl — not a teenager, now that Lily looked closer — cocked her head to one side and folded her arms over her tiny torso. "Obviously you haven't met him, or you'd know what I mean."

A low-grade headache brewed at Lily's temples. It had been a long day, and all she wanted was to find a place to stay. Not play word games with a stranger. She straightened to her full height. That, along with her heels, gave her a decided advantage over the shorter, barefoot girl. "No, I haven't met Mr. Logan. But I have an appointment with him."

The girl's face brightened. "You here to look at the apartment?"

"That's right." Now they were getting somewhere.

"Great. I hope you take it. We'll be neighbors then. My name's Maxi. Maxi North. Short for Maxine." She held out her hand and smiled again, revealing two rows of even, white teeth.

Lily frowned slightly and accepted the young woman's outstretched hand. "I'm Lily." The wary city-girl in her declined to give her full name.

"Nice to meet you." The sound of a vehicle pulling into the driveway pulled

21

Maxi's gaze over Lily's shoulder. "That's him now."

Lily turned. A battered red pickup jerked to a halt, and the driver's door swung open. Lily wiped damp palms on her jeans.

Please let things be better this time.

She checked her thoughts. That had sounded too much like a prayer. Prayer, she'd discovered long ago, got you nowhere.

"Hope to see you again, Lily," Maxi said. "Oh, and don't mind Nick. He's a bit on the serious side." With that, she waved to the man getting out of the truck before she disappeared inside.

Lily clutched her shoulder bag, mentally preparing for the dreaded tenant interview, while Mr. Logan strode up the driveway. Her internal radar zoomed in on the fact that this was not the overstuffed bear of a middle-aged man she'd pictured. Clad in a light blue shirt, snug fitting jeans, and western style boots, this man could pass for an urban cowboy. Broad shoulders complemented well-muscled arms, hinting at work that included physical labor. When he reached the stairs, he pulled off a baseball cap to reveal a thick crop of blond hair. Intense blue eyes stared into hers then crinkled at the corners. Just the sort of good-looking complication she did *not* need now that she'd sworn off men.

"Lily Draper?" His smile could stop traffic, even in a town the size of Rainbow Falls where none existed. When she nodded, he held out his hand. "Nick Logan. Hope I didn't keep you waiting." His deep voice slid over her like silk.

"No. I just got here myself."

His hand, warm and firm, dwarfed hers. The handshake of someone dependable.

"Good. I see you met Maxi. She lives on the main level." He crossed the porch to pull open the front door. "The house is divided into two apartments. The unit for rent is upstairs. Come on in."

As she entered the house, Lily tried to ignore his larger-than-life presence and concentrate on the building. The main entryway was wide and welcoming with gleaming hardwood floors. A framed mirror hung above a narrow table holding a vase of fresh flowers. She inhaled the appealing floral scent. So far she liked what she saw.

In more ways than one.

"Maxi's place is down the hall." Nick pointed toward the rear of the building. "The only thing you'll have to share are the laundry facilities in the basement."

Lily frowned as she followed him up a set of narrow stairs. He sounded as if she'd already agreed to take the place. Maybe the rent would be outrageous. Maybe the roof leaked. Maybe Mr. Logan would see right through her façade of respectability and send her packing. But instinct told her that wouldn't be the case — if only she could keep her nerves at bay.

When they reached the narrow landing, Nick unlocked the door and stepped aside to let her in. "It's nothing fancy, but it's clean and neat with lots of windows, so the lighting's good."

Lily held her breath as she entered the apartment. She wanted to like it so bad, she was almost afraid to look. His voice faded into the background while she took in the high ceilings, the sculpted crown moldings and the wide arched entrance into the living room. Good solid bones, Mama would've said.

Nick continued his commentary as she moved around the room. "You can walk into town from here. The grocery store, post office, and the church are all close by."

She gave a polite nod, though church was the last place she'd be going. Hadn't darkened the door of one since she'd left her father's tyrannical rule and didn't plan to start anytime soon.

She eyed the overstuffed green sofa and

matching chair. "Does it come furnished?"

"Yes. Unless you've got your own things."

"No. The furniture will be fine."

He raised an inquisitive eyebrow. "From out of town I take it?"

"Yes." She turned to avoid his curiosity — something she didn't need. Especially when trying to keep a low profile.

Down a small hallway, she found two bedrooms. The larger one had an airy quality, painted light blue with white lacey curtains. She gave an inward sigh, imagining herself sleeping in this beautiful setting. Quite a step up from the back room at Hank's.

The spare room was just as inviting. Nick hadn't exaggerated about the windows either. The lighting would be perfect for painting, with lots of room for her easel.

"What do you think?" Nick's voice startled her from her daydreams.

She turned to find him — and his broad shoulders — filling the doorway.

"I like it." She folded her arms in front of her, pushing back the anxiety that clawed its way up her spine. If only he'd move away from the door . . .

The sudden piercing shriek of a police siren split the silence. Lily jerked backward, smothering a scream. Her bag slipped off her shoulder, landing with a clatter on the hardwood floor.

Had Tobias found her already?

Nick strode into the room and bent to help her. "Are you all right?" A frown creased the space between his eyebrows.

"I . . . I'm fine." Her hair shielded her face as she grabbed for the lip gloss and nail clippers that had spilled onto the floor. "The noise startled me."

He gave a low chuckle. "That's the chief testing his siren. Doesn't get to use it much around here, so about once a week, he turns it on to make sure it still works."

"Oh." The elastic band around her lungs loosened a notch.

They rose together, Lily clutching the bag to her body like a lifeline. She struggled to keep her expression calm, one ear attuned to any noise on the staircase. At last, when certain the police weren't about to break in, Lily forced her muscles to relax and stepped out into the hall.

"How much is the rent?" she asked once they'd returned to the living room.

He studied her as though trying to learn the secrets of her soul. She ignored his gaze and ran her fingers over the smooth wood of the fireplace mantel, allowing the calming effects of the green-hued room to soothe her jangled nerves.

When he named the price, disappointment slid through her. The amount was more than she'd hoped. But she couldn't pass up this apartment. Not after the other horrible ones she'd seen. If it meant working two jobs, then that's what she'd do.

It'd be worth it to find her sister.

"I'll take it," she said. "If it's all right with you."

His blue eyes held hers like a magnet, and a string of tension hummed through her veins. Why did she get the feeling Nick Logan could throw a big monkey wrench into her plans if she weren't careful?

At last, he nodded. "The place is yours."

The tension across her shoulders eased. "That's great. Thank you." She rifled through her bag and pulled out a wad of bills. "I can give you a deposit right now."

Nick shifted his weight away from the living room doorframe, hands up. "Whoa. That's a lot of cash to be carrying around." He scratched his head. "Why don't you give me, say, one hundred dollars for today, and we can settle the details later."

Her hand with the money froze in midair. "What details?"

"The lease, for one thing. I'm sure you'll want to read it over before you sign it."

"Is a lease really necessary?"

His gaze narrowed. "Why? Is it a problem?"

She shifted under his direct stare. *Stay cool, Lily. Don't blow this.* "I'm not sure how long I'll be staying. A couple of months, maybe more."

"I see." Nick pursed his lips. "How about an open-ended lease then? Or a month-by-month contract?"

She took a moment to consider. "Either of those options would be fine." She handed him the deposit, which he took without counting the bills.

"When would you like to move in?"

Lily bit her lip, not wanting to appear desperate, yet not willing to waste her dwindling cash supply on another night at the Rainbow Falls Motel — a luxury she'd allowed herself after two uncomfortable nights in her car. She ran her hand over the plush back of the sofa. "I was hoping today. If that's not a problem."

His mouth fell open before he clamped it shut and scrubbed a hand over his jaw. "I suppose that'll be fine." He paused as though trying to digest the swiftness of the transaction. "Do you need help with your bags?"

"No, thanks. I can handle it."

"All right then." He fumbled in his pant pocket until he pulled out a small key ring and a slightly battered business card. "Here's the key to the front door downstairs and one to your apartment. And my contact info. If you need anything, don't be shy."

His fingers brushed hers as she took the items from him. She jerked her hand back from the heat of his touch and stuffed the keys, along with the card, into her bag.

"Thank you." She tried to manage a smile, but couldn't quite force her lips to comply.

"Welcome to Rainbow Falls, Lily." His baritone whisper resonated inside her.

He studied her for another moment, then tugged on his cap and left.

Lily stared at the door after he'd shut it behind him, allowing her emotions to settle. A few seconds later, his footsteps echoed down the stairs.

One thing for sure, Nick Logan was like no other man she'd ever met. Half an hour in his company and he hadn't even hit on her.

Lily had just finished hauling the last of her bags from the car when a loud knock shattered the silence of the apartment. Her suitcase slipped from her hand, landing on the bedroom floor with a thud that matched her heart rate. When a louder knock followed, she slipped down the hall to the entrance, wishing for a peephole in her door.

"Who is it?"

"It's Maxi. From downstairs."

The air whooshed out of Lily's lungs in one great gust. *Not the police. Thank goodness.*

"Just a minute."

Before she opened the door, she schooled her face into what she hoped was a normal expression.

"Hi," Maxi said before Lily could speak. "I noticed you bringing your things in. Does this mean we're neighbors?" Her face wore an expectant smile, her eyes friendly.

"It does."

"Terrific." Maxi whipped a container out from behind her back. "I brought some homemade cookies as a welcome."

Lily blinked, trying to reconcile the spiky-haired girl in the flowered halter-top to a person who baked cookies. "Thank you." She took the tin, as Maxi breezed past her. "I'd offer you coffee, if I had any." Lily kept close to the door, hoping her new neighbor would take the hint and leave. All she wanted right now was a hot shower, some Chinese take-out, and a good night's sleep. She'd barely closed her eyes for more than a couple of hours the past few nights.

Maxi, however, had already moved into the tiny kitchen. "Not to worry. Logan usually has some teabags kicking around here."

Dumfounded, Lily could only follow her. Sure enough, Maxi pulled teabags from a bright yellow canister on the counter and plugged in the kettle. Lily hesitated, not sure how to react. She knew small-towners were friendly, but this seemed over the top.

Maxi stopped in the middle of pulling cups out of the cupboard and grinned. "Logan used to live here until a few months ago. Whenever I had a problem, I'd cry on his shoulder, and he'd make me tea."

No wonder she acted as if she owned the place. Lily deposited the cookie tin on the counter, then leaned against it, a sudden suspicion dawning. "Are you two dating?"

Maxi set the cups on the counter with a burst of laughter. "Logan's a great guy, not to mention easy on the eyes, but he's too much of a 'goody-goody' for me. I prefer the bad boys."

An unsettling image of Curtis flashed through Lily's mind, but she pushed it away. She refused to allow thoughts of her ex-boyfriend to interfere with her new life. The kettle snapped off and Maxi poured the water over the teabags.

"You're more than welcome to go after Nick. But you'll have to arm wrestle Sarah Jane for him."

Lily's brain swam trying to keep up with Maxi's ramblings. "All right, I'll bite. Who's Sarah Jane?"

Maxi handed her a cup and opened the cookie tin. The kitchen wasn't big enough to include an eating area, so they stood at the counter.

"She's the town librarian and Reverend Baker's niece, not to mention secretary of the church women's group."

A librarian and a churchgoer. Not someone Lily would likely socialize with. Although, she had paid a visit to the library two days ago to look up past issues of the local newspaper. She tried to recall the face of the woman she'd met that day.

"Plain as a post, poor thing," Maxi continued as she dunked her teabag. "Wish she'd come into our salon for a makeover. Maybe then she'd have a better chance with Nick."

Lily suddenly remembered the unattractive hairstyle and drab attire. The woman's silver cross necklace had even made Lily wonder if she were a nun.

Maxi studied her as she sipped her brew. "Unless I'm out to lunch, I'd say you're not from around here. I'm sure I would've remembered you."

Lily's hand tightened on her cup. The girl switched topics faster than the wind changed directions. This topic, however, had taken an unwelcome turn. "No, I'm not."

"So what brings you to our humble town?"

Lily swallowed a mouthful, trying not to choke. "Needed a change of scenery." She kept her gaze averted and took another sip of hot liquid, almost scalding her tongue in the process. The weight of Maxi's curiosity made the kitchen seem smaller.

Maxi tapped a finger to her lips. "Let me guess. Man trouble? A relationship gone bad?"

Lily's shoulder muscles relaxed a fraction. "Something like that."

"Say no more." Maxi held up a hand. "Been there a few times myself." She picked up a cloth to wipe the counter. "What're you doing for work?"

At last, a safe topic. Maybe one Maxi could help her with. "I'll have to start looking for a job tomorrow. Any suggestions?"

Maxi gave her a pensive look. "I don't know what you have in mind, but there's an opening at the hair salon where I work. Nothing fancy," she hastened to add. "Reception and some tidying up. Pays better than minimum wage though."

Excitement stirred within Lily. A hair salon might be the ideal place to find her sister. Most women in town would come in there sooner or later. Maybe Chloe would, too. Lily managed her first genuine smile of the day. "Actually, that sounds perfect."

Maxi dried her hands on a striped dishtowel. "I don't know if the pay will be enough to cover the rent here."

Lily shrugged. "I don't mind working two jobs if necessary."

With the kitchen tidied, Maxi moved into the hallway. "The shop's at McIntyre and Main Street, about four blocks from here. Peg's the owner. Come by tomorrow, and I'll put in a good word for you."

Lily was amazed this girl would go out of her way for a complete stranger. Amazed and suspicious. Could she have ulterior motives, or was she just being neighborly? The risk was worth the chance of employment. "Thanks. I appreciate it."

"You're welcome." Maxi paused in the doorway and grinned, dimples appearing on each cheek. "I have a feeling we're going to be good friends, you and I. See you tomorrow."

Nick pulled into the parking lot of the Good Shepherd Community Church and cut the engine, his mind still consumed with his new tenant. A definite aura of mystery surrounded Lily Draper.

He rubbed his arms to ease the prickle of unease that sat just under his skin. Why had he rented her the apartment without checking her credentials first? Usually he asked potential tenants for references from previous landlords or employers. Sometimes he even had them sign a consent form and his friend, Police Chief Mike Hillier, would run a background check on them, especially if they were new to the area. But today he'd handed over the keys to Miss Draper five minutes after meeting her.

An uncomfortable thought made him shift in his seat. Could it have anything to do with the fact she was drop-dead gorgeous? He wouldn't be human if he hadn't noticed the long mane of dark curls or been affected by those big brown eyes. Looks like that could turn any man's head. But Nick prided himself on his ability to judge a person by their inner beauty, by their character and integrity.

So what intrigued him about Lily?

Maybe it was the vulnerability that haunted her eyes. Or the protective way she held herself. Or the skittish energy that surrounded her, like when the siren had spooked her. Lily wore the look of someone who'd known pain and who didn't trust easily. His mother used to wear the same haunted expression, thanks to his father's abuse.

Whatever the reason, he wanted Lily to trust him. And trust worked both ways. Maybe that's why he'd given her the keys. As a show of good faith.

He prayed his faith hadn't been misplaced.

Nick jumped out of the truck and strode up the walkway to the rectory situated beside the church. He looked at his watch and increased his pace. He was ten minutes behind schedule for his meeting with Reverend Baker.

"You're late, Nicholas." The gray-haired minister answered the door, peering over his reading glasses with a frown.

"I know. Sorry, sir. A new tenant."

"Well, don't just stand there. Come in. Come in."

Nick pulled the screen door shut behind him. As per the usual routine, he followed Ted into the airy kitchen where they would share a cup of tea. Sure enough, the china pot with red and yellow roses was already filled with the brewing liquid. The familiar scent of lemon cleanser and cinnamon sticks filled Nick with a sense of home. How many times had he hung out here as a rebellious teen, receiving guidance — many times unwanted — from the patient pastor?

"So what's on your mind, Reverend?" Nick leaned a hip against the counter.

The elderly man poured the beverages with a slight tremor to his hand and then passed Nick a cup. Even though Mrs. Baker had been dead for years, Ted still used his wife's fancy china for company, a quirk Nick found oddly endearing.

Ted shuffled to the worn kitchen table. "Just wanted to touch base. We haven't spoken much since your mother's funeral. You managing to keep up with those courses?"

Nick stiffened at the unexpected mention of his mom. Two months after her death, thoughts of her still tore at the raw wound. Ted was likely worried that grief had overshadowed Nick's studies. He'd been sidetracked while he nursed his mom during her last days, but now his studies had become a form of therapy, giving him something to focus on besides an empty house.

"I've caught up on the assignments, and exams start in a few weeks." Nick made a point of adding milk and sugar while he waited for Ted to reveal the real reason for this meeting. He only hoped the clergyman hadn't changed his mind about retiring.

As pastor of Good Shepherd Community Church for the past fifteen years, Ted had gained the loyalty of an adoring congregation. But due to advancing age, he planned to step down in the fall. The timing seemed divinely inspired for Nick to take over, and Ted had led him to believe he wanted that as well. After four years of studies, nothing would make Nick happier than to use his calling here in his hometown.

"So when you pass these last exams you'll be done?" Bushy gray brows met in the center of Ted's wrinkled forehead.

Nick curbed his impatience. Ted knew exactly what was required for him to achieve his Divinity Degree. But, as usual, he humored the older man. "That's right."

Ted sipped his brew somewhat noisily. "Good. Good. And how is your aunt holding up? It must be hard for her losing her sister when they were so close."

Nick blew the steam off his tea. "Aunt Sonia's taking it pretty hard. She relied on mom a lot after Uncle Leonard passed away."

"And they both relied on you. You were a good son to Marion, Nicholas. I hope you know what a comfort you were to her in her final days."

Nick blinked hard to clear his vision from the tears that sneaked up every now and then. "Yes sir, she told me all the time." He swallowed his emotion with a sip of tea, grateful he'd gotten to be with his mom when she passed away. She'd feared dying alone, but God had spared her that.

"And how are things with you and Sarah Jane?"

The sudden change in topic caught Nick off guard. He shifted on the hard wooden chair. "We've been out a couple of times." He kept his tone casual, and hoped he didn't sound bored. As bored as he felt on his dates with Sarah Jane. Right away, he berated himself for such an unkind thought. Especially about Ted's niece.

"Excellent. And when do you think you'll be getting engaged?"

Nick almost choked, recovering only seconds before he would have spurted liquid all over the table. "Engaged? I . . . I haven't even thought about it."

"Well, what's keeping you, boy? It's time to get serious." Ted stood with some difficulty and moved to the counter, his back to Nick. "Believe me, the church elders will view your candidacy for my position in a much better light if you're married, or planning on it real soon."

Married? Ted had hinted at this for a while, but to hear it verbalized in such blunt terms jarred him.

"People in this town don't take change well. Your youth won't be held against you if you've settled down." Ted turned to pin him with a watery stare. "Sarah Jane is a good woman. Reliable, honest, and loyal. There's no one I can think of who'd make a better minister's wife. Puts me in mind of my own dear Millie."

Nick used all his will power not to roll his eyes. As much as he loved Ted, if he had to hear another litany of the late Millie Baker's virtues, he didn't know what he'd do. "There's no doubt Sarah Jane is a real asset to the community, but . . ." The words stuck in his throat at the older man's glare.

"If I were you, I wouldn't let a fine woman like that slip away."

Nick struggled to keep his emotions strapped down as he drained the contents of his cup. He was not about to enter into a debate on marriage at this early stage in the relationship. "I'll keep that in mind, sir. Though I'd prefer to wait on God's timing to find a wife." He rose and took his dishes to the sink. "Thanks for the tea."

"Anytime, son. You give Sarah Jane my love."

Nick drove toward home on automatic pilot, the hot beverage still churning in his stomach. Why was Ted trying to push him into marriage? He wasn't even twenty-seven yet, for heaven's sake. A lifelong commitment like marriage required the proper level of maturity, a fact proven by his almost-engagement to Cheryl Cartwright four years ago. Both of them had been much too young to consider such a huge step. And when Nick had realized his true calling to a life of ministry, Cheryl hadn't been prepared to accept the sacrifices she felt his vocation would demand. Better they'd called it off when they did.

He made a mental comparison between Cheryl and Ted's niece and couldn't deny Sarah Jane had every quality a minister's wife should have. If only his heart would fall in line with his head.

Nick blew out a frustrated breath as he rolled to a stop at one of the town's only traffic lights. Perhaps he wasn't being fair to Sarah Jane. They'd only gone out a few times. It was possible he hadn't seen her best side yet. Maybe he should try another couple of dates just to be sure. As a favor to Ted, if nothing else.

When the light turned green, he directed his truck onto McIntyre Street. As he passed by his rental house, where a rusting Toyota now sat in the driveway, the sudden image of Lily Draper came to mind. With her dark, sultry looks, Lily couldn't be more opposite to Sarah Jane. Beautiful and mysterious — anything but boring.

And probably the last woman a would-be minister should be thinking about. Still, despite his best efforts to put Lily out of his mind, he couldn't help speculating what it would be like to go on a date with his new tenant.

2

Lily strolled down McIntyre Street the next morning and gave herself a mental pat on the back for her accomplishments. Things were going better than she'd expected. Not only had she found a decent apartment, she had a lead on a job. For the first time in weeks, the knots of tension in her shoulders became bearable. If she were on speaking terms with God, she might even thank Him for this sudden turnaround in her life. But she hadn't relied on God for anything since she was ten years old, when her desperate prayers to heal her mother had gone unanswered. His silence had been deafening then, just as hers was now.

Lily shook off depressing thoughts of the past and focused on the present. The beautiful, spring day had dawned sunny and cool. She breathed in the clean, crisp air while she walked, taking in the charming atmosphere. Large maple trees, their leaves bright with just-bloomed color, lined the main street. Hanging baskets of newly planted flowers dripped from the quaint black streetlights. She passed a bank, a convenience store, an insurance office, and the library across the street. Rainbow Falls turned out to be a pretty town, although a bit rustic for her taste.

Finally, she spotted the sign for Peg's Cut 'N Curl. Her steps slowed as sudden nerves danced in her stomach. In the window's reflection, she paused to smooth down her wind-blown hair. She eyed her flared jeans and brown corduroy blazer, hoping they were professional enough for a salon. And not just a hair salon either. Several manicure stations lined the far side of the shop.

A movement inside caught her attention. Maxi waved, motioning her to come in. Lily took a deep breath and pushed through the door, making the bell jangle.

Maxi bounded over to greet her like an eager puppy. Large triangular earrings bobbed with each step. Her bright red hair, stiffened with hair gel, spiked out in all directions. "Hi, Lily. Come and meet Peg."

Maxi led the way to a row of styling chairs where a short, round lady stood snipping an elderly client's hair. She wore her faded tresses piled on top of her head in a loose bun, with a comb sticking out from the middle. Thin, wire-rimmed glasses perched precariously on the tip of her nose. A black striped top showed off ample cleavage, but fit a little too tight on the rest of her torso.

"Hey, Peg," Maxi said. "This is Lily, the girl I was telling you about."

For a moment, Peg said nothing but continued the quick snip of the scissors. Then she turned to look over her shoulder. "Howdy, Lily. I'll be with you in two shakes, soon as I finish with Mildred here."

"No rush. I'll wait at the front."

Maxi showed Lily to the chairs by the reception desk before scurrying off to help a customer at the hair dryer. Lily drank in the atmosphere of the shop while she waited. The cheerful tangerine décor matched the upbeat music on the radio. She inhaled an appealing scent, a mixture of citrus and lavender she guessed. Maybe lime or mango. On the right, a pedicure and two manicure stations sat empty. How much call could there be for that type of pampering in such a small town? She'd never even had a manicure.

"A sinful waste of money," her father would growl. "A woman should not be painting herself up to look like a tart. No good can come of that type of vanity."

The words burned in her memory like a brand searing flesh. Would she ever be rid of the constant criticisms echoing in her head?

Approaching footsteps snapped her back to the present.

"Well now, let me introduce myself proper like. I'm Peg Hanley, owner of this great establishment."

Lily smiled and stood to shake her hand. "Lily Draper. Nice to meet you."

"Likewise. Let's head on to the back room where we can talk in private." Peg nodded in Maxi's direction and winked over her shoulder at Lily. "Not much gets by that one."

Lily smothered a grin and followed Peg's swaying hips to the back of the store into what appeared to be a staff lunch room.

"Have a seat," Peg told her before heading to the coffeemaker on the counter. "Coffee?"

"No, thank you." Lily needed steady nerves to get through this interview.

Peg poured herself a cup and came to sit on one of the mismatched metal chairs at the table. "So Maxi tells me you're new in town and looking for work."

"That's right." Lily tried not to squirm under the woman's direct gaze. Intelligent, hazel eyes, framed by a network of fine lines, warned Lily that Peg was not a woman to be trifled with.

"What kind of experience do you have?"

Lily squared her shoulders. "A bit of everything. But for the past two years I've been working as a waitress."

Peg took a thoughtful sip. "Whereabouts?"

Despite the perspiration that trickled down her spine, Lily kept her gaze even. "At the local tavern in Bismarck."

She waited for some sign of disapproval, but Peg's facial expression remained unchanged. "I'll be needing references from your last employer. Will that be a problem?"

Lily shifted in her chair. "Shouldn't be. The owner's name is Hank Deveraux. I can give you his number." Lily clasped her hands together on the tabletop. "If you could manage not to let Hank know where I'm living now, I'd be grateful."

Peg's eyes narrowed. "Why's that?"

Lily licked her lips, her heart beginning an uneven tempo as she tried to form an answer. Before her brain could make her mouth open, Peg leaned forward.

"Maxi mentioned you may've had problems with a boyfriend. That have anything to do with it?"

The tone of Peg's voice had softened

enough to let Lily know she might be sympathetic to her situation. She nodded. "Curtis and I didn't part on good terms. I'd rather not have anyone know where I am right now."

That much at least was true.

Peg leaned over to pat her hand. "Not to worry. I'll do my best to keep your whereabouts private." She paused. "Just wanted to make sure you weren't an escaped jailbird or something." She chuckled at her own joke.

Lily's blood ran cold, but she forced herself to remain calm. "No, not a jailbird. Just someone who's made a few bad choices."

The older woman raised her mug in a mock salute. "Haven't we all." She turned to a drawer behind her where she pulled out a sheet of paper. "Here's an application to fill out. I should tell you the job's part-time to start. There's a one month probation period, and if things work out, I'll consider making you full-time with an increase in pay."

"I understand." Lily hesitated. "Does this mean I have the job?"

She held her breath, waiting for the answer. Maybe it was the friendly camaraderie she sensed between the women here. Or maybe it was because the salon would be a good starting point to find Chloe. Whatever the reason, Lily wanted this job. Needed this job.

Peg smiled as she stood, revealing slightly uneven teeth. "If your reference checks out, you can start on Monday."

Some of the tension eased out of Lily's shoulders. "Thank you so much. You won't regret it."

Peg paused in the doorway. "Save your thanks 'til your first week is done. See how you feel then." She winked and disappeared back into the shop.

Lily allowed a small dose of optimism to trickle through her as she filled out the application. When finished, she picked up her bag and walked to the front where Maxi sat at the reception desk.

Maxi looked up as Lily approached. "So how'd it go?"

"If my reference checks out, I'll be starting on Monday." She smiled, hardly daring to believe it. Her plan was falling into place. She had an apartment and now a job.

Maxi grinned at her. "Super. I'm working Monday, so I can show you the ropes."

"Good to know." Lily paused on her way to the door and turned back. "Thanks for your help, Maxi. I really appreciate it."

"No problem. I told you, I've got great instincts about people."

Lily managed a weak smile, hoping Maxi didn't live to regret those words.

Bright and early Saturday morning, Nick knocked on Lily's apartment door. Although he hated that something had gone wrong with the apartment so soon, a secret part of him was happy to have an excuse to spend time with his new tenant. He offered up a quick prayer for guidance, and maybe if God didn't mind, a little help to make a good impression. Two seconds later, the door cracked open.

"Thanks for coming so fast." Lily motioned for him to enter.

He hesitated, surprised to see her clad in a short bathrobe, her hair wrapped in a towel. Long, bare legs still glistened with moisture. He cleared his throat. "No problem. It sounded serious." He tried to avoid looking at her, but the smell of her strawberry shampoo drifted past him in waves, engaging his senses.

Lily closed the door behind him. "It started off as a drip, but now it's like a small waterfall. The drain is running slow as well."

He followed her down the hall to the bathroom, relieved to have somewhere else to focus his attention. Sure enough, a light stream of water dripped from the spout in the bath into a rapidly filling tub. Setting his toolbox on the tiled floor, he turned to give her a reassuring smile. "I'll have this fixed in a jiffy."

Today, with her skin pink from her recent shower, she looked younger, more vulnerable. In the morning light, her eyes appeared almost translucent, like the color of finely polished oak. Lily reached up to clutch the lapels of her robe together but not before he caught a glimpse of some puckered skin near her collarbone. A scar of some sort. He turned away so as not to embarrass her. "Holler if you need to get in here."

He heard her footsteps retreat down the hall, followed by the distinct click of the lock on the bedroom door.

Nice going, Logan. Probably thought he was a pervert, staring at her neckline like that. He sighed, vowing to make it up to her by finishing the job in record time.

Half an hour later, with the leak stopped and the drain unplugged, Nick rolled down his shirt sleeves and packed up his toolbox. He strode into the hallway, past the empty bedroom, wondering where Lily had gone. The door to the spare room stood ajar, allowing him a view of what looked like the legs of an easel inside.

Curiosity won, and he nudged open the door. His jaw dropped at the sight before him. A large, painted landscape dominated the easel, depicting a wooded area, flanked by mountains, with a river flowing through it. Though unfinished, the magnificence of the piece was undeniable.

He pushed farther into the room. Brushes, paint tubes, and mixing palettes lay neatly organized on top of the small desk in the corner. Several more canvases leaned against the far wall. Intrigued, he crossed the space and peeked at the finished works. Vibrant colors, shadows and highlights jumped off the canvas. He gave a low whistle of appreciation.

"What are you doing in here?" Lily's ice-cold voice ricocheted in the sparse room.

Nick whirled around to find her scowling in the doorway, arms crossed. She'd changed into jeans and a brown turtleneck sweater. Her dark eyes blazed, making him feel like a kid caught with his hand in the cookie jar.

"I — I'm sorry. I caught a glimpse of the painting and had to take a closer look."

"My art is private."

Nick let her anger roll off him. "That's

too bad." He waved a casual hand toward the stack of paintings. "I'm no art critic, but I know talent when I see it."

Her features softened slightly. "You think I have talent?"

The glimpse of vulnerability surprised him. "Hasn't anyone ever told you that?"

An untold emotion passed over her face before her expression hardened. "No."

"Well, that's a shame because these are incredible."

Color bloomed in her cheeks. She looked away and toyed with a long, gold necklace hanging over her sweater. "Thank you."

"You're welcome." He bent to retrieve his toolbox. "The leak is fixed, and I unplugged the drain, so you shouldn't have any more problems."

"Thanks."

What was it about those huge brown eyes that riveted his attention like a magnet? Secrets lay within their depths. Secrets he wanted to learn more about. "My pleasure." He smiled, hoping to make her feel more comfortable. "You settling in OK?"

"I am. I've even landed a job at Peg Hanley's shop."

"So I heard. That's good news." He gave a slight cough. "Could I trouble you for a glass of water?" He hoped his ploy to stall for time wasn't as obvious as it felt.

Lily hesitated for a fraction of a second and then nodded. "Sure. Follow me." She headed down the hall to the kitchen where she pulled a bottle of water from the fridge and handed it to him.

"Maxi probably told you I used to live here." He walked into the living room and flopped onto the couch. "When my mother got too ill to live on her own, I moved back home to look after her . . . until she passed away." The familiar jolt hit his stomach and twisted. When would he get used to the fact that his mother was gone?

"I'm sorry." Lily hovered in front of the fireplace, hands hooked on her jeans pockets. "Do you have other family in town?"

He took a long swig from the bottle. "Only an aunt and a cousin I'm very close to."

Her expression turned pensive. "I don't have much family either. My mother died when I was young."

"What about your father?"

A flicker of something like fear passed over her features. "We don't get along. I haven't seen him in years."

Her jaw tightened as though clenching her teeth together. Could her father be the reason for her pain?

"So what made you move to Rainbow

Falls?" He wanted to learn everything he could about the mysterious Lily Draper. But his question obviously hit a nerve. He swore he could see the walls coming up around her as she shrugged.

"Needed a change of scenery."

He stayed silent, waiting for her to offer more.

She fiddled with the necklace again. "I broke up with a boyfriend and wanted a fresh start."

He nodded, noting she didn't meet his eyes. There was definitely more to the story than she was willing to tell.

"I'm sorry," he said. "I know it's hard ending a relationship."

She raised her head to level a direct stare at him. "Speaking of relationships, I hear you and the town librarian have a thing going."

Nick nearly choked on his water before he got control. He wiped the moisture from his chin with his sleeve. "Maxi has a big mouth," he muttered.

"Is it true?" Lily's dark gaze pinned his.

Annoyance, like an itch that wouldn't go away, crept under his skin. "Not that it's anyone's business, but no. Sarah Jane and I have been on a couple of dates. That's it."

Heat crept up his neck. Was she trying to

make him uncomfortable on purpose? If so, it was working. Maybe it was time to cut his losses. He handed her the nearly empty bottle as he stood. "Thanks for the water. Let me know if you have any more plumbing problems." He stifled a groan at the way that had sounded.

She raised a provocative eyebrow. "You'll be the first person I call."

Nick bent to pick up his toolbox in an effort to hide his embarrassment. After a quick nod, he left without looking back. Confusion swirled through his brain as he clomped down the stairs. He couldn't seem to get a handle on this woman. One minute, she appeared withdrawn and nervous around him. The next, almost flirtatious.

He threw his tools into the back of his truck and attempted to shrug off his discomfort. The image of his old girlfriend, Cheryl, flashed to mind. Sensual and fun loving, she hadn't been at all suited to a life of ministry. Was Lily a brunette version of Cheryl? If so, he needed to figure out why he was always attracted to the wrong type of woman.

He stared up at the window to Lily's apartment as though the answers would become apparent in the glass. A brief movement at the curtain made him start. Had she been watching him the whole time? With a grunt, he jumped into the driver's seat and plugged his key into the ignition. Before he could start the engine, his cell phone chimed out a welcome distraction.

"Nick. Hi, it's Sarah Jane."

Nick forced himself not to take out his bad mood on someone who didn't deserve it. "Hey, what's up?"

"If you aren't busy this afternoon, I'd like to discuss a couple of ideas for a church fundraiser."

Nick's tense muscles relaxed. This was exactly the sort of woman he needed in his life. Dedicated to her church and the community — to all the same things that mattered to him.

"Sounds good. I'll meet you in the church hall in half an hour."

3

"Your job is to answer the phone, book appointments, and greet customers," Maxi informed Lily on her first morning at the salon. "When things are slow, you sweep the floor, launder the towels, and generally do any odd jobs Peg needs done."

Lily pushed her ponytail over one shoulder, relieved Peg had handed over the rest of her orientation to Maxi. "Sounds easy enough." Anything had to be easier than hauling beer at Hank's. "And what do *you* do around here exactly?"

Maxi grinned at her. "I'm the manicurist, pedicurist, and occasional hair stylist."

"Really? You look too young to be qualified for all that."

"I started doing this part-time in high school, so I've had lots of experience." She closed the till with a bang and blew the spiky fringe of hair off her forehead. "Someday I'm going to own my own shop. Maybe even in New York City."

Lily chuckled. "That's dreaming big."

"No point in dreaming small."

The jingle of the front doorbell cut their conversation short. Two young men entered the shop. They lifted motorcycle helmets from their heads. Not exactly the types Lily expected to frequent the Cut 'N Curl. Her breath caught at one of the men's likeness to Curtis. Longish black hair swept the collar of his leather jacket. He stood, feet wide apart, staring at Lily with undisguised interest. Before she could ask either one what they wanted, Maxi let out a squeal and raced over to hug the lanky red-head in the ragged denim jacket.

"Jason, what are you doing here?"

"Just came to say hi," he said. "Plus Marco wanted to check out the new girl."

Marco's eyes had not left Lily's face except to roam slowly over her body. A queasy sensation swirled in her stomach, like she was back in Hank's bar with the customers leering at her.

Maxi waved a hand in her direction. "Lily, these are my friends, Jason Hanley and Marco Messini. Guys, this is Lily."

Lily managed a polite smile. "Nice to meet you."

"Likewise." Marco flashed her a grin,

revealing a dimple on either side of his mouth.

"Aren't you working today?" Maxi gazed at Jason in undisguised adoration.

"Nah. Tony gave us the day off. Not much happening."

"Jason and Marco work at Tony's auto body shop," Maxi explained.

"Oh." Lily squirmed under the intense scrutiny of Jason's cohort. "I should get back to work." She sent Maxi a silent apology and headed to her desk.

To her dismay, Marco followed, helmet tucked under one arm. "So, Lily, you have a boyfriend or anything?" He wiggled his eyebrows in a suggestive manner.

Lily remained standing, not willing to give him the advantage. She crossed her arms and looked him in the eye. "Not right now. Just left a big, mean one back home."

Marco gave a loud laugh, apparently not the least intimidated.

A door slammed in the back.

"If you're not here for a haircut, Jason Hanley, I'd appreciate you letting my staff get back to work," Peg bellowed from the rear of the shop.

Jason looked sheepish. "OK, Ma."

Ma? Seemed everyone in small towns *were* related.

"If you're not working today, there's a list of chores at home that need doin'."

"Geesh. Embarrass me in front of the women, why don't you?" Jason's face flushed as red as his hair.

Peg grinned, leading Lily to believe the woman's annoyance was mostly put on for Jason's sake.

"I need to get my own place," he grumbled. "No one to boss me around."

"Go right ahead, young man. I'll help you pack."

With a growl, he pulled on his helmet. "Come on, Messini. I don't need this hassle."

Marco followed Jason to the front door and winked at Lily. "See you again soon."

Maxi watched out the store window until the motorcycles roared away. She wandered back to the desk and sighed. "Isn't Jason wonderful?"

Lily stifled a laugh. "He seems nice."

Maxi leaned a hip against the desk. "He is." She lowered her voice, glancing over to where Peg had gone back to work. "But I have to be careful around Peg. She's a tad overprotective."

"Really?"

"Yup. But I'll take my chances if Jason ever notices me that way. Hey, you want a coffee or anything? I'm going down to the diner for a muffin."

Maxi jumped from one topic to another like a butterfly flitting from flower to flower.

"Coffee would be great. Thanks."

Once Maxi had taken Peg's order and left the shop, Lily took the opportunity of a quiet moment to flip discreetly through the appointment book. All the entries were made in pencil, some harder to read than others. Three pages later, she came upon the name she'd been looking for, only half expecting to see it. *Chloe Martin* appeared next to a 3:30 PM manicure on Thursday. Lily's pulse galloped. Could she really be lucky enough to find her sister this soon? The odds were in her favor. After all, how many Chloe's could one small town have?

Lily closed the book, determination straightening her spine against the hard back of the reception chair. Whatever it took, she would be here on Thursday afternoon when Chloe Martin arrived.

I'm doing the right thing.

For courage, Nick repeated the mantra all the way to the library. Courage to do what his head told him he should. Then why did his collar seem too tight and his feet feel like lead?

Pushing his doubts aside, he opened the heavy oak door to the Rainbow Falls Library and stepped inside. He allowed a moment for his eyes to adjust to the indoor lighting and reminded himself once again of all Sarah Jane's good qualities. Her many hours of volunteer work, her faithful devotion to the church, and her unwavering support of Nick's bid to take over her uncle's ministry when he retired.

She'd proven her commitment again the other day with the good ideas she'd proposed for several summer fundraisers — fun events that would bring in some much needed revenue for their small parish. No one could fault Sarah Jane for her dedication to the church.

Nick inhaled the comforting scent of old books as he walked toward the information desk where Sarah Jane stood speaking to Mr. Dennison. She took the elderly man by the arm and led him down one of the aisles. Nick waited several minutes, shuffling from one foot to the other. Maybe he shouldn't bother her while she was working. He'd come back later, or better yet, call her at home tonight. He'd taken two strides toward the main door when he heard his name called.

"Nick? What are you doing here?"

Plastering a smile on his face, he turned to face her. "Hi, Sarah Jane. I came to talk to you, but if you're busy, it can wait."

A quizzical expression joined the slight blush on her cheeks. She fiddled with the buttons on her blue cardigan. "I have a free minute now. Do you need help finding a book?"

"No." He shoved his hands into his pockets.

"Do you have a question about the fundraiser?"

He took that crumb and ran with it. "Yeah. I'd like to discuss the summer fair with you in more detail. I was wondering if you were free on Saturday night . . . for dinner." There, he'd done it.

A bright smile creased her face, making her plain features seem almost attractive. "I'd love to have dinner with you."

"Good. I'll pick you up about six."

"I look forward to it."

A sour sensation burned in Nick's stomach moments later as he jogged down the steps of the library to the sidewalk below. Shouldn't he be feeling a lot happier when the girl he'd asked out had accepted a date with him? He raised his eyes to the clear blue skies above.

Lord, if it's Your will for me to marry Sarah

Jane, I'd sure appreciate Your help to feel a bit more enthusiastic come Saturday.

Wednesday morning, Lily sat on the side of her bed, tapping one bare foot on the braided floor mat. With a free morning, she could've enjoyed the luxury of sleeping late, but instead found herself unable to relax. Her mind worked overtime, replaying the life-changing events of the last few weeks like a repetitive slideshow.

She pushed off the bed and padded to the window where she peeked through the curtains at the dawn breaking over the quiet community. She wished the new light seeping over the trees could illuminate her memory of the past. Why didn't she remember anything about this town where she'd apparently spent the first five years of her life? She ran an absent finger over the scar on her collarbone. Could her mind have blocked out not only the tragedy that had occurred here, but the existence of her birth family as well?

A force beyond her will compelled her to the nightstand beside her bed where she once again retrieved the yellowed newspaper clipping. She slipped back onto the bed, unfolded the page in her lap, and smoothed out the creases. Her hands trembled as they had the moment she'd taken it out of her father's hiding place. Her desperation at that moment, the bone-deep hopelessness of being broke and homeless, rushed back with a chill that had nothing to do with the early morning coolness of her room.

Lily fingered the locket she always wore around her neck. Mama had given it to her when she was six — told her they'd found it in the pocket of her clothing in the hospital. Inside, the photo of a smiling young woman was thought to be her birth mother. Lily clicked open the locket and traced the edges of the worn picture. If only she could remember this woman who'd lost her life in such a tragic manner.

Lily refolded the fragile newspaper and tucked it away in her night table. With a determined huff, she pushed off the bed, straightened the blankets, and headed for the shower. Time to go back to the library to see what else she could find out about the deaths in her family. Maybe something there would jog her frozen memory.

An hour later, she approached the Rainbow Falls Public Library, an impressive stone structure standing majestically against the clear sky. A set of steep cement stairs led up to the oak doorway. Lily walked inside, soaking up the atmosphere of the historic building. At this early hour, a reverent hush hung in the air. She suspected she was the first customer of the day.

The same woman as before sat behind the information desk. This time Lily paid closer attention to her appearance, remembering what Maxi had said about her interest in Nick. She wore her brown hair pulled back into a tidy knot at the nape of her neck. Not a speck of makeup adorned her very pale face. If the girl had any eyelashes at all, they were invisible, even behind the magnification of her black-rimmed glasses.

She looked up as Lily approached. "Good morning. May I help you?"

Deliberately pushing Nick out of her mind, Lily managed a brief smile. "You must be Sarah Jane." Lily offered. "Maxi North told me you were the librarian. I'd like to look at your archived newspapers on microfilm again please."

Sarah Jane removed her glasses and set them on the desk in front of her. "Of course. What dates would you like today?"

Lily couldn't tell if the sour expression on the woman's face was meant for her, or if maybe her hair was pulled a touch too tight. Lily gave her the dates she needed.

"If you'll come to the back room, I'll pull the films for you."

Lily followed Sarah Jane past the rows of books to the back of the building where they entered the small, glass-paneled room with several microfiche workstations. While Sarah Jane slipped into a locked area, Lily sat down at one of the tables and removed a notebook and pen from her shoulder bag.

A few minutes later, Sarah Jane returned with the films.

"Thank you." Lily turned her attention to the viewer and threaded the film with quick movements, trying to ignore the other woman who hovered nearby.

After several tense moments, Sarah Jane spoke. "You're new in town, aren't you?"

Lily lifted her head from the viewer. "Yes."

The pale eyes narrowed. "You're Nick Logan's new tenant."

"That's right. I'm Lily Draper."

Sarah Jane managed what looked more like a grimace than a smile. "I'm . . . Nick's girlfriend."

The possessive tone did not escape Lily. Nor did the air of disapproval. Lily stiffened on her chair, as painful memories surfaced. Memories of harsh accusations from other jealous women over the years. "Funny, Nick never mentioned he had a girlfriend."

In fact, he denied it.

Sarah Jane's lips thinned. Her eyes hardened into a cold glare as she folded her arms across her thin frame. "That's odd since . . . well, we're practically engaged."

Engaged? Lily fought to keep her jaw from dropping. Either Nick had misrepresented their relationship, or Sarah Jane was exaggerating . . . a lot.

The bold statement, as well as the woman's antagonistic stance, sparked old hostilities in Lily. Sarah Jane was no different than the self-righteous high school girls who'd waged constant war against her. Lily lifted her chin. She wasn't sixteen any more, and she refused to be intimidated, especially when she'd done nothing to antagonize this woman.

"Engaged?" Lily echoed. "So are you two living together?" Maybe Nick had failed to mention that pertinent detail as well.

Beet-red blotches appeared on the girl's horrified face. "Of course not. That wouldn't be proper."

"Why not?"

"Well . . . I . . . we haven't been dating that long . . ."

Lily raised an eyebrow. "And you're practically engaged?"

The girl's mouth opened and closed, reminding Lily of a fish out of water. "Um . . . not quite. But I hope to be . . .

very soon."

Bingo. Major exaggeration. "I'll have to congratulate Nick the next time I see him."

Sarah Jane's eyes widened. "Oh, no. Please don't say anything." She clutched the neck of her blouse as though she were suffocating. "Excuse me. I have to get back to the front."

If it weren't for the small prick of guilt hovering on the edge of Lily's conscience, she would've found the woman's bolt from the room almost comical. Sarah Jane must have some severe insecurity issues if Lily's five minutes in town threatened her relationship with Nick. Lily shook her hair back in a deliberate attempt to push the remorse aside and concentrate on the articles instead.

A few minutes later, her efforts were rewarded. *"Local Girl Succumbs to Injuries."*

Lily's hands trembled as she focused the lens and read each word. The article recapped the horrible events of the day David Strickland had killed his family and ended with the news that the five-year old daughter, Addie Strickland, had lingered in the hospital for several weeks but had finally died from her injuries.

Lily jerked hard on the wooden chair. Addie had died? She swallowed. All this

70

time, everyone in town had assumed she was dead. How could such a horrible mistake have been made? Who would have declared her dead? The newspaper wouldn't print something unless the reporter was sure of his facts.

Lily rubbed her eyes, trying to remember something — anything — about those early years. About her biological father. Surely a five-year-old wouldn't forget her family.

Over the years, vague, disturbing flashes of memory had haunted her, but the details always shimmered just out of reach. Her doctor had diagnosed her with post-traumatic stress, saying she'd blocked out everything about the ordeal, then thought to be a fire. Her hand fluttered to the ridge of the scar — a wound she'd never believed had come from a fire.

The beginning of a headache thumped at her temples. Despite the throbbing, she scanned a few more films, hoping to find further follow-up articles. One more item caught her attention concerning the Strickland home, which had been up for sale since the tragedy. No one wanted a house with such a terrible history. The article concluded that the house on Elm Street would be boarded up and left as is.

Lily stretched her neck and turned off the

machine. A visit to her childhood home appeared to be the next logical step. Maybe seeing the house again would trigger some of those memories that hovered maddeningly out of reach.

A cold chill crept up her spine as the thought of the violence she might remember caused tremors to race through her body.

On second thought, that adventure could wait for another day.

4

By noon on Thursday, with business at the salon slowed to nothing and Peg gone home for lunch, Lily's nerves stretched taut, like the strings of a violin about to snap. How would she endure the time until Chloe's three thirty appointment?

She barely managed to eat a bite of her sandwich, feeling as though the lunchroom walls were closing in around her. To keep her sanity, she found a broom and busied herself with mindless cleaning.

"Hey, super girl, slow down. You're making the rest of us look bad." Maxi appeared beside Lily and pulled the broom out of her hands.

Lily grabbed it back with a scowl. "I'd like to keep busy, if you don't mind."

She didn't dare tell Maxi she was as nervous as a cat in a dog kennel. And although she'd love to ask Maxi a million questions about her next client, Lily couldn't afford to arouse Maxi's suspicion — not with so much uncertainty surrounding the situation.

Maxi followed her around the shop as she swept. "How about doing me a favor, then?"

"What kind of favor?"

Maxi's face lit up. "You know I'm the 'nail queen' around here, but I'm also learning to do hair."

Lily resumed sweeping with vigorous strokes, her ponytail swaying with each movement. "You are *not* cutting my hair."

"I won't cut it —"

"You're not dying it either." She cast a wry glance at Maxi as she worked. "Unlike you, I like the color God gave me."

Maxi put her hand on the broom. "Can I get a word in?"

Reluctantly Lily stopped to give Maxi her full attention. "OK, shoot."

"I need to practice my up-do's, you know, for weddings and grads. I figured your gorgeous locks would be perfect to practice on. And since we have no other appointments at the moment . . ." She raised her eyebrows in a pleading manner.

Lily sighed. "What exactly would this involve?"

"Just some big curls and a few strategically placed pins. If you don't like it, I'll take it right out. Promise."

Lily wavered, the sudden temptation for a bit of pampering overcoming her good sense. "You don't think Peg will mind?"

"Not as long as there aren't any customers."

Lily shrugged. "Why not? It's got to beat sweeping."

A few minutes later, Lily found herself in a stylist's chair with her hair pinned up in various places. Maxi chattered an incessant stream while manipulating the curling iron to create large, loose ringlets.

For the first time in weeks, Lily allowed herself an unguarded moment to relax. The tension slowly eased from her stiff shoulder muscles while Maxi prattled on. After exhausting the local town gossip, most of it concerning people Lily had never met, Maxi set the iron back in its stand.

"Tell me again what you thought of Jason." She twisted a curl around her fingers before pinning it in place.

Lily smirked. The girl was definitely obsessed. "I only met him for a few seconds."

"But you must've got some impression?"

Lily caught Maxi's hopeful expression in the mirror. "He seemed nice enough."

Maxi beamed, patting and poking the

back of Lily's hair. "He *is* the nicest guy in the world, with just the right touch of 'bad boy' in him."

"The best of both worlds?"

"Exactly." Maxi wedged two bobby pins between her teeth.

"Are you two dating?" Lily dared to risk the detailed explanation that might follow.

"No, but a girl can dream." She plucked a pin from between her teeth and pushed it into Lily's hair. "By the way, I think Marco likes you. How do you feel about him?"

The innocent-sounding question didn't fool Lily for a minute. Maxi was fishing for info. She met her eyes in the mirror. "He reminds me too much of my ex-boyfriend."

That got Maxi's full attention. She took the last hairpin out of her mouth. "Really? The leather jacket, motorcycle type?"

"Pretty much."

"Cocky, too?"

"Worse." So much for relaxing. Lily's muscles tightened just thinking about Curtis. "He had a vicious temper. Especially after a few beers." Which was one of the reasons Lily never touched alcohol. She'd seen too many people become monsters under its effect. Working at Hank's hadn't improved her opinion.

Maxi pinned the last curl in place, her

mischievous twinkle replaced with a solemn expression. "Did he hit you, Lil?"

Lily dropped her gaze to her lap. "He got rough a couple of times but never actually hit me. Put a nice hole in my wall though. My landlord evicted me the next day." Lily bit her lower lip, recalling the horrible scene and the terror that had robbed her of breath, wondering if she'd be the next recipient of his fist. She blinked to erase the memory and shifted in her seat.

"Do you think he'll come after you?" Maxi grabbed a can of hairspray off the shelf behind her.

Lily fingers curled around the arm of her chair as the familiar swirl of anxiety returned. "I hope not, but I'd rather play it safe."

"He sounds like a creep." Maxi gave the can a hard shake and squirted a mist over Lily's head. "Marco's a bit of a womanizer, but I don't think he'd ever hurt anyone on purpose. What will you do if he asks you out?"

Lily tried not to choke in the haze of hairspray. "I don't know. I'm not sure I'm ready to date anyone right now."

The bell at the front jangled, and Nick Logan strode in, tool belt slung low on his hips. He stood inside the doorway for a moment before he turned to look in their direction. His eyes widened when he spotted Lily.

Time slowed to a standstill as the intensity in Nick's gaze made Lily's mouth go dry. Her cheeks heated. She must look ridiculous with her hair all done up like she was going to a prom or something.

"Hey, Nick," Maxi called out. "I'm practicing my skills on Lily."

Nick's gaze never left the mirror. "Looks good. Real good."

Lily's face burned even hotter. She pushed out of the chair, and whipped off the stylist's cape.

Nick turned to address Maxi. "So where's this broken dryer?"

Maxi gestured toward the back of the room. "It's the same one you fixed last month. The sink's backing up again, too."

Lily returned to the reception desk, doing her best to calm her erratic pulse. What was it about Nick Logan that reduced her to an awkward adolescent? With all the boyfriends she'd had over the years, she'd never experienced this type of reaction, never allowed emotions to dictate her actions. This out-of-control response was definitely *not* a welcome sensation.

Nick gripped the wrench and squeezed

hard, attempting to quell the knot of tension in his gut. Lily looked prettier than a package tied up with a bow. He almost swallowed his tongue when he saw her — those huge eyes riveting his gaze.

Focus on the drain, Logan. At least in the back of the shop, he wasn't able to see the object of his fascination. He winced as the pipe suddenly let loose a stream of water that hit him square in the forehead. If that didn't cool him down, nothing would.

Nick finished with the sink and moved to a bank of hair dryers along the wall. He set the tool box on the floor, allowing himself one quick glance at Lily seated up front with her back to him. Was she at all affected by his presence or merely annoyed?

The bell jangled and Justine Henderson swept inside the shop, her three-year old daughter, Jenny, howling in her arms. The imp's face was blotched with tears, her light brown curls a tangle on top of her head. Nick smothered a smile. It seemed little Jenny had a severe objection to getting her hair cut. He dusted his hands off and headed to the front of the shop, thinking he could help distract the toddler.

Maxi beat him to the door. "Hey, Justine. Hi there, Jenny. What can we do for you?"

Justine huffed. "Can you take an emer-

gency? She got gum in her hair — again."
The exasperated woman rolled her eyes
while the girl wailed louder.

Nick slowed his stride as Lily pushed up
from her chair. Undaunted by the howls and
the storm of tears, Lily lifted a tentative
hand to one of Jenny's curls.

"Hello, pretty girl."

The child's shrieks became a whimper as
she contemplated Lily.

"Bring her over here," Maxi called from
the first stylist chair.

Jenny cowered against her mother, looking as if another bellow was imminent.

Lily smiled and pointed to her own head.
"Look, honey, Maxi just did my hair. Do
you like it?"

Jenny poked her thumb in her mouth
which temporarily stopped the noise. Her
eyes widened, seeming mesmerized by Lily.
Nick could totally relate.

"Would you like Maxi to do yours like
this? Like a princess?"

Jenny's thumb came out. "With a crown?"

Lily exchanged glances with Maxi who
nodded. "Yes, with a crown."

The little girl considered the idea and then
held out her arms to Lily. Justine's eyebrows
shot upward, mirroring Nick's own surprise.
Lily hesitated for a second, before gathering

Jenny to her. Over the toddler's head, Nick saw Lily's lids flutter closed. She pressed her nose to the girl's hair, appearing to breathe in her scent. When her eyes opened, a sheen of love glistened there. Nick's heart did a slow roll in his chest.

She deposited Jenny gently in the chair, and Maxi swooped in to take over.

"Thank you, so much." Justine pushed wisps of bangs off her forehead. "You have a real knack with kids. Have any of your own?"

A force compelled Nick to move closer.

Lily lifted her gaze — a swirl of longing and despair. "Not yet but maybe someday."

Lily waved at Jenny as she left with her mama, her newly-trimmed hair topped with a plastic tiara that Maxi had stashed in the back. Such a precious little girl — one who brought unbidden yearning to her soul. Lily remembered wondering if she were pregnant once during her rocky relationship with Curtis. For a week, she'd had time to imagine what it would be like to have her own child, a tiny being to love uncondition- ally, who would love her in return. But it turned out to be a false alarm, and a secret part of her mourned the loss of that fragile dream.

She sighed. Now knowing Curtis's true nature, it was probably for the best. No child deserved him as a father.

The front door swung open again, jangling Lily out of her daydreams. Marco Messini swaggered up to the desk. Sunglasses hid his eyes until he pulled them off and whistled. "Look at you, Lily-belle, all gussied up. Must've known we were going out tonight."

She pushed all thoughts of babies from her mind to focus on her customer. Behind her, the clanging of tools on metal ceased abruptly. In the tense silence, Lily became hyper aware of Nick's movements in the background.

She smiled at Marco. "What can I do for you?"

He winked. "You can join me for dinner tonight."

Though she found Marco's easy-going confidence amusing, Lily had no interest in going out with him. But before she could think of a polite excuse, a shadow loomed over her right shoulder.

"Why don't you do Lily a favor and leave her alone?"

The underlying warning in Nick's gruff voice raised the hairs on the back of Lily's neck.

Marco's smile changed to a scowl. "How is this any of your business, Mr. Handyman?"

Lily glanced over her shoulder. A nerve pulsed in Nick's jaw, while his eyes stayed trained on Marco.

"Just looking out for Lily's best interests — which means staying far away from you."

In the midst of the heated male emotions swirling around her, Lily's own temper rose. The last thing she needed was another male meddling in her life. She'd had enough of her father's interference.

Pushing up from her chair, she glared at Nick. "I'm perfectly capable of deciding whom I will or will not date. The fact that you're my landlord does not give you a say in my social life."

Nick pinned her with a look somewhere between hurt and anger. "My mistake. I thought we were becoming friends."

When he stalked back to the dryer, shame squeezed the air from Lily's lungs, but a second later, annoyance flared. How dare he make her feel guilty? She could go out with whomever she wished. She turned back to Marco. "I'd love to have dinner with you tonight." She made sure her sugar-sweet voice was loud enough for Nick to hear. The clanking of tools increased behind her.

Marco beamed, all evidence of ill-humor gone. "Great. I'll pick you up at six."

He waved to Maxi — who Lily thought had shown remarkable restraint staying out of the conversation — and sailed out the door, whistling off-key.

Lily sank back onto her chair and let out a long breath, still not entirely sure how she'd ended up agreeing to a date with Marco Messini.

The next few hours passed in a blur, and the time for Chloe Martin's manicure arrived. Peg had turned up for her shift just as Nick left and was now busy with a color job. Lily could barely concentrate long enough to answer the phone or take down appointments. Every few minutes, she had to wipe her damp palms on her skirt and remind herself to breathe in a normal fashion.

Maxi hovered near the reception desk, chatting about what Lily should wear to dinner with Marco, but Lily didn't hear a word. When the door jangled open at precisely three thirty, Lily's gaze flew to the front. An attractive dark-haired girl burst in, her focus glued to the cell phone in her hand. Lily stared, drinking in every detail of the girl's appearance — the light brown eyes, high cheekbones and chin-length bob. From her attire and the hefty pack on her back, she appeared to be a high school student — just the right age to be her sister.

The girl looked up from her phone and smiled past Lily. "Hey, Maxi. How's it going?"

"Hi, Chloe. Just peachy. Hope you haven't been biting those nails again."

Chloe grinned as she held out her hand for inspection. "Nope. I've been good."

As though sensing Lily's scrutiny, Chloe turned her head, a slight frown bringing her thin eyebrows together. Lily rose from her chair on shaky legs. She tried to speak, but her dry throat closed up.

"Oh, sorry." Maxi waved a hand in her direction. "Chloe, this is Lily, our new receptionist and my new neighbor. Lily, this is Chloe."

Lily forced her trembling lips into a smile. "Nice to meet you, Chloe."

"Same here." With a brief nod, Chloe dismissed her and turned her attention to Maxi. "Can we get started? I gotta help Mom before I can go out tonight."

The rest of her words trailed away as Chloe followed Maxi to the manicure area.

Lily's rubbery legs gave out from beneath her. She sank onto her chair and forced herself to focus on the appointment book so she wouldn't stare.

The same heart-shaped face, the same wide eyes and dark hair. The resemblance was undeniable. An arc of electricity raced through Lily's system, her body confirming what her brain had only started to comprehend.

Lily had just met her sister.

5

Nick couldn't concentrate on his studies that night. First, the hard spokes of the kitchen chair bit into his back, and no amount of shifting alleviated his discomfort. Then a powerful need for a cola had him rummaging in the fridge. Finally, the incessant drip of the kitchen tap magnified to sound like a form of Chinese water torture.

He slammed the textbook closed and pushed up from the table to pace the linoleum. The real problem — the one he'd been trying to avoid all evening — sat like the weight of a rock on his chest.

Lily's ridiculous date with Marco Messini.

He rubbed his neck and looked up at the wooden clock on the wall. Eight thirty. Would she be home yet? Knowing Marco as he did, Nick doubted it. His hands fisted as images of that slime ball putting the moves on Lily filled his imagination.

Lord, watch over Lily and protect her from

Nick stalked into the living room, hoping the familiar wallpaper and tattered couches would calm him. He hadn't had the courage to change a thing since his mother passed away. Now, as he forced his thoughts from Lily, Nick took a long look around. His childhood home needed some serious renovations. The outdated furniture, worn carpeting, and peeling wallpaper all had to go.

He still hadn't decided whether to sell the place or make it his permanent residence. This house held so many memories, both good and bad. It would be hard to let it go. But if he did become the minister of Good Shepherd Church, he'd have the rectory to live in.

Nick ran his hand over the smooth mahogany mantel. Selling this house could give him the capital to realize his long-held dream of building a shelter for women. After suffering his father's abuse, Nick had vowed long ago to make sure Rainbow Falls one day opened such a haven. He let out a deep sigh. No matter what he decided, this house would need a major overhaul, but all of that would have to wait until he finished his exams.

He moved to the roll-top desk in the

corner of the room where his glance fell on the copy of Lily's rental agreement. His pulse rate jacked up. Just the excuse he needed to go over and make sure she was OK. Nick grabbed the lease, pulled on his jacket, and raced out the door.

He set out on foot, hoping the fresh evening air would clear the cobwebs from his brain, but his anxiety level heightened two blocks later as he turned onto McIntyre Street and spied the battered Ford in Lily's driveway. He prayed she hadn't allowed Marco up to her apartment, not even for an innocent cup of coffee.

Nothing involving that womanizer was innocent.

Nick's steps slowed at the sight of two people on the front porch, standing much too close together for his liking. He clenched the papers in his hand until they crumpled. What should it matter to him if Lily got friendly with Marco?

The fact that you're my landlord does not give you a say in my social life. Lily's angry words flashed through his mind. Though harsh, he couldn't discount the truth of her accusation. It certainly wasn't Lily's fault she brought all his protective instincts to the surface. Then again, she didn't know Marco Messini the way he did.

Nick debated whether to turn back and bring the papers over the next day, but the unease at the back of his neck intensified. Something about the scene didn't sit right. Nick moved closer to get a better view. Marco had Lily pinned tight against his chest, and she seemed to be struggling.

"Let go of me."

The hint of fear in Lily's voice lit a match to Nick's temper. The papers fluttered to the ground as he made a wild dash across the lawn and up the few stairs. With the element of surprise on his side, he pulled Marco up by the collar of his leather jacket and flung him onto the grass below. Marco landed heavily on his back. Nick glared over the railing. "When are you going to learn to keep your hands to yourself, Messini?"

While Marco crawled to his knees, Nick turned his attention to Lily, expecting a show of gratitude or relief.

Instead, a dangerous light blazed in her dark eyes. "What do you think you're doing?"

The adrenaline surge still sang through Nick's body like a jolt of electricity. "Saving you from that punk's wandering hands."

"I had the situation under control," she snapped. "I don't need any would-be hero acting all macho —"

"Could I speak to you in private for a minute?" Nick said through gritted teeth.

At the wary look in her eyes, he took a calming breath and made an effort to relax his shoulders. "Please? It's important."

Lily darted a glance at the ground where Marco had started to pull himself up. She bit her lip and lifted her chin. "All right. You have five minutes. Then I want you gone."

Nick nodded and followed her inside, making sure to lock the front door behind them. They made their way up to her apartment in silence. Lily unlocked the door and motioned him inside. He noted she left the door wide open. Was she afraid of him now? A tug of remorse sat under his skin as he walked into the living room and pushed his hands deep into his pant pockets.

"You probably think I'm acting like a lunatic," he said, "but I have my reasons."

"Such as?" She flayed him with a scathing glare, arms crossed in mutiny.

"Let's just say I know all about Marco's dating techniques."

"What does that mean?"

Nick faltered, torn between explaining himself and keeping a personal confidence. He walked to the fireplace and stared into the pit of ashes, as though the solution

91

would magically appear.

Lord, give me the right words to make her understand.

He turned back to face her. "Someone I'm close to had an unpleasant experience on a date with him. From that, and from other women I've talked to, I know how he operates. He expects . . . repayment . . . for the price of the meal he buys."

Instead of appeasing her, Lily seemed even angrier. She stalked to the other side of the room. "I've dated a lot of guys like Marco," she bit out, "and I've always managed just fine." The last words were fierce in their intensity. "I've been looking out for myself since I was ten years old. I don't need any help from you."

He took a cautious step toward her, as though approaching a wounded animal. "What happened when you were ten?"

The unexpected question seemed to catch her off guard. She bit down on her quivering bottom lip, before turning toward the fireplace, her face shielded by a curtain of hair. For a minute he thought she wouldn't answer. "My mother died," she said at last.

The sorrow in her voice tore at his heart, bringing his own grief roaring to life. "I'm sorry. I know how hard that is."

He watched her attempt to get control of

her emotions, astonished at how much he wanted to take her in his arms and comfort her. "What about your father?" He remembered she didn't get along with him. Maybe now he'd find out why.

She snapped her gaze upward, boring into his. The anguish on her face nearly undid him. "Any affection he had for me died with my mother. He blames me for her death." Her chin quivered. "I don't know why I'm telling you this."

His ability to hold back vanished. He reached for her and gently pulled her stiff form into his arms. "You were only a child," he murmured. "You weren't responsible."

How could any father burden a child with that type of guilt? Visions of his own father's face, twisted with rage, came to mind. *How could any parent beat their own son?*

When her breath hitched, Nick gathered her closer, reaching up to caress her soft hair. The subtle scent of her perfume invaded his senses. He fought to keep a clear head, relieved when her muscles relaxed and the trembling subsided. He held her silently, enjoying the sensation of closeness, and the fact that he could help in some small way.

"Did your father . . . mistreat you?" he asked after a few minutes.

As if coming out of a reverie, she blinked

and moved away from him. He crossed his now empty arms as she took a seat on the couch.

"Yes." She pulled a cushion against her like a shield. "I tried to run away several times, but he always had the police bring me back."

Harsh memories from Nick's own childhood rose up inside him as he joined her on the sofa. "I know that helpless feeling. My father used to beat me when he drank." He couldn't keep the bitterness from his voice. "I tried to run away, too, only the beatings got worse when he found me."

She reached over to lay a tentative hand on his arm. The sorrow in her eyes told him everything she wasn't saying.

"I guess that's why I can't take it when a man is abusive in any way, especially to a woman."

She nodded, seeming to understand. "Who was it that Marco . . . ?"

"My cousin. She's like a little sister to me."

Even now, his gut tightened with the memory of her hysterical phone call, begging him to come and get her at the edge of town where teenage boys liked to park after a date. Only sixteen at the time, she'd gone out with Marco, who was several years her senior, against the express orders of her mother.

"Was she OK?"

"Yeah. When she wouldn't give Marco what he wanted, he abandoned her out in the country. Good thing she had a cell phone."

Lily remained silent for a moment. "I understand now why you reacted the way you did. I'm sorry I got so angry."

The knot of tension in his stomach loosened. "I'm just glad you're all right." He paused. "You won't be going out with him again, will you?"

She shook her head.

He released the breath he'd been holding. "Good."

The velvet depths of her eyes held him captive. He found it hard to tear his gaze from hers, but he knew he had to go — before he did something stupid, like kiss her. He squeezed her hand and reluctantly pushed up from the couch.

She followed him to the door. "Thank you for looking out for me. I guess I'm not used to dealing with a genuinely nice guy."

Before he could respond, she raised herself on tiptoes to kiss his cheek. Silky strands of hair brushed his face. He held her gaze for a second, fighting the overwhelming urge to kiss her. But to take advantage of her vulnerability after what she'd been through would be lower than low. He'd be sinking to Marco's level.

"Call me if he gives you any more trouble."

"I will."

"And lock this door when I leave."

"I always do."

They stood in the hallway with the door open.

"Good night, Nick."

He paused, wanting to stay longer but unable to find another excuse to linger. " 'Night, Lily."

On the landing, he waited for her to close the door behind him, listened for the click of the dead bolt, and started down the stairs. When he exited onto the porch, Nick was relieved to find the Ford gone and no sign of Messini. At the same time, an unmistakable prickle of guilt nagged at his conscience. As a future minister, he couldn't go around losing his temper and manhandling people — even if they did deserve it. His behavior needed to be above reproach, a shining example to his parishioners.

He sighed and began the walk home, mentally preparing an apology for the morning.

■ ■ ■ ■

Lily sank back in the bathtub, allowing the hot water and fragrant bubbles to soothe her frazzled nerves. What a disastrous night. Not only was Marco a boring date, but he *had* expected compensation for their meal. She should have known better. A plate of spaghetti was not worth getting groped.

All she'd gotten for her trouble was one tidbit of information about Chloe Martin. Marco told her that Chloe lived with her frail, widowed mother, a devout woman who kept Chloe on a tight rein. From his description, Mrs. Martin sounded surprisingly similar to Tobias. For Chloe's sake, Lily hoped not.

Lily laid her head against the tiled wall, her thoughts turning to Nick Logan. She didn't know what to make of him. Could he really be as genuine as he seemed? Of all the men she'd encountered in her life, only Hank had ever treated her well. Working at the tavern, she'd mastered the art of deflecting men's advances.

Lily pulled the plug, and the soft gurgle of draining water filled the room. Once dried, she pulled on sweatpants and a T-shirt and shook her hair out of its clip. With a large hairbrush, she began the nightly ritual of untangling.

As she did so, she contemplated her image in the slightly warped bathroom mirror. What did Nick see when he looked at her? Did he find her attractive? Her dark eyes and her long, thick hair had always been her best features. Yet many men preferred blue-eyed blondes. Was he one of those?

Most males found her curvy figure desirable, a fact she'd used to her advantage over the years to survive living on her own. She shuddered to think how Nick would view her less-than-stellar past. All the more reason she should put Nick Logan right out of her mind.

Still, she couldn't deny her attraction. Nick's novelty was a big part of his appeal, yet after the time she'd spent with him tonight, the danger he posed became very real. The safety and comfort she'd experienced in those few, brief moments in his embrace were nothing but a beautiful deception. She'd learned the hard way never to count on a man to bring anything but trouble.

Nick Logan was an illusion she could *not* afford to believe in.

"Hey, Mike. It's Nick. Sorry to bother you

so late."

"It's not late. Not for a cop anyway." His friend laughed at his own joke. "What can I do for you?"

Nick swiveled at his desk in the living room, tapping a pen to his lips. After his encounter with Lily, he was churned up and restless, haunted by the feel of her in his arms. He needed to know more about this woman who continued to wreak havoc with his emotions.

"I've got a new tenant I'd like you to check out for me. The name's Lily Draper." He ignored the unease in his chest. He wasn't snooping. Merely protecting his interests — in more ways than one.

"I wondered when you'd get around to that. Folks are talking about what a looker she is."

Nick gripped the arm of his chair, thankful Mike couldn't see his face. "What's that got to do with anything?"

"Nothing. Except you usually get me to check out tenants *before* they move in."

Mike's tone had Nick's defenses kicking in. "Look, I felt sorry for her. I got the impression she was a bit desperate."

"Un-huh."

Mike implied something Nick didn't want to hear. "Are you going to help me or not?"

Mike chuckled. "Don't I always?"

"Yeah."

"OK. So where is Lily Draper from?"

"Up north. Bismarck, I think."

"A city gal. Wonder what she's doing down here?"

Nick leaned back in his chair, which squeaked in protest. "I wondered the same thing."

"I'll see what I can find out."

"Thanks, Mike. Oh, and keep it under your hat, will ya? No need to spread her business around town."

"Always do."

6

The next afternoon, Lily juggled two bags of groceries on the front porch while trying to pry her keys from her pocket. To her surprise and relief, the door flew open.

Maxi poked her head out. "Need a hand?"

Lily blew wisps of hair off her forehead. "Thanks. You're a lifesaver."

Together they lugged the groceries up the flight of stairs to Lily's apartment. Maxi set her load on the kitchen counter and strolled into the living room.

"Hey, I love what you've done with the place. Where'd you get the fantastic artwork?"

Lily peered around the corner where Maxi eyed the paintings Lily had hung on the walls. "They're mine."

"Yours, as in you painted them?" Maxi's mouth gaped as she pulled a stool up to the pass-through counter.

Lily gave a casual shrug. "It's a hobby."

She turned and opened the fridge. "Want a soda?"

"Sure."

Lily handed her a cola and pulled out a can of her own. This was the first chance she'd had to talk to Maxi since meeting Chloe. Lily itched to pump her for information but wasn't sure how to bring up the topic without arousing Maxi's curiosity. "You working tonight?"

"Nope. Tonight's my youth group meeting."

Lily popped the lid and took a sip from her can. "What's that?"

"A group Nick started to keep kids out of trouble. We meet in the church hall every other week."

Nick volunteered with teens? This guy really must be a saint.

Maxi's eyes widened. "Hey, you should come with us. It's a great way to meet people."

Lily bit her lip and set down her can. "I don't think I'd feel comfortable. I'm a little old for that."

Maxi laughed. "There's no age restriction, Methuselah. The older volunteers mentor the younger kids."

Lily's shoulders stiffened. "I don't think

so. I'm not into religion." *More like allergic to it.*

"Oh, it's not religious." Maxi waved a casual hand in the air, bangle bracelets clanging. "We just use the church basement as a meeting place." She pursed her lips. "Well, Nick does say a prayer, but that's about it. We have discussions, go on outings, raise money for charities, that sort of thing."

Lily turned back to her task. Maxi didn't strike her as the type to be interested in such mundane activities. There must be another incentive. "Does Jason go to these meetings?"

"Sometimes. But I usually go with Chloe. You met her at the shop the other day."

Lily's heart rate kicked into overdrive, knocking as loud as the old motor in her refrigerator. She focused on keeping her hands steady as she put away her eggs. "The brunette?"

"That's her."

Lily closed the door with a careful click. "How are you friends? Isn't she still in high school?"

Maxi sipped her drink. "She's very mature for her age. Probably because she's been through so much — losing her dad, and her mom getting sick."

"The poor kid." Lily had hoped Chloe was having a glorious, carefree life, unlike her own horrible childhood.

"Yeah. She has a lot on her shoulders helping out at home."

"Does she have any . . . siblings?" Lily tried not to choke on the word.

"Nope. An only child." Maxi looked at her funky silver watch. "I'd better go eat and get ready. Let me know if you want to tag along." She threw Lily a wicked grin. "I'm sure Nick wouldn't mind."

Lily turned away to hide the warmth that rushed into her cheeks.

Maxi hopped down from the stool. "That reminds me. How'd your date with Marco go?"

Lily hesitated, remembering Marco was Maxi's friend. "Not so great. He got a bit too . . . friendly . . . for my liking."

Maxi only laughed as she opened the front door. "That's Marco for you. Don't take it personally." She paused to wink over her shoulder. "Let me know if you change your mind about tonight."

After Maxi left, Lily finished putting away the last of the groceries, her mind returning to the fact that Chloe would be at that meeting. If Lily joined the group, she'd have a perfect opportunity to get to know her sister better. As a friend and peer.

Only one huge obstacle held Lily back. She swore she'd never go near a church again. But how could she pass up this chance?

She wiped her damp palms on her jeans and stiffened her spine. The least she could do was give it a try. If the situation became intolerable, she could always leave.

Grateful for the remaining prepaid minutes on her cell phone, she took Maxi's number off the fridge and dialed.

Nick looked over the group of rambunctious teens assembled in the church hall and a satisfied smile stretched across his face. He'd started the group over a year ago with only a handful of kids, but attendance had steadily increased, and they now boasted a crowd of between twenty to thirty kids.

Nick loved providing a safe environment for adolescents to air their opinions and grievances. The fact that he got to mix some faith in with their fun was an added bonus.

Ignoring the din of excited voices, he pulled the material for tonight's meeting from his briefcase and set it on the rickety table beside his laptop.

"Good evening, Nick."

Nick looked up as Sarah Jane walked by, a

tray of baked goods in her arms. His mood plummeted as he remembered their upcoming date. The idea held about as much appeal as stripping wallpaper.

She turned from placing the treats on a side table, caught him watching her, and smiled. Remorse roared to life as he smiled back, thankful she couldn't read his mind.

The sound of footsteps descending the basement stairs gave Nick an excuse to look away. Maxi dashed into the hall, a bundle of vibrant energy. Nick chuckled at her outrageous hair, bejeweled top, and platform shoes. Nothing subtle about Maxi North. His gaze moved past her, expecting to see Chloe.

Instead, the tentative figure of Lily Draper entered the hall. She hesitated in the doorway, hands stuffed into her jeans pockets, and looked around like a doe scouting the forest for enemies. Her dark hair fell in a soft cloud around her shoulders. Dressed in slim, hip-hugging jeans that flared over pointed, high-heeled shoes, she drew the attention of every male in the room.

A spurt of excitement shot through Nick's system, infusing him with new enthusiasm. The evening had just become a lot more interesting. Lily's gaze traveled around the room until she locked eyes with him. She flashed him a smile that made his pulse jump four notches.

Oh man, he was in trouble if a mere smile could do that to him.

Nick's familiar face became Lily's beacon in the storm of nerves cascading over her. She tried not to stare as she dodged the circle of metal chairs to cross the room. Tonight, instead of his usual handyman attire, he wore dress pants and a brown sports jacket, giving him the air of a professional businessman — not her type at all.

So why did her heart hiccup when his blue eyes met hers?

"Hi, Lily. Glad you could come tonight." Nick grinned so wide that tiny lines crinkled around his eyes.

"Maxi invited me." She clasped her damp hands together to hide their trembling.

Get a grip, Lily. It's only a church hall.

"Well, I look forward to hearing your opinion of the group."

"You might not like it."

He winked at her. "Trust me. You won't be able to resist my charms."

Before she could untangle her tongue long enough to think of a comeback, someone flew up beside them, creating a stir in the musty basement air.

"Hey, Nick." The girl threw her arms around his neck.

"Hi, brat." Nick's eyes warmed with apparent affection as he returned her embrace.

Lily's eyebrows shot up. The girl draped over Nick was none other than Chloe Martin.

He untangled himself but kept an arm around the girl's shoulders. "Lily, this is my cousin, Chloe."

Lily's mind swam. Nick's cousin? How could that be?

Chloe smiled. "We already met the other day at the salon."

Lily swallowed. "Th-that's right. Nice to see you again, Chloe."

"Same here. I guess Maxi dragged you out." Amusement shone in her whiskey-colored eyes as she tugged off her bomber jacket.

"Yeah. She thought I needed to meet more people." Lily attempted to focus her whirling thoughts and concentrate on what Chloe was saying.

"Good idea. You'll have to be part of our discussion group then."

"I divide everyone up for discussion purposes," Nick explained. "Speaking of which, we'd better get started."

He excused himself to walk to the front of

the room. "Good evening, everyone. Could you please take your seats, and we'll begin with a short prayer."

Dread saturated Lily as she sank onto a chair between Maxi and Chloe. Since moving out of her father's home, she'd avoided all contact with religion.

Until now.

She clenched her hands together on her lap and fused her gaze to the floor.

"Lord, bless all of these wonderful young people gathered here this evening for fellowship in Your name. Enlighten our hearts and minds to serve You and each other to the best of our ability. Amen."

Lily raised her head. Surely there had to be more. Tobias would have gone on for half an hour. Instead, Nick gave a brief recap of the last meeting and outlined the topics of discussion for the night.

With determination, Lily set aside her nerves and the myriad of questions rioting through her brain, and focused on the evening's activities. To her relief, the meeting proved most enjoyable. The teenagers expressed their views in an enthusiastic manner. Lily paid particular attention to everything Chloe said and found her articulate and funny.

Her mind still struggled with the fact that

Chloe was Nick's cousin. Just how were the two connected? Through Chloe's adopted family? It had to be. If not, she and Nick could be related. She shifted in her seat and put that unwelcome thought out of her mind. One thing for sure, she'd have to watch herself around Nick. She wasn't ready to let anyone in on her secret just yet. Not until she'd had time to get to know Chloe and to figure out more about their family's murders.

After a quick closing prayer, Nick helped Sarah Jane serve the refreshments. Laughter filled the large room as everyone mingled. Lily stood on the sidelines, content to watch the various interactions, until Nick came up beside her, coffee in hand. His arm brushed hers, sending a flutter of warmth through her body.

He gave her shoulder a playful nudge. "So, what's the verdict?"

She glanced over at him. "I have to admit I'm impressed. I like the way the kids are free to express their opinion with no judgment calls." Totally unlike her own upbringing.

"That's the whole idea. To give adolescents a forum to express their ideas and to learn from each other in an accepting atmosphere."

"I think you've accomplished your goal."

He smiled, seeming pleased by her answer. "Does that mean you'll come again?"

The hopeful expression on his face made the blood rush to her cheeks. She looked at him from under her lashes. "I think I could be persuaded."

A grin spread over his rugged face. The vivid blueness of his gaze drew her in like a hypnotist's watch. She couldn't seem to look away until a movement on the outskirts of her vision became more insistent. She shifted her gaze, only to find a very unhappy-looking Sarah Jane standing beside Nick, clutching his sleeve in a possessive manner.

"Hello, Miss Draper." The words sounded as tight as Sarah Jane's lips. Her sour expression did nothing to improve her features.

"You two know each other?" Nick's eyes widened. His puzzled, almost guilty expression made Lily want to laugh.

She nodded. "We met at the library."

"Oh." He pulled at the neck of his shirt and glanced at Sarah Jane. "Maxi invited Lily so she could meet more people."

A prickle of irritation erased Lily's amusement. He was trying to let Sarah Jane know *he* wasn't the one who'd invited her. For

111

someone who swore Sarah Jane was *not* his girlfriend, he sure acted like a guilty man.

The tension clogging the air between them became more than Lily cared to endure. She stepped away from Nick's magnetic pull. "I should see if Maxi's ready to leave. Maybe I'll see you next time."

She swung her hair over her shoulder, confident Nick Logan would be watching her walk away. That thought gave her a small measure of satisfaction.

Like a ship adrift on unfriendly seas, Lily sought shelter with Maxi and Chloe, who stood munching cookies by the refreshment table.

"You and Nick looked cozy over there." Maxi wiggled her eyebrows in a suggestive manner and grinned. "Seems you ruffled Sarah Jane's feathers the wrong way though."

Lily fastened the buttons on her jacket. "She's got nothing to worry about."

Chloe smothered a laugh. "I don't know. Judging by the way my cousin was looking at you, I'd say she has a lot to worry about."

Maxi's laughter joined Chloe's giggles, drawing a bit too much attention to them. Lily tossed her paper cup in the trash and frowned. "I wasn't trying to create problems."

"Someone with your looks never has to try," Maxi said. "It just happens. Come on. I'm driving Chloe home."

Lily followed the girls out the door, grateful to escape Sarah Jane's dark glares. As an added bonus, she'd get to spend some extra time with Chloe and see where she lived. Several minutes later, they pulled up in front of a small bungalow. From what Lily could tell in the dark, it looked like a cozy, well-maintained home.

Chloe let out a groan when Maxi shifted into park. "Now I have to study for a math mid-term next week. If I don't pull my mark up, I may not get into college."

Maxi gave her a sympathetic pat on the arm. "Sorry, kiddo. Can't help you there. Math was not my best subject."

"I got good grades in math." The words were out before Lily thought it over. Her brain raced ahead, envisioning another way to get closer to Chloe. "If you want, I can help you."

Chloe turned in her seat to look back at Lily. Suspicion lurked in the depths of her brown eyes. "We can't afford a tutor."

"I don't want any money," Lily assured her. "Why don't you bring your books by the salon? I'll take a look and see if I know the material."

Chloe hesitated, glanced at Maxi, and then shrugged. "OK. I'll come by tomorrow. Thanks for the ride, Maxi."

"See you, kiddo."

Lily released a pent up breath and moved up to take the vacated front seat, fiddling with the seat belt to avoid Maxi's curious eyes.

"That was unexpected," Maxi remarked as she pulled away from the curb. "Why would you want to tutor Chloe?"

Lily scrambled for a plausible answer, settling for a version of the truth. "She reminds me a lot of myself at that age. If she's anything like I was, she could use some help, not to mention a friend."

Maxi pursed her lips. "You're pretty perceptive. Chloe hasn't always hung out with the best crowd. That's part of the reason Nick asked me to bring her to the youth group. To meet a different set of kids." She signaled a right-hand turn. "At first I thought the whole youth thing was a corny idea, but I did it for Nick. I owed him, you know, for renting me the apartment. Now Chloe and I are good friends."

"Is it helping her?"

"I think so. At least she's not getting into trouble at school anymore."

Lily smiled. "Chloe's lucky to have you in

her corner."

Maxi shot her a sidelong glance. "Looks like now she'll have you, too."

7

Nick cut into the succulent steak on his plate, and his mouth watered in anticipation.

"I don't like her." Across from him, Sarah Jane sat, hands folded in her lap, her grilled chicken untouched before her.

"Like who?" Nick shifted his weight on the plush seat and grimaced inwardly. His choice of dining establishment had turned out to be a huge error in judgment on his part. *Giorgio's* romantic music and dim lighting gave entirely the wrong impression.

"Your new tenant. She's very . . . nervy." Sarah Jane wrinkled her nose. Horizontal frown lines creased her forehead. "Do you know she asked me if we were living together?"

Nick grabbed a napkin to cover his mouth before food spewed out. "Why would she ask you that?"

The blush on Sarah Jane's face told him a lot.

"I *may* have indicated we were . . . a couple. But she jumped to her own wild conclusions."

"A couple?"

Her color deepened. "Well, it may have been more like we were . . . engaged."

Nick reached for his glass of water, sloshing back a quick sip. Sarah Jane told Lily they were engaged after he'd sworn they'd only dated once or twice? "Why did you tell her that?"

She kept her gaze glued to her plate. "I don't know. It just slipped out. I'm sorry."

Nick didn't know whether to be upset with her fib or with Lily's outrageous question. At least Sarah Jane had the good grace to look remorseful. "Don't worry about it. I'll straighten it out when I see Lily. I'm sure you handled her question with your usual tact."

She fiddled with her peas. "I tried."

He couldn't picture Sarah Jane making a scene or doing anything the least bit outrageous. Sensible and predictable would be the best adjectives to describe her behavior. Tonight, however, she'd stepped out of character and made some small concessions to her appearance — presumably to impress him. She'd worn a more feminine dress and high heels. With her hair loose around her face and a smattering of lip gloss, she looked almost attractive. Unfortunately, Nick didn't feel any type of spark. He hadn't even kissed her yet and had no desire to do so.

Nevertheless, she was honest, loyal, and upright — qualities that had caught his interest in the first place. The extreme opposite of Cheryl, a non-believer, who'd dropped him at the first hint of inconvenience to her selfish pleasures. Nick could see now how far he'd swung in the opposite direction.

Too far apparently. Because, on this third date with the reverend's niece, Nick would give anything for an excuse to cut the evening short. He pulled his attention back to Sarah Jane as she rambled on about a fussy library patron. He did his best to show concern for her difficulty in satisfying Mrs. Sheppard's obsession with Martha Stewart, but when his cell phone vibrated at his hip, a tidal wave of relief washed over him.

"Excuse me. I'd better take this." He snapped open his phone like a man on death row given a reprieve.

"Nick?"

At the sound of Lily's voice, Nick's pulse sprinted.

"I'm sorry to bother you," she said, "but there's a problem with the fridge."

"The fridge?" His spirits brightened. "You can't fool around with that. I'll be right over." He ignored Lily's sputtering protest and disconnected.

"Sorry about that," he told Sarah Jane. "There's an emergency I need to take care of."

He signaled the waiter for the bill, hoping he looked suitably disappointed.

Lily hated to bother Nick on a weekend, but the motor on the fridge had given out with a loud bang. It seemed only fair to let him know right away.

Now, with the appliance pulled out at an odd angle so he could get at the back, he'd effectively trapped Lily in the kitchen. She blamed her nerves and mild claustrophobia on the small space, not on the proximity of her handsome landlord.

To keep busy, she continued drying her dishes from dinner. At least the fridge blocked Nick from her line of vision, eliminating the strong temptation to stare. He'd arrived looking especially attractive in a navy suit and tie, giving credence to Maxi's gossip that he'd been out on a date with Sarah Jane.

A twinge of some uncomfortable emotion churned in Lily's stomach. Had to be the lumpy meatloaf she'd had for dinner.

"You didn't have to interrupt your date, you know. It could've waited 'til the morning." She reached up to put a plate in the cupboard.

The noise behind the fridge stopped. Nick's frowning face appeared around the side. "How did you know I was on a date?" He pushed the sleeves of his shirt farther up his arms.

Lily quirked one eyebrow. "Did you forget I work with Maxi?"

"Maxi." The word came out as a groan.

"Yup." Lily picked up a saucepan to dry. "I guess Sarah Jane wasn't too thrilled when you left to come over here." She hoped her tone sounded casual, not like she was fishing for information.

"The date was pretty much over anyway." Nick gave her a long look, one that made her pulse trip, before he ducked behind the appliance.

Lily stared at the fridge, heat working its way to her cheeks as she imagined Nick kissing Sarah Jane good night. The thought made her twist in her sneakers. She rubbed the already dry dish a little harder, then opened the oven to store the clean pot inside. Her nose wrinkled at the charred odor that puffed out — a remnant of the pork chops she'd burned the other night. Lily straightened, hung the towel over the stove handle, and leaned back against the counter.

"This is probably none of my business, but why are you dating a woman you don't seem that interested in?"

The silence of the tools told her she'd struck a nerve. She bit her lip, wishing she could take back the impulsive question, but before Nick could answer, an electric buzz sizzled through the overhead light. The bulb flickered once, and the next second the kitchen plunged into total darkness.

"Hey —" A loud bang erupted from behind the fridge.

Instant panic seized Lily by the throat. "It's OK," she said, more to reassure herself than Nick. "The bulb must have burned out. I think I saw some spare ones under the sink."

Fighting to overcome her childish fear, she reached out a hand toward the lower cupboard while her eyes fought to adjust to the inky blackness. When her fingers brushed the cool metal handle, she pulled the door open.

"Hang on," Nick said. "I have a flashlight

in my toolbox."

He came out and shoved the fridge back a bit. She could just make out his figure coming toward her. Being alone in the dark with Nick unnerved her even more than the lights going out. A thin pencil of illumination beamed into the room. Nick aimed it inside the cupboard for her.

"Found them." She straightened with a box of bulbs. "Is there a step ladder around?"

"Sorry, no. I took it when I moved out."

"I'll get a stool then."

Grateful she could now see better, Lily scooted by him into the living room, turned on a lamp and grabbed one of the stools. She returned to set it under the kitchen fixture. The tiny space seemed to shrink with Nick's large frame taking up so much room.

"Here. Let me do that." Nick tried to take the box of bulbs from her, but she shook her head.

"The stool won't take your weight. Just hold it steady for me." She pushed one bulb into the pocket of her sweatshirt and started to climb.

Maybe she didn't want him to see her irrational fear of the dark. Or maybe she wanted to prove she wasn't a helpless female. Whatever the reason, she needed to do this. She'd been tackling far greater problems on her own for the past six years. She could certainly handle a light bulb.

Rising on her tiptoes, Lily managed to reach the metal fixture and began to unscrew the bulb, until a horrible grinding sound made her flinch and her fingers met with resistance.

"That socket can be tricky." A hint of impatience laced Nick's voice. "Why don't you let me try?"

"I've got it." The stool jiggled under her feet, and fear leapt into Lily's throat.

"Watch it."

Nick's warm hands grasped her legs to steady her, but it had the opposite effect. Her hand jerked, promptly shattering the bulb. Pieces of glass rained down on them. She cried out as she lost her battle with gravity and tumbled off her perch.

Nick's strong arms broke her fall. He pulled her tight against his chest. "Are you all right?"

Lily startled at the feel of his warm breath in her hair. "I — I think so."

Slowly he lowered her feet to the floor. She leaned back against the counter, too unsteady to stand on her own.

Glass crunched under Nick's shoes as he

retrieved the flashlight he'd dropped when he caught her. In mere seconds, he replaced the broken bulb with a new one and flipped the switch. Lily shielded her eyes against the blinding glare.

"Hey. You're bleeding." Nick took hold of her arm where a trail of blood dripped from a gash in the fleshy part of her thumb. He turned her hand over to inspect the wound. "You've got a piece of glass in there."

She stared at the jagged shard in disbelief, amazed she hadn't felt any pain.

Nick scooped her up and deposited her on the shard-free counter beside the sink. "I have a first aid kit in my toolbox," he said. "Don't move." He returned seconds later with a white plastic box and flipped open the lid.

The pain had set in now, roaring to life like a fire-breathing dragon. She sucked in deep breaths to cope with the searing heat shooting up her wrist.

Nick turned on the cold water and reached for her hand, his expression apologetic. "Sorry. This is going to hurt."

She squeezed her eyes shut at the initial burst of pain. When she opened them a second later, the stinging receded as she focused on the face so close to hers. The intoxicating scent of his spicy cologne surrounded her. Nick turned off the tap and examined the injury, tiny ridges of concentration creasing his forehead. When he raised his head, their noses almost touched. The air backed up in Lily's lungs.

For a moment, he simply gazed into her eyes. "I'm going to take the glass out now. Let me know when you're ready."

"Got a bullet to bite?"

He chuckled. "That's one thing I *don't* have in my toolbox."

Then with one quick jerk, he pulled the shard out of her thumb. Lily bit her lip to smother a cry of pain. Blood spurted down her wrist, and though she tried to be brave, her body rebelled with tremors that raced through her torso.

Nick clamped his hand down over the gash to stem the flow. Lily fought the longing to lay her head on his shoulder and let the warmth of his body ease the chill that made her teeth chatter. Was it the shock of her wound or Nick's touch that caused her trembling?

When the bleeding slowed, Nick patted the area dry with a towel, applied salve with careful skill, and wrapped a gauze bandage around her hand. The warmth of his steady fingers sent soothing tingles up her arm. It had been a very long time since anyone had treated her with such kindness. No one, except her beloved mother, had ever made her feel so cared for. The bittersweet memory caused hot tears to burn behind her lids. She blinked hard to keep them at bay.

At last, Nick looked up. "Do you have any aspirin? Because this is going to throb like the dickens later on."

Her throat, thickened with emotion, made speech impossible. She could only nod.

He peered at her, apparently noticing the dampness of her eyes. "Is the pain that bad?"

She shook her head, hating this display of vulnerability. Despite her efforts, a lone tear escaped and trickled down her cheek. Nick reached over to brush it away, his thumb a whisper over her skin. The absolute tenderness of the gesture undid her. She couldn't pull her gaze from his.

"Thank you," she whispered.

"You don't have to thank me."

"Yes, I do."

"Lily, I —"

On impulse, she jerked forward and cut off his words with a kiss. His lips were soft and warm, tasting of coffee and peppermint. She stilled, shocked by her own recklessness, but Nick folded strong arms around her and pulled her closer to deepen the kiss.

She fisted her hands in the soft cotton of his shirt as waves of pleasure flooded her system. Nick's gentle fingers moved to caress her cheek, as though she were something infinitely precious.

Which of course she was not.

Lily stiffened as reality crashed in, returning her to sanity. Hadn't she promised herself not to get involved with another man? She flattened her hand against Nick's chest, aware of his heart beating hard against her palm, and pushed him back.

"I'm sorry. I shouldn't have done that." Her gaze fused to the blue buttons of his shirt, unable to look at him for fear of the disgust she might see there.

"Why not?" His voice was husky. "I've wanted to do that for a while now."

She jerked her head up. The look in his eyes, now a dark navy, told her he was dead serious. How could this man make her heart stop with one glance?

Lily shook her head. "The timing's all wrong for one thing. I've just come out of a bad relationship. And you've got a girlfriend. Or should I say fiancée?"

"Sarah Jane is *not* my girlfriend. And we are definitely *not* engaged."

A flicker of hurt flashed across his face, but she steeled herself against it. Better to hurt him now and nip this . . . whatever this was . . . in the bud.

"Then why did you take her to *Giorgio's* tonight?" she demanded. "According to Maxi, the place isn't exactly platonic."

He broke eye contact and stepped away. "That was a mistake." With jerky movements, he repacked his first aid kit and snapped the lid closed.

Lily twisted the soiled towel on her lap, fighting the urge to break down and weep.

He pinned her with another searing look. "The truth is, the whole time I was out with Sarah Jane, I was thinking about you."

Before she could wrap her brain around the implication of that statement, he turned away from the sink. "I'd better finish this repair."

He disappeared behind the bulky appliance leaving Lily sitting on the counter, bandaged hand in her lap. Her wound throbbed in time with the headache beginning at her temples. What had she done? Initiated a mind-blowing kiss and hurt Nick's feelings all in one fell swoop.

Disgusted with herself, she hopped down from the counter, her feet crunching over the bits of glass on the floor. With a sigh, she bent to retrieve the broom and dustpan.

If only it were as easy to clean up the other mess she'd made.

8

"Are you guys ready for a break yet?" Maxi's plaintive voice drew Lily's attention away from the textbook in front of her.

"What's the matter? You bored?"

"As a matter of fact, I am." Maxi wandered over to look out the front window of the salon, her arms wrapped around her waist.

Lily shrugged and returned to the books. Her second tutoring session with Chloe was going well. Peg had been a good sport about letting them use the shop when they weren't busy. "Why don't you go and grab us some burgers then?" Lily glanced up at the metal wall clock that ticked out each second. "By then, Chloe should be finished with this chapter. You want anything, Chloe?"

The girl's dark head was bent over her notebook, a well-chewed pencil clenched between her teeth. She looked up and blinked. "What?" She pulled the pencil out.

"Oh, no. Thanks. Mom will have dinner waiting for me."

"I'm not hungry," Maxi said, "but I'll get you something if you want."

The melancholy tone finally registered with Lily. She got up and walked over to give Maxi's shoulder a nudge. "What's up with you? You're never depressed."

Maxi's gaze remained fixed outside. "Love stinks. That's what."

Lily bit back a smile at Maxi's dramatic expression. "Is this about Jason?"

Misery darkened Maxi's features as she turned and nodded. "He has a new girl-friend."

Chloe and Lily gasped at the same time. How had Lily not realized that Maxi's feelings went far deeper than a mere crush?

"I'm so sorry." She put her arm around Maxi's shoulder. "Maybe it isn't serious."

Maxi blinked back tears. "I think it is. You should see his face when he talks about her."

Chloe abandoned her books and followed Lily and Maxi to the cushioned bench in the waiting area. "Who is she? I'll get the dirt on her."

Maxi shook her head. "Thanks, but that's not necessary."

Her friend's sorrow triggered a wave of compassion in Lily. "Have you ever thought of telling Jason how you feel?" she asked. "Maybe he feels the same way and hasn't realized it yet."

Maxi picked at her painted fingernails. "I tried once, but I couldn't do it. I'm scared it might ruin our friendship."

Lily threw a desperate glance at Chloe who only shrugged. Completely out of her element, Lily fell back on her own coping mechanisms. "You know what you need? A super-decadent chocolate sundae with whipped cream and cherries. That always gets me through my men problems."

Maxi managed a laugh while dabbing a tissue to her cheeks. "Tempting. But we can't leave the store."

"Then I'll bring the sundaes here. You watch the phones, and I'll be back with the supplies." Lily yanked her purse out of the desk drawer. "And you," she pointed at Chloe, "keep working until I get back."

Ten minutes later, Lily returned with a tub of rocky road ice cream, a can of whipped cream, chocolate sauce, and cherries. "OK troops, to the lunch room. We have thirty minutes before the next customer arrives."

They proceeded to transform the staff room into a make-shift ice cream parlor, and by the time they finished, Lily was grati-

fied to see a smile back on Maxi's face —
well worth blowing her grocery budget.

"Mom is going to kill me." Chloe giggled
around a huge spoonful of ice cream. "Talk
about ruining your appetite."

Lily glanced over at Maxi and burst out
laughing at the chocolate sauce lining her
mouth. "You look like a clown with a bad
makeup job."

The three of them laughed and sprayed
more whipped cream. Looking around the
ugly Formica table, Lily stilled at an unexpected realization. She was having a normal
girl moment with her sister and new best
friend, something she'd missed out on during her teen years. For the first time in a
long, long time, the crushing weight of
loneliness ebbed, and tears of gratitude
threatened.

"So, are you coming to the next youth
meeting?"

Chloe's question startled Lily out of her
thoughts. She blinked back the unexpected
tide of emotion. "I'm not sure. Why?"

"Because we want you there."

Lily hesitated, rubbing a pensive finger
over the bandage on her thumb. Since the
kiss in her kitchen, she'd avoided Nick,
unsure how to behave around him.

"Come on," Chloe coaxed. "What else

133

have you got to do?"

"Another date with Marco?" Maxi teased.

Lily snorted. "Not likely. I haven't heard from him since Nick knocked the wind out of him." She bit back a groan the minute the words were out.

Chloe's mouth dropped open. "Nick did what?"

Heat scorched Lily's face as she pushed her chair back, the metal legs scraping the floor. "It was no big deal. He caught Marco getting a little too friendly, and well, he put a stop to it." She dumped her dishes in the sink and turned on the hot water.

"You never told me that part," Maxi accused. "This totally confirms my suspicion. Nick has a serious crush on you."

Lily shrugged. "He said he knew what Marco was like and was just looking out for me."

Chloe's expression sobered. "Yeah, Marco tried that with me once. I thought Nick was going to kill him."

"See, simple explanation. Now can we forget about Marco, please?" Lily moved to clear the table and prayed for a change in subject.

Chloe rose with her dishes, a slight frown creasing her forehead. "I think Maxi's right. I've never seen Nick act so protective with anyone but me." She turned on the tap and shot Lily a penetrating look. "How do you feel about my cousin?"

Images of their amazing kiss popped into her head. Lily swallowed hard, willing the color away from her cheeks. She grabbed a cloth to wipe the tabletop. "Nick's very sweet. Unfortunately he's not my type at all." She half expected a lightning bolt to strike her at any moment. Instead, the familiar panic began to build in her chest.

I cannot be falling for Nick Logan.

Maxi stood and pushed her chair in. "You're probably right, Lil. Somehow I don't see you as a minister's wife."

The cloth fell from Lily's hands with a wet plop. "Wh-what did you say?"

Maxi's eyes widened. "Hasn't he told you? Nick's studying to be a minister. Wants to take over for Reverend Baker when he retires."

The blood drained from Lily's head and pooled in her feet. She grabbed the back of one of the chairs to steady herself. "A minister?"

"Yeah. You OK?"

Maxi and Chloe both stared as if she'd suddenly sprouted horns.

"Do you have a problem with that?" Chloe demanded.

Lily hesitated. These girls were her new family. She owed them some sort of explanation for her reaction. She sank onto one of the chairs. "My father is a minister, and he's, well, let's just say we don't get along." *Understatement of the year.* "I swore off anything to do with religion when I left home."

Maxi's eyes narrowed. "What did he do to you?"

Lily shook her head. "It's not what you're thinking." How did she describe the type of neglect and emotional abuse she'd endured? "He didn't like me — and constantly let me know it."

Chloe gasped. "What kind of father doesn't like his own child?"

The two girls sat beside her, and Chloe put her hand over Lily's.

"One who's forced to adopt a child he doesn't want. Things were fine while my mother was alive, but once she died . . ." Lily trailed off, the steady drip of the tap breaking the silence.

"I didn't know you were adopted, too." Sympathy swamped Chloe's expressive eyes. "Something else we have in common."

Lily bit her lip and held herself rigid on the seat, afraid of blurting out the truth.

"Did your father hit you?"

Lily picked up a napkin and crumpled it into a ball. "Sometimes. He quoted the Bible whenever he did. Seems he had a verse to justify everything."

Maxi laid a hand on Lily's arm. "That's horrible. But you know Nick is nothing like that, right?"

Lily stiffened her spine, along with her resolve. "It doesn't matter, because Nick and I will never be anything more than friends." She rose abruptly. "I'd better get back to work now."

As she stalked back to her desk, Lily clamped her mouth into a firm line. This was just the information she needed to keep any feelings she might have for Nick from blossoming.

A minister would be the absolute *last* person she would ever get involved with.

Nick slammed the door to his truck with more force than necessary as he got out in front of the church. Frustration still hummed in his veins two days after fixing Lily's fridge. He'd finally shared a kiss with her — a kiss more amazing than he'd ever imagined — and she'd pushed him away. From her initial reaction, Nick was sure she'd felt the same spark. She'd kissed him until something had changed, and for the life of him, he couldn't figure out what.

Now Reverend Ted had summoned him to a meeting at the church, and judging by his tone over the phone, it was not going to be a pleasant conversation. No cups of tea this time.

Nick paced the rector's office, waiting for Ted to arrive, and eyed the tired décor. The first thing he'd do when he took this position would be to modernize the office. The furniture and curtains had to be twenty years old or more — as outdated and stuffy as the air in the room.

"Nicholas. Please have a seat." Ted entered the room and closed the door with a sharp click. The scowl on his weathered face only confirmed Nick's fears.

He waited for Ted to take his seat behind the scarred wooden desk before pulling up one of the guest chairs.

"I'm somewhat at a loss for words, young man," Ted began. His bushy eyebrows drew together in a straight line over his glasses.

"What about, sir?"

Ted shuffled a pile of papers to the corner of the desk. "Word has it you've been spending time alone with your new tenant — a young woman of questionable morals."

Shock speared through Nick. Who would spread such vile rumors about him and

Lily? "I believe you've been misinformed," he replied in a cool tone.

The eyebrows now rose in a question. "So you deny you left during a date with Sarah Jane to rush over to this young woman's apartment?"

Nick gripped the arms of the chair, straining to remain calm at this assault on his character. "There was a problem with the refrigerator that needed to be handled right away."

"It must have been serious. Apparently, you were alone with the woman for almost two hours."

The last strip of Nick's patience evaporated. He vaulted to his feet. "What did Sarah Jane do? Follow me and watch the building until I left?"

Ted's gaze shifted, and Nick knew he was right. Sarah Jane must've followed him to Lily's, watching and imagining all sorts of sleazy things going on. He thought about the kiss then, and anger burned in his gut. It was not something he planned, and he would not feel guilty about it. He paced the room like a prisoner in a cell.

"Calm down, son. We're just trying to get to the truth here."

Nick sent him a piercing glare. "Whose version of the truth?"

Ted inclined his head. "Why don't you sit down and tell me your side of the story." His voice was gentler this time, less accusatory.

Nick waited a beat before complying. Then he told Ted the bare facts of what had transpired, leaving out the kiss. "For some reason, Sarah Jane has taken an instant dislike to Lily. I know Lily can be a bit abrasive at times, but I think it's a defense mechanism, stemming from her traumatic childhood."

Ted remained silent for a moment. "Seems you know quite a lot about this woman."

Nick bristled. "I've had a few conversations with her. There's nothing sordid going on." The hard spokes of the chair bit into his back as Ted studied him.

"I believe you, Nicholas. Just be careful. You don't need to give the gossipers any fuel for talk. As a minister, your reputation is worth everything."

The fight drained out of Nick as quickly as it had risen. "I know, sir. I know." With a weary sigh, he rose, and started toward the door. He paused with his hand on the knob. "About Sarah Jane and me . . . I'm afraid things aren't working out between us. She's a very nice girl, but —"

Ted raised a hand to stop him. "Don't

burn any bridges just yet, Nicholas. You may be sorry."

9

Nick pushed the documents across his aunt's dining room table. "Is this really necessary, Aunt Sonia?"

After his talk with Ted yesterday, Nick thought nothing could worsen his mood. Reading his aunt's new will, however, had done just that — making him realize how far her illness had progressed. The same heart condition that had taken his mother's life a few months ago would soon claim her only sister.

His aunt's blue-veined hands moved the papers back across the oak tabletop in front of him. The oxygen machine behind her chair clicked every few moments, as if it marked the time when the Lord would call Sonia home. "You know it is, dear. With the state of my health, I can't put it off any longer."

"Sonia is doing the smart thing, Nick." Clyde Summerhill, the top estate lawyer in the area, nodded his head toward Aunt Sonia. "It's best to get everything down in black and white while she's still up to it." He handed Nick a pen. "If you'll sign on the appropriate line, we'll wrap this up and let you get back to your day."

Nick looked from his aunt's pleading face to the placid gaze of her lawyer and huffed out a loud breath. "If it will make you feel better, then, of course, I'll do it." With steady hands that belied his inner turmoil, he signed the dual copies, then aimed the pen at his aunt in mock sternness. "This doesn't mean you get to give up. You still have to fight this illness as long as you can."

Moisture rimmed her eyes. "I won't leave you and Chloe while I can still draw breath. But I feel better knowing you're in charge of Chloe's inheritance until she's mature enough to handle it."

Nick swallowed the lump in his throat. It hurt to think of his already small family shrinking even more. "I'll take good care of it — and her."

Sonia patted his hand. "I know you will, honey."

Clyde gathered the papers and put one set in his briefcase. "Thank you, Sonia. Thank you, Nick. I'll be in touch." He stood and shook Nick's hand.

"I have to go, too." Nick bent to kiss his aunt's cheek, noting the paper-thin skin and bluish tinge to her lips, evidence of the truth he was trying to deny. "Call me if you need anything else."

His aunt reached for his arm. "There is one more thing you can do."

"Sure. What is it?" Nick helped her stand, and they made their way to the front hall. The portable oxygen machine afforded his aunt the flexibility to move around the house.

"Help me convince Chloe to attend college in the fall. I won't have her putting her life on hold while I get worse." Her chin quivered.

Nick frowned. "I didn't know she was having doubts about going."

Aunt Sonia nodded. "She used to talk about college all the time. Now she won't discuss it." Her fingers clutched Nick's arm. "She listens to you. Tell her I'll be fine here with you and my friends to watch out for me."

Nick reached for his jacket on the hall tree. "I'll do my best. College is just what Chloe needs."

She gave a soft sigh. "I agree. At least she's trying to improve her marks. A new friend — Lily I think her name is — has been tutoring her."

Nick's eyebrows shot up. "Lily's helping Chloe?"

"Yes. At the salon after school." Aunt Sonia gave him a curious look. "Isn't she your new tenant?"

"That's right."

"What do you think of her?"

Nick tugged the door open, suddenly anxious to be on his way. "She seems very nice." *Good noncommittal answer, Logan.* "Anyway, don't worry. I'll talk to Chloe."

"Thank you, dear." She patted his arm, and he dropped another kiss on her cheek.

"See you on Sunday."

Nick climbed into his truck but didn't turn the engine on right away, his thoughts too unsettled. Events seemed to be spiraling out of his control lately. Chloe's life was about to change drastically in more ways than one, starting with her eighteenth birthday in a couple of weeks when she'd officially inherit her late parents' estate, including an abandoned house Chloe had no idea belonged to her. A house Nick hoped to one day use for his shelter. How would his aunt ever explain the tragic history associated with that building?

Nick let out a gusty sigh. The bigger worry was Aunt Sonia's health. Losing her would be like losing his mother all over again. He closed his eyes, reminding himself that none of this was under his control. He would have to wait and see what God had in store for them. He bowed his head over the steering wheel in a quick prayer.

Lord, give me strength and wisdom to do Your will, whatever it may be. Help me to be a source of love and support for Aunt Sonia and Chloe, no matter what happens. Amen.

Apprehension marred Lily's enjoyment of the glorious morning sunshine. She'd put off this unpleasant chore long enough, but if she wanted answers to her past, visiting her childhood home was the best place to start. Now, with a rare day off from the salon, she had no excuse to prevent her from going.

As she walked down Elm Street, Lily drank in the charming atmosphere of the neighborhood where she must have played as a child. She admired the Victorian-style houses, the white-washed fences, and the tall mountain ash trees that shaded the sidewalk. Farther down the street, the manicured residences gave way to a large lot with overgrown hedges. Lily's steps slowed as she neared the old house on the property. She didn't need to check the number hanging askew on the porch post to know it was the right address. Something deep inside her had quivered in recognition the moment she saw it — the brick walkway now obscured by weeds, the old wrap-around porch, the carved oak door.

After scanning the street to make sure no one was watching, she climbed the rickety steps and reached out to try the door, expecting it to be locked. When the knob turned under her hand, she jumped. The hinges groaned in noisy protest as she pushed inward. Her heart pounded in her ears, blocking out all other sounds. On the other side of the threshold, Lily hesitated, the musty smell of an unused residence assaulting her senses. She found herself in the middle of a tiled foyer with an enormous staircase leading up to the second story. Her eyes followed the stairs upward, but courage failed her at the thought of facing the bedrooms.

Instead, she headed toward the back of the house where the huge kitchen spanned the entire width of the building. Snatches of sunlight slipped past the grime on the window, illuminating the once homey room. With a start, Lily found she could picture it exactly as it had looked eighteen years ago. A glimpse of a pretty woman in a white apron stirring something on the stove skirted across her memory.

She crossed to the kitchen counter where a ceramic cookie jar sat covered in dust. She lifted the lid and looked inside. The years vanished and suddenly she was a child reaching into that container for a cookie. A ball of emotion rose in her throat as memories crashed over each other like waves against a rocky shore. Memories of fighting with her brothers over the cookies in this very jar. Memories of her mother stepping in to smooth the waters. The lid slipped from her nerveless fingers and clattered onto the counter, cracking in two. She stared at the broken crockery overcome by the fact that, for the first time, she'd remembered her two younger brothers. They'd been mischievous imps, always teasing her and fighting with her.

She clutched her necklace with shaking fingers and turned to focus on the kitchen table. A strong impulse compelled her to run her hand over the grimy surface. She remembered breakfasts at this table, milk being spilled and a dark-haired baby in the high chair, banging a spoon.

That baby was Chloe.

Lily bit down hard on her lip to stop the quivering. The dusty air became suffocat-

148

ing. She tightened her grip on her purse and headed back to the entry where the stairs loomed ahead of her. Reaching out, she steadied herself on the newel post. Could she face going up there? If she'd already started to remember her family, would she also remember the devastation that occurred in those rooms?

She closed her eyes and rested her forehead against the wooden rail. Though terror threatened to overwhelm her, she refused to let it take hold. This could be her chance to find out what had really happened that day so long ago. She took a deep breath, stiffened her spine and started up the steps.

Nick was halfway home when his cell phone went off.

What now? He pulled his truck to the shoulder of the road and flipped open the device.

"Logan."

"Nick? It's Peg Hanley. Sorry to bother you."

He frowned. It wasn't often Peg called him. "What's up?"

"You keep an eye on the old Strickland house for your aunt, don't you?"

"Yes. Why?"

"I just drove by there, and I think the front

door's open. I would've stopped to check, but I'm late for an appointment."

Nick scrubbed a hand over his face. "Thanks for letting me know. Probably teenagers but I'll swing by and see."

He pocketed his phone, checked his mirrors, and pulled a U-turn, heading the truck toward the outskirts of town. He hadn't been by the property in a while. He usually liked to drive by every few weeks to keep his goal at the forefront of his agenda, as well as to save Aunt Sonia from having to worry about it.

Nick slowed his speed as he neared the estate. The acreage of land sprawled around the house was dotted with trees and overgrown bushes. Yet he could picture with vivid clarity exactly how it would look when he'd transformed it into "The Logan Shelter for Women" — the manicured lawns, colorful gardens, and the children's playground he planned to build. The house itself would need extensive repairs, having been left empty for so many years. Luckily, he enjoyed that type of work.

He pulled to a stop at the curb in front of the rundown structure. Peg was right. The front door stood slightly ajar, and there was no car in sight. In all the times he'd been by to check, it had never been open. Maybe a homeless person had taken refuge inside. Or maybe kids were using it as a hangout. He turned off the engine and got out of the cab.

As a safety precaution, he pulled a crowbar from the back of his truck. With a quick prayer, he climbed the stairs, crossed the wide porch, and stepped through the front doorway.

He scanned the empty foyer, and his eyes narrowed at the distinct pattern of footprints visible in the dust on the floor. From the size of the shoe, his theory about teen intruders could be correct. He paused for a moment to listen for any movement that might give away their whereabouts — if they were still here. A muffled noise caught his attention. It seemed to come from upstairs. Senses on high alert, he crept up the staircase, one step at a time. Dust motes danced in the musty air. Cobwebs draped down from the corners above him.

When one stair creaked loudly beneath his foot, he stopped dead. Beads of sweat popped out on his forehead. Had they heard him? He stilled, holding his breath in the silence. Then an undistinguishable sound echoed through the empty structure from above.

Palms slicked with sweat, Nick continued

his slow ascent. When he reached the upper hall, he turned to the left, almost tiptoeing down the carpeted hallway. One door stood wide open and sounds like muffled weeping drifted out. Shaking off unsettling thoughts of rumors that the house was haunted, he tightened his grip on the crowbar and entered a child's room. Shock halted his feet. A woman knelt huddled on the ground beside a crib, her dark head bent over her hands. She rocked back and forth, weeping softly.

Nick lowered the crowbar to his side as his brain struggled to make sense of the details. The jeans . . . the shoes . . . the familiar brown jacket . . . "Lily?"

She raised a tear-streaked face to him. The pupils in her brown eyes were dilated and unfocused. "Nick? What are you doing here?" She seemed dazed.

"I was about to ask you the same thing." He leaned toward her, alarm spiking through him. "What's wrong? Why are you crying?"

She didn't answer, only lowered her head into her hands. His pulse thudded an erratic warning. He set the crowbar on a dusty dresser and went to kneel beside her.

"Lily, what is it?" He kept his voice as gentle as possible while trying to imagine what she was doing in this abandoned house that belonged to his cousin.

She wiped her face on the sleeve of her jacket and went to stand. He rose with her, steadying her with a hand under her elbow. Her eyes now appeared more focused, less hazy. She gripped his arm and looked up at him.

"This used to be my home," she said in a shaky voice.

Nick could only stare. She wasn't making sense.

"Bad things happened here, Nick." Her free hand flew up to grab her necklace like it was an anchor in a storm. Her eyes mirrored the same storm raging within her.

"I know," he said in his most soothing voice. "A terrible tragedy occurred here. But that was a long time ago." Maybe she'd been studying the history of the house. Sarah Jane said she'd been reviewing archived news articles at the library.

Her nostrils flared. "Not that long ago."

He frowned, an uneasy sensation rising in his chest. "What do you know about it?" Dread filled him, as if he knew the answer would be inconceivable.

Life altering.

"I lived through it."

The pain on her face revealed the truth of

her words.

"My name used to be Lily Strickland."

10

Lily stared out the window of Nick's truck while the scenery sped by in a blur. She couldn't stop the flood of memories crashing over her with relentless fury. Her body still shook with uncontrollable tremors. Standing in her old bedroom, she'd relived the terror she'd felt as a five-year-old girl facing a man with a gun. She re-experienced the horrific explosion of pain in her chest. Those feelings were as real to her now as the ridge of her scar. But more worrisome was her inability to recall the gunman's face. The fact that it could've been her biological father haunted her.

The motion of the truck stopped. Nick shifted into park and turned off the engine. "Come on. I know a place we can talk."

Lily allowed him to help her out of the vehicle. He kept an arm under her elbow as they walked. After a few minutes, the sound of rushing water penetrated her consciousness. As if coming out of a fog, Lily realized they were walking across a grassy area toward the river.

"I thought I'd show you our town's namesake," Nick said. "The falls are beautiful, even without the rainbow."

They followed the river until they rounded a bend, and the sheer majesty of Rainbow Falls hit her full force. She stopped to take in the sight, allowing the wonder of the cascading water to banish all the bad memories for the moment. The smell of the evergreen trees, the soothing gurgle of the water as it flowed, the sunlight glinting off the river, all acted as a gentle tonic to her soul.

"There's a log we can sit on over there." Nick pointed to a fallen tree near the water's edge.

After they sat, Nick pulled a bottle of water from the pocket of his jacket and handed it to her. She thanked him and took a long swallow to ease her parched throat.

"This is my favorite spot," he said. "I come here when I need to think or pray, to feel closer to God."

Lily concentrated on each minute detail of the landscape, hoping the numbness inside would last a little longer. Because if it didn't — if she allowed one hint of emotion to leak out — the floodgates would open, and she'd fall apart completely.

They sat in silence for a long time, until her muscles stiffened from her rigid posture. Nick must have a million questions, but he'd respected her privacy enough not to pry, to wait until she was ready to open up. The problem was she didn't have a clue how to begin.

"If you want to talk, I'm a good listener," Nick said quietly.

When she looked into his sincere blue eyes, every instinct told her she could trust him. She needed to tell someone about her past, about this horrific discovery. She'd borne the burden alone since that fateful night at her father's.

She licked her dry lips and exhaled. "I always knew I was adopted. My parents told me my family had died in a fire, and I'd been the only survivor. I found out a few weeks ago that wasn't entirely true. A tragedy took the lives of my family, but it wasn't an accident. They were murdered."

"How did you find out?"

She frowned. Why didn't he seem more shocked? "I found a newspaper clipping about the Rainbow Falls murders at my father's house. I didn't understand the connection until I found my birth certificate underneath." She took another quick swallow of water before twisting the cap back on. "When I realized I had a sister, I knew I had to find her."

She glanced over at Nick, his face a mask of resignation.

"Chloe's your sister," he whispered. "That's why you've taken such an interest in her."

She nodded. The sadness oozing out of him made her wish the answer could be different. "Did you know your cousin was adopted?"

"Yes. Chloe knows, too. She just doesn't know the details of her past." Alarm leapt into his eyes. "You're not going to tell her, are you?"

Lily jerked to her feet and moved to the edge of the river. The water cascaded into the pool below, the churning water mirroring her inner turmoil. Nick's simple question summed up her whole conflict. How could she rip Chloe's world apart with a story so horrific? Yet how could she remain silent?

"I'm not planning to say anything yet." She kept her back to him and sensed him rise from his perch on the log.

"But you will at some point?"

She wouldn't lie to him, not even to ease

his mind. "When the time is right, yes."
After several minutes of silence, she turned
to face him. "Did you know Chloe had a
sister?" The breeze pushed a strand of hair
across her face, catching in her eyelashes.
She reached up to pull it away as she waited
for Nick's reply.

He came toward her, stopping inches from
where she stood. "No, I didn't. I remember
hearing pieces of the story as a child. But
from what I understood, the whole family
had died — except for Chloe."

Lily's life had always been shadowed by
half-truths, secrets, and hypocrisy. Yet, in
the core of her being, she knew he spoke
the truth. She wanted to trust him — she
just wasn't certain she could yet.

Nick must have seen the struggle playing
across her face. He scrubbed a hand over
his chin. "My aunt may know more about it
than she's told me. But right now she's very
ill. I don't want to upset her by bringing up
that painful time."

Lily fought back a tide of disappointment.
She'd hoped to talk to Mrs. Martin to see
what she knew about the Stricklands. But
that would have to wait. Instead, she voiced
the question that haunted her. "The newspaper says I died. How is that possible when
it's not true?" She pressed her lips together

to stop the quivering.

Nick drew closer, and without hesitation, pulled her into his arms. "I have no idea, but I'm sure we can find out. Together."

She inhaled the male scent of him, relishing his warmth. Gradually his body heat helped dispel the chill that had enveloped her ever since she'd entered the house.

"If I help you, will you do something for me?" Nick asked.

She backed away to look at his face. "I'll try."

"Keep this between us for now. Please."

Lily's gaze moved past Nick to a sparrow as it flew from one branch to another above their heads. Was sharing her burden with Nick worth the loss of control she now felt? Still, she couldn't deny Nick's stake in the situation. "I guess I can do that. For now." She narrowed her eyes as a sudden question hit her. "What were you doing at the house anyway?"

"Peg called to say she saw the front door open. I thought maybe some neighborhood kids had broken in, but I must have forgotten to lock it the last time I was checking on it for Aunt Sonia."

She frowned. "I don't understand. What does your aunt have to do with the house?"

He shoved his hands deep into his pockets.

"When my aunt and uncle adopted Chloe, they become guardians of the Strickland estate, and Chloe's trust, until she turns eighteen."

Lily's mind whirled to keep up. "What trust?"

"The house and property, plus whatever money your parents left, all belong to Chloe. Or at least they will when she turns eighteen." He paused. "I guess now it will have to be divided in two." An air of suspicion hung in his voice.

"You make it sound like I'm here for the money."

He exhaled in a loud gust. "Look, I'm sorry. I'm having trouble processing all this."

She waved aside his apology, her mind still reeling. "How is your aunt going to explain this sudden inheritance to Chloe in a few weeks?"

"I have no idea."

They began to walk back along the riverbank in silence.

"I'm sorry," Nick said again after a few moments. "I've been thinking about Chloe and my aunt, and forgetting how hard this must be for you."

She sighed. "You have no idea." She shuddered as the visions began to intrude on her consciousness again. The screams of her brothers, gunshots echoing in the hallway, footsteps coming into the room where she was hiding in the closet . . .

"Do you remember getting shot?"

The gentleness of his voice nearly undid her tightly-held control.

"I don't want to talk about it." She jerked ahead across the grass as if she could outrun the memories. She sensed him come up beside her again. He took her by the arms, halting her steps, and drew her close.

"I want to help, Lily. For your sake as well as Chloe's."

The intensity of his gaze held her in place. Then, almost in slow motion, Nick bent toward her. His warm breath fanned her face as his lips hovered above hers. For one brief moment, Lily yearned to be transported beyond the pain, the loneliness, and the fear. To feel safe and cared for.

He's going to be a minister — just like your father. The thought hit her like a physical slap, awakening her out of the fog she'd been in, reminding her she couldn't afford to let her defenses down.

As though sensing her withdrawal, Nick stepped back and shoved his hands into his jacket pockets. His eyes shone with remorse. "I'm sorry. I seem to be doing everything wrong today."

She shook her head, sadness weighing down her shoulders. The wind whipped her hair around her face, and she pushed it back with a resigned sigh. "We don't belong together, Nick. We're too different."

"How so?"

"You're going to be a minister for one thing."

A scowl darkened his features. "What does that have to do with anything?"

She lifted her head, determination giving her strength. "I don't want any part of religion. I've had my fill of that hypocrisy, thanks to my father, and I never want to be part of that world again." Before he could say anything, she turned toward his truck, following the river's edge. A ball of emotion lodged in her chest — a toxic mixture of sorrow, regret, and longing.

"Wait one minute." Nick's footsteps pounded up beside her, but she kept up her quick pace until he reached out to grasp her arm. "Hold on. You lost me back there."

With quiet dignity, she turned to face him. "My father is a minister. I think that about sums it up."

His eyes turned dark with intensity. "I realize you have issues with your father, but I resent being tried and convicted by his mistakes. Don't I deserve to be judged on my own merit?"

She felt herself softening and stiffened her backbone along with her resolve. "To be honest, I can't find one fault in you, Nick. I'm the one who's flawed. I'm damaged goods. You don't need that in your life."

"We're all flawed, Lily. In one way or another."

She held up a hand to ward off his words. If he knew the real her — the true state of her sinfulness — his opinion of her would shatter. "I'm not worthy to be involved with someone as good as you. Believe me, your congregation would never tolerate it."

She could feel his frustration as he ran his hands through his hair, leaving it standing up in golden tufts.

"Aren't you getting ahead of yourself?" he finally asked, shoulders sagging.

She shook her head. The wind tugged at her jacket and hair as Nick's sadness tugged at her heart. "Just trying to save us both a lot of pain." She took a shaky breath. "Now I'd like to go home, please."

Nick sat at the kitchen table the next morning nursing his third cup of coffee, necessary due to the sleepless night he'd spent mulling over the enormity of Lily's situation. He still couldn't believe Chloe had a

sister. She would be thrilled to find out —
if only he could tell her without having to
reveal the tragic circumstances of her
family's deaths.

Without upsetting Aunt Sonia.

Nick had only been eight or nine at the
time and remembered very little about
Chloe coming into the family, except for his
aunt's and uncle's excitement at getting a
new baby. Years later, he'd overheard his
mother and aunt discussing the "terrible
tragedy" of Chloe's family, but the details
had been vague. He took a long swig of
strong coffee, vowing to find some other
way to help Lily discover the truth around
her family's deaths.

He scrubbed a hand over his stubbly jaw,
recalling how he'd almost kissed her by the
falls. Not one of his proudest moments.
Comforting her was one thing. Taking
advantage when she was off kilter and
vulnerable was entirely another.

Lily's words haunted him. No wonder she
was so leery of getting involved with a future
minister. Her father had tainted her whole
view of God and religion. How could he
ever undo that type of damage?

The phone rang, pulling Nick out of his
tortured thoughts.

"Hey, slacker. Must be nice to sleep in."

Nick chuckled. Mike always had a way of making him laugh. The gruff man's gentle humor had helped a confused boy take one step away from breaking the law. Without Mike, who knew where he'd be today? "Try no sleep at all and a pot full of caffeine."

"What's got your boxers in a twist?" Mike snorted. "Or should I say who?"

Nick ignored the jab. "Family stuff. Got any news for me?

"Not what you're hoping, I'm afraid."

Now what?

"The only trace of Lily Draper I could find was that she worked at a bar called Hank's Tavern. When I tried to follow up, nobody would talk, except to say she'd recently quit."

"No family in the area? A father maybe?" Nick wondered if Lily had moved away from the area where her father lived, given their estrangement.

"Nope. And none in the nearby towns. Did she tell you about any other family members?"

Nick shoved the cordless phone between his ear and one shoulder as he took his cup and plate to the sink. "Her mother's dead. Her father's a minister, but they don't get along. Hasn't had any contact in years."

There was a moment of silence on the

other end. "I hate to say this, buddy, but maybe *she's* the wild card here. A minister is usually a solid citizen. And the place where Miss Draper was working isn't exactly the pillar of the community, if you get my drift."

Even though Mike's remarks made sense, Nick bristled. "You wouldn't think that if you knew her the way I do." He ran a stream of water over the dishes and flicked off the coffeemaker. He'd had enough caffeine for the time being.

"Is there something you aren't telling me?"

For a minute, Nick considered telling Mike the whole story and asking his advice about what legal steps Lily could take to get herself declared "undead." But, instinctively, he knew Lily wouldn't want him to say anything, and he wasn't willing to fracture the fragile trust that existed between them. "I've found out some things about Lily on my own."

"What kind of things?" The suspicious cop-voice had kicked in. Nick could picture his friend sitting in his office, scratching his salt-and-pepper goatee, scowling into the phone.

"I can't say. You'll have to trust my judgment on this." He leaned back against the kitchen counter, legs crossed.

Mike growled on the other end. "Hope you know what you're doing, pal. Because my instincts are telling me there's a lot more to this woman that she's not telling you."

"Yeah, well, thanks for the effort. I appreciate it."

"I'll keep digging to see what else I can find." He paused. "Now to totally change the subject. You still want me to talk at the next youth meeting?"

Nick grinned into the receiver. "Definitely. It never hurts to put the fear of God, or the fear of the law, into teenagers."

11

Lily's alarm went off, dragging her out of sleep. With a groan, she hit the OFF button and swung her legs over the side of the bed, only to find her head swimming. The lack of sleep last night must be catching up with her.

Even a hot shower didn't help. Nausea rolled in her stomach, but she forced herself to get ready for work. She had to go in. It was her turn to open the shop — the first time she'd been entrusted with the task. Two days ago, Peg had called her into the backroom for a chat. Filled with trepidation over some imagined transgression, Lily had nervously awaited Peg's lecture.

But instead of the expected reprimand, Peg had praised her work and rewarded her by offering her full-time hours along with a pay raise. Giddy with relief, Lily had accepted, thankful she no longer had to find a second job before next month's rent came due.

After her employer's show of good faith, Lily could not afford to be ill. She couldn't — *wouldn't* — let Peg down.

She ate no breakfast, stopping only to buy a cup of herbal tea at the diner on the way. By eight thirty, Lily sat at the reception desk, head in her hands, hoping Maxi would be on time for her shift and wishing the room would stop spinning around her. If this kept up, she'd have to cancel Chloe's tutoring session that afternoon.

Lily looked at her watch and groaned. Maxi wasn't due for half an hour yet. Maybe keeping busy would help. She tried to muster the energy to make her way to the storage room in back and top up the towels and other supplies for when the shop opened. But as she stood, the room spiraled around her and a wave of nausea rose in her throat. Clutching a hand to her mouth, she raced to the bathroom, barely reaching the toilet before her stomach heaved.

When the retching stopped, she wiped her face and flushed the toilet. Her body trembled, perspiration beading on her brow. She tried to pull herself up to the sink, but her weakened limbs collapsed beneath her. Sweating and shaking, she sank to the floor and curled into a fetal position. The room became darker and darker until nothing remained except the cold tiles against her cheek.

The incessant ringing of the phone disturbed Nick in the middle of studying. He slapped his pen down onto the desk and blasted out a loud sigh at the interruption.

"This had better be important," he grumbled.

"Nick, it's Maxi. Can you come down to Peg's right away?"

The panic in her voice had Nick's senses on instant alert. "What's wrong?"

"It's Lily. She's out cold on the floor. I don't know what to do. I can't move her."

Nick jumped to his feet, knocking papers to the ground. "Call Doc Anderson. I'm on my way."

The short drive over to Peg's was a blur. He burst through the front door, saw Maxi waving from the back, and sprinted over. Lily lay sprawled on the bathroom floor, a rolled towel under her head. The small area reeked of vomit.

"Has she come-around at all?"

"No, but she's breathing OK." Maxi's huge eyes were wracked with worry. "I didn't know who to call."

171

Nick checked Lily's pulse. "I'm glad you thought of me. Did you get a hold of the doc?"

"He's on his way."

"Good. Can you get a cold cloth for her head? She's burning up."

Maxi bounded off, returning seconds later with a wet towel, which Nick used to gently wipe Lily's pale face. An irrational fear gripped his insides and twisted hard as he administered the cloth — a fear he knew stemmed from the impotence he'd felt as he cared for his mother day after day on her sickbed, unable to do anything but watch her die.

Please, Lord, let this be a minor illness.

A powerful instinct to protect her surged through his chest. He scooped her limp form off the cold bathroom floor and carried her out to a cushioned bench in the waiting area. Maxi followed, hovering near Lily's head while Nick knelt beside her and continued to bathe her face.

A few minutes later, the bell jangled as Percy Anderson bustled through the door. The large man dabbed a handkerchief on his moist, balding head and then stuffed the cloth back into his jacket pocket.

Nick stood to greet him. "Hey, Doc. Thanks for coming so fast."

"Sounded urgent." He pulled out a stetho-scope to listen to Lily's heart, took her temperature, and then clucked his tongue. "She's got a high fever and her heart rate's erratic."

"Is it the flu?" Maxi clutched her arms around her middle, a worried frown creas-ing her forehead.

"Could be. There's a pretty bad one going around right now, and she's got all the symptoms. I'm giving her a shot to keep her from vomiting. Then she'll need lots of rest and fluids."

He pulled a syringe out of his leather bag and asked Maxi to roll up Lily's sleeve.

Nick paced the reception area as Doc administered the needle. "What now?" He hated feeling so helpless.

"It's not serious enough for the hospital, but she'll need careful monitoring for the next couple of days." Doc looked up at them as he repacked his bag. "Dehydration is a big risk with this type of illness."

Nick scrubbed a hand over his jaw and made a quick decision. "I can do it. I'm studying for exams, which I can do any-where."

Doc Anderson raised an eyebrow. "She has no family nearby?"

Nick shook his head. "Only an estranged

father somewhere up north." Doc had to be thinking about the propriety of the situation. The image of a scowling Reverend Ted came to mind, and Nick's shoulders slumped. No matter how innocent the situation, some people would misconstrue it. For the sake of Lily's reputation, as well as his own, he had to set his feelings aside and make sure his actions were above reproach.

"Maxi will help me when she's not working, won't you, Max?" He sent her a pleading look, grateful she lived so close to Lily.

"Of course. And I'm sure Chloe will help, too."

Still, that didn't solve the immediate issue of getting Lily home. "Could you call Peg and explain the situation? See if she can cover the shop while you help me with Lily."

"Sure. Give me five minutes."

While they waited, Doc monitored Lily's pulse one more time and jotted some notes on a small pad of paper. "Remember to take her temperature every hour. If it goes up much higher, call me immediately. We may have to take her to Kingsville Memorial Hospital if we can't keep it down."

Nick nodded. "I will."

Maxi returned. "We're good to go. Peg's heading over right away, and I've rescheduled my morning clients."

A measure of relief loosened Nick's tense muscles. As crazy as it sounded, he was glad he wouldn't bear the responsibility for Lily alone.

Doc buttoned his jacket. "Keep me posted on her condition. I'll drop by later today to see how she's doing."

"Thanks, Doc, for all your help."

"Not at all, my boy. That's what I'm here for." He picked up his bag and walked out the front door.

Nick turned to Maxi. "Thanks, Max. I feel better knowing Lily will have both of us looking out for her."

Maxi nodded, her expression serious. "She's my friend, too. I want to help."

"Let's start by getting her home." He lifted Lily's inert figure, gently cradling her head against his shoulder.

Maxi rushed to open the door for him. "I'll get her things and lock up. Be right behind you." She patted his arm as he stepped outside. "Don't worry, Logan. We'll get her through this."

Nick walked to his truck, put Lily inside, and reclined the seat, using his jacket to pillow her head. As he buckled her in, he tried to force the image of his sick mother out of his head. He told himself Lily only had the flu, and it wasn't that serious, but his anxiety level refused to listen. On the way over to the apartment, he prayed her temperature would not go up even one more degree.

Nick jolted awake from some kind of nightmare, his heart pounding, his mouth dry. In the dim light, it took him a second to figure out where he was, until his gaze fell on the still figure under the bedcovers. He was supposed to be watching Lily while Maxi caught a few winks on the couch, but he'd dozed off. Nick blinked, rubbed his eyes, and stretched. His stiff back felt like it would crack in two if he straightened up fully. *That's what you get for sleeping on a chair, Einstein.*

He reached over to feel Lily's forehead. What if her temperature had risen while he was asleep? He'd never forgive himself. To his relief, she was no worse.

Nick hobbled to the bathroom where he moistened a washcloth, then made his way back to the bedroom. For a moment, he simply stared at Lily as she lay beneath the patterned blue comforter, her dark hair spread over the pillow. His heart expanded in his chest as he gazed at her. Against the pallor of her skin, her long lashes created shadows on her cheek. Her full lips, usually rosy, were cracked from dryness. He remembered the washcloth and bent to wipe her face in gentle strokes.

It had been more than twenty-four hours now, and she hadn't awakened for more than a few minutes at a time. When she did, she hadn't seemed coherent, and Nick had called Doc Anderson. Patient man that he was, Doc had come over twice to check on her. "She's holding her own" was all he'd say. Not exactly the reassurance Nick needed.

Lord, grant Your healing graces to Lily. Please let her get better — soon.

He squeezed the cloth out into a bowl on the nightstand and laid it gently on her forehead. The muted glow from the lamp cast soft shadows over her face. Despite the violet smudges under her eyes, she was indescribably beautiful to him. The unbearable temptation to touch her proved too great, and he brushed a finger down her cheek. Her skin was softer than the satin of her pillowcase. He closed his eyes, unable to deny the truth of his feelings any longer.

For better or worse, he was falling in love with Lily.

He bent his head and murmured a few more prayers. As usual, prayer gave him strength, filled him with purpose. Lily *would* get better and when she did, he'd make up for lost time. He was determined to win her heart — for him and for God — no matter how long it took.

An incessant knock on Lily's front door forced his attention back to the present. Who could that be? Doc wouldn't be back until later. When the banging continued, Nick went to answer it. His stomach sank to his shoes at the sight of a somber Reverend Ted Baker on the landing. This would not look good to his mentor. Not good at all. Thank goodness he'd had the foresight to ensure he had a chaperone.

He swallowed his apprehension and managed a smile. "Hello, Ted. Glad you could come by. Lily could use some extra prayers right now."

Ted's mouth flapped open and shut. Before Ted could say a word, Nick ushered him inside.

"She's still asleep. Barely opened her eyes in the last twenty-four hours. We're waiting for the fever to break." He glanced into the living room where Maxi stirred on the couch, pushing the blanket back. "It's Reverend Baker, Maxi. He's here to see Lily."

She yawned. "Hello, Reverend Baker."

Ted's eyes widened. "Hello, Maxine."

She rose from the couch and stretched. "I'll put on a pot of coffee."

"Thanks. We won't be long." At least Nick hoped they wouldn't be.

He guided Ted down the hall to Lily's room and prayed she wouldn't choose this moment to regain consciousness. Seeing a minister in black shirt and white collar standing over her could frighten her.

Ted removed his hat and stood twisting it in his hands.

"If you don't have your prayer book, I can lend you mine," Nick offered, grateful he'd left his on Lily's dresser.

He held it out to Ted, who waited a beat before accepting the book. He hung his hat over the bedpost, opened the missal and began to read. Nick bowed his head, hoping he'd dodged a bullet. But when Ted finished, he handed Nick the book and motioned him outside. "I'd like a word with you, please."

"Of course."

Nick led the minister to the living room. They'd just sat down when Maxi came in with a tray of coffee mugs, a carton of creamer, and the coffeepot. She set it on the table and straightened. "I'm going to run downstairs and change into some clean clothes. Give you two a chance to talk." She shot Nick a look that seemed to warn him to behave himself. "Back in a few minutes."

"Thank you, Maxine."

Nick rubbed his damp hands on the legs of his jeans as Maxi left and waited for Ted to start the conversation, praying for the grace to handle the situation well.

"I hope you realize talk is flying all over town." Ted's mouth formed a grim line.

Pouring coffee in two cups, Nick pretended not to understand his implication. "I imagine it made quite a story — what with Lily passing out cold in Peg's shop."

"That's not the part people are gossiping about." Ted's accusing stare could peel paint off the walls.

"Isn't gossiping a sin?" Nick struggled to control the annoyance that percolated as strong as the coffee he was pouring.

"I'm only repeating what the community is saying so you can rectify the situation."

Nick reached for the cream and sighed. Maybe coffee wasn't the best idea. His nerves were already frayed around the edges. "OK, Ted. Why don't you tell me what's going on?"

The man fingered the brim of the hat on his lap. "Folks are saying you've been here with the Draper woman . . . day and night."

Nick's gaze remained steady. "They're

partly right. I have been here since yesterday, along with Maxi, Chloe, and Peg Hanley." He paused to enunciate the next part. "I've never been alone with Lily. Not that it matters since she's been *unconscious* the whole time."

Ted had the good sense to look uncomfortable as he refused the coffee Nick offered. "Nonetheless, this whole situation doesn't sit well with the folks around here."

"You mean it doesn't sit well with Sarah Jane." Nick realized his tone was as cold as the carton of creamer he held in his hand. He thought he'd made his position clear to her in their last conversation, but apparently, she'd chosen to ignore him.

Ted's agitation showed in the tick of his jaw. "She's not the only one who's upset. The whole women's auxiliary is up in arms."

Nick fought to keep calm. "You tell the ladies I'm helping a person in need. Isn't that one of our Christian mandates? To minister to the sick?"

Ted shot to his feet and shook his finger at Nick. "Don't twist the words of the Bible, young man." Shoving the Fedora on his head, he proceeded into the hall, turning to pin Nick with an ominous glare. "Mark my words, Nicholas. If you're not careful, this girl will be your undoing."

12

Lily's head felt as if someone had wrapped it in cotton, muffling her senses. She attempted to open her eyes, but her lids refused to cooperate. Heavy with fatigue, her whole body ached and burned. It hurt to take air into her lungs. Her dry lips stung, but the effort to do anything about it proved too much for her to attempt.

The next time she drifted into consciousness, she became aware of a cooling sensation on her face. Then someone spooned ice chips into her mouth. The chilly wetness felt wonderful on her tongue. When she managed to open her eyes at last, the glow of a bedside lamp made it hard to focus. She blinked several times before she adjusted to the light, still unable to tell if it were day or night. Realizing she was in her own bedroom, she attempted to pull herself to a sitting position. The effort left her gasping for air.

"Whoa." Strong arms guided her gently back against the pillows. "Take it easy now."

When the room stopped reeling, Lily squinted. Nick's face peered at her, a mirror of anxiety. He held a glass of water to her lips, which she sipped, grateful for the cool lubrication.

A myriad of questions charged through her brain. How had she ended up in bed with the weight of a brick on her chest and Nick bringing her water?

"What happened?" Her voice sounded like a rusty hinge.

Nick set the glass on the nightstand. "You took sick at work. Maxi found you and called Doc Anderson." He pulled the chair closer to the bed and perched on the edge.

"Oh." She had a vague recollection of feeling ill at work. "Why are you here?"

Nick leaned his elbows on his thighs and locked his fingers together. "Maxi called me. She was worried and didn't know what else to do."

Lily tried to make her sluggish brain work. She pushed some stray hair off her face. "How long . . . ?"

"Almost forty-eight hours. But the good news is your fever is finally down. Can I get you anything?"

She nodded, fighting the overwhelming

drowsiness that swamped her. "Some juice please."

"Coming right up."

When she awoke again, she found Nick dozing on the chair by her bed. Once her eyes focused, she took the opportunity to study him. Her heart swelled at the vulnerability he showed as he slept. His tussled blond hair stood up in several places, and a few days' growth of stubble shadowed his jaw. Why was he taking care of her like this — like she mattered to him?

As if sensing her scrutiny, Nick roused to life. He opened his eyes and stared right into hers. Lily dropped her gaze to the blankets, allowing a fall of hair to hide her discomfort.

Nick stretched as he rose from the chair. "How are you feeling now?"

"Better, I think."

His face broke into a smile which made her senses reel.

"That's good news." He reached over to the nightstand and picked up a glass of orange juice. "You never did get the drink you wanted." He helped her sit up and held the glass to her lips.

She took a long swallow before slumping back onto the pillows. "Thank you."

"You're welcome." He set down the cup.

"You've had us all very worried, you know."

She frowned. "Who's us?"

He bent to straighten the blankets. "Doc Anderson, Maxi, Chloe, Peg — they've all been here." He checked his watch. "In fact, Peg just left for work, and Maxi is cleaning up the kitchen."

Gratitude, embarrassment, and disbelief warred within her. "I don't know what to say."

"How about telling me what you'd like to eat. You must be hungry after two days."

"You've been here that long?"

He gave a sheepish grin. "Yeah, well, it gave me a chance to catch up on my studying."

Words failed her. Not since her mother had nursed her through the chicken pox had she felt so cared for. It was more than she could comprehend.

"Think I'll whip you up some chicken soup," Nick said. "That's always good when you're sick."

A while later, he returned with a tray. Lily studied him from under her lashes as she drank the soup. Dark shadows under his eyes told her he hadn't had a decent sleep in a while. A twinge of guilt surfaced with the realization that she was responsible.

"That was good. Thank you." She patted

185

her mouth with a napkin.

"If you like that, wait 'til you try my homemade turkey soup." He bent to pick up the tray, shooting her a mischievous grin that made her head spin.

"Quit trying to impress the girl, for heaven's sake."

Color bled up Nick's neck as he scowled at Maxi standing in the doorway.

She sauntered in and plopped down on the end of the bed. Her hair, which today contained several streaks of purple, was slicked back behind her ears. "Nice to see you awake again, Lil."

"Nice to be awake." Lily looked from the cross-legged girl on her bed to the man standing awkwardly at her side. What had she done to deserve friends like these?

Maybe God did care about her after all. Her throat constricted at the thought.

Nick plucked the tray of dirty dishes off the dresser. "I'll go and let you two talk." He practically ran out the door.

Maxi let out a long laugh, making her earrings dance. "It's funny to see Nick out of control when he's *never* out of control."

"What do you mean?"

Maxi shook her head. "You don't have a clue, do you? Nick's so infatuated with you, he can't see straight."

Lily's mouth fell open. She shook her head in silent denial.

"When I found you on the floor at Peg's, he broke every speed record getting over there, and he's barely left your side since." Maxi sighed. "If that's not devotion, I don't know what is."

Lily's lip trembled at Maxi's implication. "I didn't want this," she whispered. Her eyes darted to the open doorway as if Nick might appear any moment.

Maxi's smile faded. "What's the matter? Nick's a great guy."

Lily reached over to clutch her arm. "There's no future for us. He needs a good woman to be a minister's wife. And that's not me."

Maxi leaned forward on the bed. "I won't let you talk like that, Lily Draper. You're as good a person as anyone else. And just as deserving of happiness."

The words hit Lily like a slap in the face, shocking her with a truth she'd never allowed herself to examine. *She didn't believe herself worthy of anything good in her life.*

Tears burned at the back of her throat. Weakness, both physical and emotional, overwhelmed her.

At that very moment Nick appeared. He took one look at Lily's face and strode to her side. "What's wrong?" Frowning, he placed his palm on her forehead. "Are you in pain?"

Lily swatted away his hand, unable to cope with his nearness.

Nick turned accusing eyes to Maxi. "What did you do to upset her?"

"I'm sorry." Maxi looked miserable. "I didn't mean to —"

"It's not her fault," Lily whispered.

Nick crossed his arms and scowled at Maxi. "Lily needs peace and quiet. No more talking."

Maxi shoved off the bed. "Fine. But I'm supposed to be relieving you. You need to go home."

"I'm not going anywhere —"

"Please stop," was all Lily could manage before sinking under the covers, waves of exhaustion washing over her.

Nick hustled Maxi out the door by the arm. "We'll settle this out here. Lily, you get some rest."

When Lily awoke next, Chloe was seated on the chair with a textbook on her lap, twirling a strand of hair around her finger. Lily breathed a sigh of thanks that Nick was nowhere in sight.

"How's the studying coming?"

Chloe jumped, almost dropped her book,

and laughed. "You're awake. Feeling better?"

"I think so."

When Lily struggled to sit up, Chloe rushed to help her with the pillows. "We were all so worried. Doc was here at least three times. And Nick —"

Lily held up her hand to ward off another account of Nick's saintly qualities.

"What's wrong?" Chloe's forehead wrinkled.

"Could you help me to the bathroom? I'd like to take a shower."

Chloe's puzzled expression changed to one of purpose. "Good idea. That'll make you feel better."

A hot shower and clean clothes gave Lily a new lease on life. Maybe she'd live after all. When she emerged from the steamy bathroom, an enticing aroma lured her out to the kitchen where Chloe stood stirring a large pot on the stove.

"What smells so good?" Lily twisted her damp hair into a braid.

"Nick's turkey soup. He had some in his freezer at home and dropped it off earlier." Chloe smiled as she ladled the liquid into two bowls. "I'll bring a tray to your room."

Lily wanted to argue she'd been in bed long enough, but her weakened limbs betrayed her. Chloe followed her into the bedroom with the tray. Once Lily was settled, Chloe returned with her own food, and together they shared French bread with the homemade soup. It was the most delicious meal Lily had ever tasted. "Nick is a great cook."

"Yeah. Maybe he'll make this for the people in his shelter."

"His what?" Lily's hand stilled on the spoon.

"Hasn't he told you about his plan?"

Lily shook her head.

Chloe tore a piece of bread in half. "He wants to open a home for abused women and children."

"Because of his father," Lily murmured, recalling his confession the night he'd hauled Marco Messini off her. She understood immediately how perfect this would be for him. To provide others with the protection he'd needed when he was a child.

"He told you about that?"

"A little, yes."

Chloe wiped her mouth with a napkin. "He has a property in mind for the shelter. An abandoned house that's been in our family for years. I don't know much about it."

Reality clicked in Lily's brain, like the

tumblers of a lock falling into place. That's why Nick was at the Strickland house that day. Why hadn't he told her the whole truth?

Chloe rose to put her dishes on the dresser before removing Lily's tray. She fixed Lily with a curious gaze. "I hear you and Maxi had a bit of a . . . disagreement yesterday."

Suddenly zapped of energy, Lily sagged back against the pillows. Her eyelids begged to close. "It was nothing."

"Maxi didn't seem to think so. She was pretty upset."

Lily's fought the cowardly urge to hide under the covers. "It wasn't her fault. I over-reacted to her pushing Nick on me. I'll apologize when I see her."

Chloe stacked more dirty glasses on the tray, watching her. "Nick's getting to you, isn't he?"

Faced with Chloe's frank amber gaze, Lily found she couldn't deny it. "I guess so."

"Why does that make you so miserable? I'd be thrilled if a wonderful guy like Nick was interested in me." Shadows from the bedside lamp danced over Chloe's pretty features.

Lily sank farther into the bed and sighed. "I'm no good at relationships, Chloe. Mine always end in disaster. And I care about Nick too much to put him through all that

191

ugliness." Her bones melted into the mattress. "We're better off as friends."

Chloe studied her for a moment. "Maybe you've been dating the wrong guys."

Though Lily found taking romantic advice from a teenager somewhat ironic, she appreciated Chloe's efforts. "I'm afraid my father has ruined me from ever having a normal relationship. Proven by all the jerks I've been involved with since I left home."

Chloe came to sit beside her on the bed and laid a sympathetic hand on her arm. "I think you're scared to try a decent guy for a change. Scared it could actually work out, and you might even be happy."

Lily shook her head as a wave of sadness washed over her. "I haven't been happy since my mother died. At least, not until I met you . . . and Maxi." *And Nick.*

"Well, it's a start. I'll be praying for you, Lily. That God will heal your wounds." Chloe reached over to envelop her in a warm embrace.

The clean scent of Chloe's perfume filled Lily's senses. She hugged her back, her heart squeezing with love. And for one glittering moment in the arms of her sister, Lily allowed herself to believe happiness was an actual possibility.

13

Doc Anderson came back to check on Lily the next morning. Though she'd been told he'd taken care of her for two days while she was in a semi-conscious state, this was the first time she'd actually talked to him. His soothing manner and kind air soon put her at ease. After checking her vital signs, Doc pronounced her ninety percent recovered, but recommended another full day of rest.

"If you push yourself too soon, you'll end up in the hospital," he said. "You don't want to ruin all our hard work, do you?"

The twinkle in his eyes allowed Lily to relax. "No, sir." She smiled and settled back against the pillows, amazed a modern doctor made house calls. She found herself liking this gentle, jolly man. Still, could she trust him enough to question him about her family's tragedy?

"When you do go back to work, start with

short shifts. You'll tire quickly at first." He packed his stethoscope into his bag and snapped it shut.

"I will."

"Excellent. Glad to see you looking so much better, my dear." He turned toward the door.

"Wait. Can I ask you something?" The words were out before Lily could take them back. But she couldn't pass up this opportunity to see what Doc Anderson might know about the Strickland murders.

He stilled, his hand on the doorknob. "Certainly."

"I understand you've been the doctor here for a long time."

He turned to face her. "Close to thirty years. Why?"

She swallowed back her nerves and willed her voice to remain steady. "Were you called to the Strickland house the night of the murders?"

His brows shot together, creating a wreath of wrinkles on his forehead. "I was there, along with the paramedics, the coroner, and the police. Why? What do you know about the Stricklands?"

She weighed her answer carefully. "They were . . . relatives of mine. One of the reasons I came to Rainbow Falls was to find out more about what happened to them."

A guarded look shuttered his face. "I see." He came back into the room and lowered himself onto the chair by her bed. "I don't know how much help I can be."

She licked her lips that had suddenly gone dry. "From what I've been told, the mother, father, and two boys were shot, one girl was seriously injured and a baby survived unharmed." Nerves swam through her system. She wanted to trust this man with the truth, but fear held her back.

"That's right," Doc said. "Saddest thing I ever saw."

"Is it true Mr. Strickland was responsible for the murders?" Lily blurted the question before she had time to formulate her words.

"You'd have to ask the police."

"But in your opinion," she pressed, "do *you* think he did it?" She leaned forward and waited for his answer.

Sadness dripped over his features. "Yes. I believe David Strickland was responsible."

The air *whooshed* out of her lungs as she sank back. Her own father had put that bullet in her.

Doc Anderson rose to leave, his grim expression indicating he was unwilling to continue the conversation.

"Someone adopted the baby, but what

happened to the other daughter?"

Doc Anderson's expression changed to one of puzzlement. "You mean little Addie?"

She nodded. "No one seems to know what happened to her."

Doc gave her a hard look and suddenly Lily realized he must have seen her scar. Would he figure out who she was?

"The child was still alive, but barely. They took her to the hospital in Kingsville." He paused. "She died a few weeks later."

Lily's fisted hands tightened on the blankets. It was true then. Everyone believed she had died from her injuries.

"I'm sorry if you've been hoping your relative was alive," he said kindly, "because that's not the case." He picked up his bag. "Good day, Lily."

Nick opened the door to Lily's apartment, juggling a casserole dish and his keys. He found her standing in the kitchen stirring a cup of tea, her hair swept off her face in a loose bun. Even in an old sweat suit, she lit up the room.

"Nice to see you on your feet."

She whirled around, hand at her throat. "Nick. You scared me half to death."

"Sorry, I'll have to remember to knock now that you're no longer comatose." He grinned, his relief at seeing her so improved making him giddy. "I'm glad you didn't try to go in to work today."

She plucked the teabag from her cup and threw it in the trash. "Not quite up to that yet. Doc said I could go back for a few hours tomorrow."

"That's good news." He held up the dish in front of him. "I thought you might be getting sick of soup, so I brought some homemade mac and cheese."

"You have to stop spoiling me like this, Mr. Logan."

The sound of her light laughter did crazy things to his pulse.

"Maybe I like spoiling you." He opened the fridge and placed the casserole inside, then stuffed his keys into his pant pocket.

Lily watched him, cup in hand, a solemn look on her face. Devoid of all makeup, the pureness of her inner beauty shone through. Nick couldn't fathom how she viewed herself as a bad person.

"Could we talk for a few minutes?" she asked.

"Sure." He grabbed a bottle of water and followed her into the living room, where he took a seat beside her on his old green couch.

"I need to ask you about something Chloe

told me." She curled one leg underneath her.

Her somber expression sent warning bells off in his head. "Go ahead."

"Chloe said you want to open a shelter for women."

"That's right." *So far, so good.*

"Which is totally admirable. I understand how important that would be to you because of your childhood."

Nick sensed a major "but" coming and chose his words with care. "Exactly. I want to provide a haven for victims of abuse — something my mother and I never had."

Her brown eyes were direct and honest. "Why didn't you tell me you're planning to use the Strickland house for your shelter? That's why you were there that day, wasn't it?"

Nick was momentarily stunned. He had no idea Chloe knew anything about the property. "Chloe told you that?"

Lily cupped the mug in her hands. "She told me you had an abandoned house in mind. I just put it together."

Relief coursed through him. Chloe didn't know the gruesome details of her family history. Not yet anyway. On the other hand, he had to explain his actions to Lily without ruining the delicate trust that had developed between them. He twisted the cap off the bottle. "I'm sorry I wasn't completely up front with you. That day, I was too busy trying to process the fact that the house had been your childhood home. I didn't think it appropriate to tell you my plans right then. Especially since you'll now be a co-owner with Chloe."

Her eyes widened. "I never thought of that."

"Look, don't worry about the house. If it's God's will, He'll help me find a place when the time is right. That's a few years off yet anyways."

She took a sip of her tea, silent for several seconds, as if digesting his words. "How will you run a church and a shelter?"

He took her interest in his future plans as a positive sign. "I'm not sure. I may have to hire someone to manage it if I don't have time to do both."

She nodded. "I wish there'd been a decent shelter when I left home. Things might've been a lot different for me."

The pain on her face swamped Nick with sympathy, and he fought the urge to move closer to her. "Where did you go when you left your father's?"

Maybe she'd share some of her past with him, now that she trusted him more.

She shifted on the couch to set her tea on the side table. "At first I stayed with a friend from school until her older brother started making moves on me. By then, I was working at a donut shop, and the lady there let me rent a room from her. That didn't last long either. She hated my boyfriend and wouldn't let him come over." She paused, and her gaze slid away.

He sensed her discomfort, but he needed to know all she'd been through in order to understand her better. "What did you do then?" He took a pull of water from the bottle.

She picked at her sleeve. "Danny had his own place, so I moved in with him."

Nick clenched his jaw together, trying to hide his dismay at the thought of such a young girl having to choose between the streets and living with some low-life boyfriend. "I take it things didn't work out," he said carefully.

She shook her head, tucking a wisp of hair behind one ear. "Danny got involved with drugs. I ended up moving in with another guy I worked with. I thought Todd was a friend, but he wasn't much better." Her troubled gaze lit on his face for a second and then skittered away. "You sure you want to hear all this?"

A band tightened around Nick's chest, and he squeezed the bottle in his hand. For both their sakes, he had to. "What happened next?"

She drew her knees up under her chin. With no makeup and her hair coming loose from the bun and falling softly around her face, she looked as innocent as a child.

"Todd got drunk one night, and when I wouldn't do what he wanted" — a flush spread over her face — "he beat me up and threw me out."

Nick's free hand curled into a white-knuckled fist on his lap. The thought of anyone beating Lily made him want to forget his Christian beliefs and show the jerk just what it felt like to be a victim.

"I eventually got a better job at a tavern," Lily continued. "The owner, Hank, was a decent guy. He made sure no one bothered me. The tips were great, and I was able to rent a small apartment. It wasn't much, but at least it was mine."

Nick's own childhood seemed idyllic compared to this brave girl out in the world on her own, facing danger and depravity. "What changed?"

She shrugged, her eyes trained on the floor. "The usual. I got involved with another loser. I loaned Curtis money a few times, which he never repaid. Then one night he came over, spoiling for a fight. He wanted more money, but I didn't have any since he'd already drained my account. So he got rough. Put a hole in the living room wall. The landlord freaked out and had me evicted." The death grip of her hands clenched around her knees belied her matter-of-fact tone.

Nick couldn't stay seated. He rose and paced to the other side of the small room. "What about your father? Did you ever go to him for help?"

Lily's face hardened, her lips pressed into a thin line. "Once. But he refused. Called me a whore and told me never to come back again."

"I'm so sorry," Nick whispered. His heart wrenched with pain for her. Rejected by her father, she'd had no one in the world to trust or love. He longed to offer her comfort, but her body language screamed "do not touch."

"No wonder you're skeptical of religion. Sounds like your father has a twisted version."

Lily pushed to her feet. "I don't want to talk about my father." She snatched up her cup and strode out to the kitchen.

His mood plummeted. He'd tried so hard

to say the right thing, but he'd still upset her. He found her at the sink, rinsing the cup with shaking hands.

"Lily." He moved toward her, fueled by a need to show her how much he cared. To make her understand she was no longer alone. He came up behind her and rested his hands on her shoulders. "I hope you know how much I . . . we all . . . care about you. It can never make up for what you've been through, but . . ."

Her muscles stiffened beneath his palms. Then she pulled away and turned to face him. "I appreciate everything you've done for me, Nick. Really I do. I've never had friends like you before." She took another step back. "And I'd like to keep it that way."

Nick straightened, feeling the sting of rejection but recognizing the cause. She simply wasn't ready for anything more. The fear in her eyes told him that. "I understand," he said at last. "Just know I'm here if you need anything."

"Thank you. And thanks for the macaroni."

"You're welcome." He forced himself to resist the overwhelming urge to touch her cheek, to kiss away the sorrow on her face. "Take it easy, OK?"

She nodded, avoiding eye contact.

His soul heavy, he turned and left the apartment.

14

On the night of the next scheduled youth meeting, Lily arrived at the church hall early, hoping to catch Nick before the others arrived. Her footsteps echoed through the basement as she crossed the tiled floor of the eerie, empty room. The carefully wrapped package tucked under her arm weighed almost as heavily as her guilt over the way she'd treated Nick. Guilt that demanded restitution. The gift wasn't much, but she hoped it would go a long way to soften her rejection.

Under a flickering florescent light, she debated whether to leave the package on the table or wait and give it to Nick another time.

"You're early."

She whirled around to find Nick in the doorway. He looked so wonderful in his jeans and sports jacket, his hair ruffled from the wind, that it hit her anew, like a physical ache, how much she'd missed him. "I wanted . . . I have something for you."

"You do?" An expression of pleasant surprise crossed his features. He paused to set some papers on the front table and then came toward her.

Tentatively, she held out the package. "My small way of saying thank you for everything and to apologize for the way I acted the other day."

He stared at her without moving. "You didn't have to do that."

"I wanted to." She pressed the gift into his hand. "I hope you like it."

The hall seemed to shrink in size as she waited for him to open it. The overhead lights buzzed, breaking the silence. She'd never given away one of her paintings before, a gesture far too personal. Now, as she waited for his reaction, she felt naked and vulnerable.

He slid a finger under the wrapping, folded it back, and stared. Not a smile, not a frown, not a blink.

She stuffed her hands into her pockets to hide her nerves. When at last he raised his eyes to hers, the intensity of emotion there stalled her breath.

"One of your paintings?"

She could only nod. She'd painted a small

landscape from their time at Rainbow Falls. She hoped it would mean as much to him as it did to her.

"It's stunning. You captured the very essence of my favorite spot. The spiritual beauty there."

A jumble of relief and elation spilled through her. Right away, he'd understood what she'd been trying to portray.

"I love it. Thank you." His eyes bored into hers. "I know how hard it is for you to share your work."

She nodded again, still mute. Her pulse stuttered as he took a step toward her and leaned in to kiss her cheek.

"I will treasure this always."

The now familiar scent of his aftershave teased her senses. She managed a shaky smile. "I'm glad you like it."

A noise from behind them broke the intimacy of the moment. Lily tore her gaze from Nick in time to see Sarah Jane enter the hall, her face as rigid as the metal cake pan in her hand. Lily's mood plummeted. She'd forgotten about Sarah Jane's hostility.

Lily threw a desperate glance at Nick. *Please don't show her the painting,* she pleaded silently.

As if reading her mind, Nick wrapped the paper back around the canvas and slid it into his bag under the table. "Hello, Sarah Jane."

This time Nick's words weren't laced with guilt. He was calm and pleasant, as he would be with any member of the group.

"Hello, Nick." The iciness of Sarah Jane's voice spoke volumes. She turned to Lily. "I see you've recovered from your illness."

"Yes. I'm feeling much better. Thank you."

Sarah Jane marched over to place her dessert on the table, and Lily followed Nick.

"Can I do anything to help?"

His smile was worth enduring Sarah Jane's unpleasantness.

"Sure. You can put one of these sheets on each chair for me." He handed her a pile of papers.

Glad to be busy, Lily made her way around the circle of folding chairs. Halfway through, a deep voice bellowed through the hall, startling her. A tall, middle-aged man with graying hair and a well-trimmed goatee clapped Nick on the back. The two men hugged and laughed. Whoever he was, he seemed far too old for the youth group.

Then Lily noticed his police uniform. Her body went numb as icy fingers of panic clutched her throat.

Nick led the officer in her direction. Papers fluttered from her nerveless grasp.

Run, an inner voice screamed. But fear held her frozen to the spot.

"Lily, this is my good friend, Mike Hillier. Mike, Lily Draper."

The man smiled and extended his hand. She swallowed hard and forced herself to accept it.

"So this is the new girl in town."

Why did his tone sound ominous?

Nick bent to retrieve the papers from the floor. "Mike's our police chief. He's giving a talk tonight on 'Youth and the Law.' " Nick winked at her. "I like to scare the pants off the kids at least once a year."

Mike's hand went to his holster. Lily swallowed again, trying to ignore the beads of sweat that snaked down her spine.

"Are you OK?" Mike's eyes narrowed. "You look a little shaky."

Lily couldn't afford to make him suspicious. Or Sarah Jane, who stood at the far side of the room watching her every move. She managed a weak smile. "I'm fine. Still getting my strength back after that flu."

Nick frowned. "Maybe you'd better sit down. I'll finish handing these out."

Lily didn't argue. "Thanks." She moved to sit on one of the chairs and forced herself to take deep, calming breaths. He wasn't

209

here to arrest her. Only to give a talk to the kids.

A few minutes later, Maxi and Chloe arrived. Lily had never been so happy to see them.

"Hi, Lily. Glad you could come." Chloe dropped into the vacant chair beside her. Then she spotted Mike and groaned. "Oh, no. Not the 'scared straight' talk again."

Maxi grimaced as she took a seat. "Maybe he'll change it up a bit this time."

"One can always hope."

They both chuckled at their private joke until the smile froze on Maxi's face. Lily turned her head. Jason Hanley had just walked in with a pretty blonde at his side, smiling up at him with a look of puppy-dog adoration on her face.

To make matters worse, Marco entered right behind them. Lily hadn't seen him since their disastrous date. This had all the makings of a terrible evening.

"I should've known he'd bring Susie here." Maxi's eyes remained riveted on Jason.

Lily squeezed her friend's arm, wishing she could do something to help. When Nick began the opening prayer, she sighed in relief.

Despite the undercurrent of tension, Lily

relaxed enough to enjoy the chief's talk —
maybe because she hadn't heard it before.
He spoke with authority and a great deal of
respect for the kids. It was obvious from
their reaction they respected him just as
much.

When everyone got up to enjoy the refreshments, Lily's uneasiness returned.
Thankfully, Marco ignored her. Jason on
the other hand, brought Susie, over to talk
with Maxi and Chloe. After several minutes
of idle chatter, mostly on Susie's part, Lily
stepped in to drag Maxi away.

"Thanks for the save. All Jason does is
laugh at everything she says." Maxi grimaced.

"I noticed. Come on. Let's get some lem-
onade."

They were pouring the drinks when Mike
Hillier sauntered over, hands on his belt.
Lily tensed, willing her fingers to remain
steady.

"Hello, Maxi. Lily." Mike poured coffee
into a Styrofoam cup.

"Hey, Mike. Nice speech," Maxi said.

"Thanks. So, Lily, how are you liking
Rainbow Falls?"

The intense look in his eyes set her nerves
on edge.

"I like it very much. Everyone has made

me feel welcome." *Well, almost everyone.*

"You'll find we're a friendly place." He took a sip of coffee. "I understand you're from up north. Bismarck, is it?"

How did he know that? Had he been asking about her?

"That's right." Lily gulped down a tart sip. The drone of voices in the background made her head spin.

"You have family up there?"

"Not really." She searched for a way to escape, but her mind blanked.

"What made you move to our fair town?"

"Whoa, Mike, this isn't an interrogation," Maxi cut in. "We usually try to make newcomers feel welcome, not scare them off."

Mike gave a sheepish smile. "Sorry about that. Force of habit, I guess."

"No problem."

When Nick joined them a few minutes later, Lily could have wept with relief. There were some extremely uncomfortable vibes in the air tonight, draining what little energy she had left.

"If no one minds, I think I'm going to head home. I'm still not feeling 100 percent."

Concern shot into Nick's eyes. "Let me drive you."

She shook her head. "It's OK. I have my car."

"Well, at least let me walk you out."

"Thanks. I'd like that."

Lily said her good-byes, and Nick accompanied her out to the parking lot. The cool night breeze ruffled her hair, a welcome relief from the heat of the church hall. At her car, she fumbled with her keys, and they dropped to the pavement. Her encounter with Mike Hillier had rattled her more than she wanted to admit. Nick quickly retrieved them and opened the driver's door.

He pressed the keys back into her hand. "I want to thank you again for the painting. It means a lot to me."

Lily tried to shrug off the praise, as well as Nick's touch, but he kept a gentle grip on her fingers. She couldn't help but look up into his tender gaze. Warmth spread through her torso. "It was the best way I could think of to show my appreciation."

"It's perfect." A slow smile spread across his face. "Now I'll show you mine."

He bent his head and kissed her gently on the lips. It was a sweet kiss, and Lily fought a wave of disappointment when he drew away.

His blue eyes brimmed with emotion. "I know you're not ready for a relationship right now, but whenever you are, I'll be waiting."

Words eluded her. She clenched the keys between her fingers, letting the hard bite of metal crush the sudden longing to bury her face in his shoulder, to let him be her anchor in the storms of life.

He brushed a strand of hair off her cheek, and his expression softened. "I'd better let you get home."

She fought the urge to capture his hand and hold it against her face. Instead, she slid into the car and started the engine. Nick gave a final wave, then turned back toward the church. She watched him go, her insides a churning mass of confusion.

What on earth was she going to do about her feelings for Nick Logan?

15

Lily looked up from the appointment book when Chloe flew into the salon on Monday afternoon, bringing with her the smell of sunshine and summer air. The teen waved a paper in front of her like a victory flag.

"I got a B-plus on my mid-term."

"That's fantastic." Lily swelled with pride.

"Congratulations!" Maxi hopped up from her seat at the manicure station, leaving poor Mrs. Harris with her hand in mid-air.

"Thanks." Chloe grinned. "If I do well on my final exam, I'll end up with a B average. And it's all thanks to you." She bent to give Lily a fierce hug.

Lily waved aside her sister's thanks. "You did all the work. I only helped a little."

"We have to celebrate," Maxi interrupted. "Maybe ice cream sundaes over at Ruby's."

Mrs. Harris's loud clearing of her throat had Maxi rushing back to her client. "Sorry, Mrs. H."

Chloe pulled two envelopes out of her backpack. "Speaking of celebrations, you're both invited to my birthday party a week from Saturday."

Maxi whooped. "A party. That's just what we need around here."

Mixed emotions swirled through Lily as she slid the invitation out of its envelope. The party would be held at Rainbow Falls Community Center, which meant a big crowd would attend. The thought of being scrutinized by so many of the townspeople dampened Lily's enthusiasm at being included in Chloe's milestone birthday.

"I hope you'll come."

Under Chloe's expectant gaze, Lily smiled, swallowing her unease. "I wouldn't miss it."

"Nick will be there," Chloe whispered with a wink.

Lily kept her expression neutral. "What about Sarah Jane?"

Chloe rolled her eyes. "Not if I can help it."

Thank goodness. Lily had faced enough of the woman's constant hostility. Still, she couldn't imagine Sarah Jane letting Nick attend a party without her.

Later, as Lily packed up her desk, she fingered the invitation before stashing it in her purse. The fact that her sister wanted her at her birthday gave Lily a warm feeling inside. Their relationship was progressing far better than she'd ever hoped.

She glanced at the sunburst clock on the wall. Five minutes to closing. Peg, Maxi, and the other part-time stylist had all left. The shop sat in silence with only the ticking of the clock for company.

The front bell jangled a few seconds later, startling Lily out of her musings. She swiveled in her chair — ready to tell whoever it was they were closed — when Nick strolled through the door, a single white rose in his hand. Pure pleasure flooded her system like liquid gold.

"Hey, beautiful."

"Nick. What are you doing here?"

He smiled and held out the bloom to her. "Just wanted to see your gorgeous face."

Warmth bled into her cheeks, and she lifted the fragrant petals to her nose. The thought of their brief kiss in the church parking lot made her stomach quiver.

"There is another reason I came by." He stuffed his hands deep in his pockets. "I have a favor to ask."

"Oh?" Why did she get the feeling this was something big? Maybe because Nick seemed nervous, and Nick was never nervous.

"As part of my final course evaluation, I have to preach at the service this Sunday." He paused, fixing her with a serious gaze as he leaned over the desk. "I was hoping you'd come — for good luck — and to give me your opinion."

Was he serious? He wanted her to go to church? She opened her mouth to say no but couldn't bring herself to destroy the hopeful look on his face.

"I know it will be hard, given the history with your father. But I think if you come, you'll see not all ministers are the same." His mouth lifted at the corner.

She wanted to say yes. If only her body didn't quake with fear at the thought of walking into that church with Sarah Jane Miller and the rest of the congregation staring at her.

"Don't answer right now. Just think about it and get back to me."

She managed a smile. "I — I will."

"In the meantime, can I buy you a soda?"

The phone rang, and she picked it up, giving herself a minute to regain her composure. She jotted down an appointment and then turned her attention back to Nick who'd wandered over to the window.

"I'm closing tonight," she said. "Can you wait five minutes?"

She was playing with fire, no doubt about it, but she couldn't resist spending more time with him.

His lazy grin made her heart beat double time. "I can wait."

At precisely nine o'clock, Lily turned off all the lights, grabbed her purse, and locked the front door of the shop. They strolled down McIntyre Street until Nick stopped in front of Ruby's Diner. "You're going to love this. Ruby makes incredible ice cream sodas." He held the door open and ushered her inside.

The interior reminded Lily of a true fifties-style diner with red vinyl booths and a chrome counter flanked with round stools. An old-fashioned jukebox sat in the far corner cranking out Patsy Cline's "Crazy."

Nick nodded to a couple of guys at the counter as he led her to a quiet booth at the back. After a waitress had taken their order, Lily sat back against the cushioned seat, feeling suddenly like she was on a real date with Nick — a feeling both thrilling and terrifying.

"How's your aunt doing?" she asked in an attempt to remain casual.

A frown marred his brow. "About the same."

"Do you think she's up to Chloe's big

party?" Lily unfolded a paper napkin onto her lap.

"Not really. I tried to talk her out of it, but her mind is made up."

"Maybe Maxi and I can help." *Where had that come from?*

Nick gave her an approving smile. "I'd appreciate that. Thank you. The ladies from the church are providing the food, but maybe you could help with the decorations."

"I'll talk to Maxi, and we'll call your Aunt Sonia tomorrow."

Uncertainty crept into his eyes.

"Don't worry. I won't say anything about Chloe being my sister."

He let out a relieved sigh. "Thank you."

The waitress arrived with their chocolate sodas. While Lily enjoyed the frosty treat, she took the opportunity to change the subject. "Where would the nearest hospital be?"

Nick blinked. "Memorial Hospital in Kingsville. About thirty miles from here." An expression of concern crossed his face. "Is Doc sending you for tests?"

"No. Nothing like that."

He frowned. "Then what's this about?"

She swirled her straw through the chocolate liquid. "I talked to Doc about the

Strickland murders."

One of Nick's golden eyebrows shot up in surprise. "What did he say?"

"He was called to the house that night." She took a spoonful of chocolate into her mouth, relishing the cool burst of flavor.

"Did he tell you anything new?"

"Not really. But he did confirm that the older daughter, Addie, died in the hospital several weeks later."

"That makes no sense." Nick set his glass down with a thump. "Wait, who's Addie?"

She shrugged. "My middle name is Adelaide."

His slow smile made her senses spin like the swirls of chocolate in her glass. "Pretty, but I prefer Lily." He sobered. "Still, the fact remains that you didn't die."

"Someone from the hospital must have told him I did. That's why I need to go there and see what I can find out." She looked at Nick as she took another sip through the straw.

"I hate to disappoint you, but I doubt they'll tell you anything."

"Why not? They're my medical records."

He held her gaze. "If they even have records back that far, I'm pretty sure there are rules about who can access them. You'd likely need photo ID matching your

221

records."

She stilled. Photo ID was out of the question. Her driver's license still bore her adopted name, before she'd taken her mother's surname when she moved to Bismarck. And she had nothing with the name Strickland, except her birth certificate. Lily slumped back against the seat, fighting a surge of disappointment. Those records would tell her if she'd been actually declared dead by the hospital or if she'd been released.

Nick reached a hand across the table to squeeze her fingers. "What if we get Doc on board? He has privileges at Kingsville."

"What makes you think he'd help me?"

"If we both talk to him, I think we can convince him."

Lily ignored the tickle of fear in her belly at the thought of telling Doc who she really was. But what choice did she have? "OK, if you're sure we can trust him."

Nick nodded. "I'm sure. I'll call him tomorrow."

When they'd finished their drinks, Nick paid the bill, and they started home. Lily loved being able to walk most places in town, especially now that the weather was so nice. She glanced up at the dark night sky, noting the cascade of stars out in full force.

"Look, you can see the Milky Way." Nick pointed with one hand and draped the other around her shoulder.

She tried to concentrate on his words, despite the delicious warmth of his nearness. A star streaked across the night sky, and Lily gave a cry of delight. "I've never seen a shooting star before. Aren't you supposed to make a wish or something?"

"I think you're supposed to do this." Nick put a finger under her chin and pulled her close for a kiss.

She forgot all about the stars as she melted into his embrace. For once, she didn't fight him. Instead, she enjoyed the sensations washing over her. The tingle of every nerve. The way her senses all came to life and magnified.

When they finally drew apart, Nick tucked her hand in his, and they continued on to Lily's house. She glided on feet that barely touched the ground. For the first time in her life, she felt cared for and protected by a man. Maybe it wouldn't hurt to relish this feeling for as long as it lasted, without overthinking the situation.

They climbed the steps to her front porch, and Nick waited while she unlocked the door.

"So you'll let me know about coming to church on Sunday?" He looked like a little boy asking for a puppy.

She took a deep breath and then a leap of faith. "I'll come." Her insides quaked as she said the words, but his lightning smile beamed her reward.

"You will?"

She nodded. "It's the least I can do after all you've done for me."

He took her hand in his warm one. "Thank you. This means a lot to me."

Despite her trepidation, a warm glow spread through her body. It had been a long time since anyone had looked at her with such approval, and it felt good. *Really good.* She smiled back, wishing the moment could last forever.

When his gaze settled on her lips, her breath caught in her throat. "Aren't you going to kiss me good night?" she whispered.

A slow grin stretched across his face. "As you wish, m'lady."

Her pulse jumped in anticipation. He took his time, first raising a hand to smooth the hair off her cheek. His touch sent shivers all through her. Under the glow of the porch lamp, his eyes appeared dark and mysterious. Her own eyes fluttered closed as his lips met hers. Unlike the earlier sweet kiss, the intensity of this one made the blood sing in her veins. Nick cupped her face with both hands as though she were a precious gift. For once, she pushed fear aside and kissed him back with all the emotion bottled inside her. When they finally parted, he looked as dazed as she felt.

"See you on Sunday," she said. "Unless we can see Doc Anderson before then."

He blinked twice. "OK. See you then."

Still smiling, Lily moved across the porch to open the front door and then turned to catch one last glimpse of Nick on the sidewalk. He'd waited to make sure she got inside safely, a chivalrous gesture that warmed her from the inside out. She stepped into the foyer and watched through the screen door until Nick was out of sight. She was about to close the door, when the loud squeal of tires caught her attention. A dark sedan roared away from the curb across the street, leaving a trail of dust in its wake. Lily caught a glimpse of the driver who looked a lot like Sarah Jane.

A chill chased goose bumps down Lily's arms. Just how far would that girl take her obsession with Nick?

Lily hoped she'd never have to find out.

16

Sunday rolled around far too quickly for Lily's liking. She awoke to the twitter of birds, and despite the lazy spill of sunshine peeking through the lace curtains, she couldn't enjoy the moment. Nerves the size of hummingbirds fluttered in her stomach.

Why had she ever agreed to attend church?

Maybe she could fake a headache or a relapse of the flu. She groaned and pushed aside the bedcovers. No, that wouldn't be fair to Nick. She'd given her word, and she would keep it.

Resigned, she made her bed and headed for the shower.

Twenty minutes later, she stood before her closet, staring at her meager supply of clothes. What did she have that was suitable for church? Nothing but one black knee-length skirt. Panic undid the calming effect of the hot shower and wreaked havoc with her nerves. What was she going to do?

Maybe Maxi had a top she could borrow.

Dressed in old jeans, her wet hair pulled back in a loose ponytail, Lily raced down the staircase to Maxi's apartment. Her urgent knocks finally resulted in some movement on the other side of the door.

"Who is it?"

"Lily. I need your help."

Maxi pulled open the door, her eyes wide. "What's the matter?"

Lily rushed past her into the cozy living room, suddenly realizing it was the first time she'd been inside Maxi's place. "I need something to wear to church," she blurted.

She turned to look at Maxi, and the woman's disheveled hair and hot pink pajamas made her consult her watch. Six thirty AM? How could it be that early? "I'm so sorry. I didn't realize what time it was."

Maxi scrubbed a hand over her spiky hair. "Hey, who needs sleep anyway? It's highly overrated. Come on. Let's get some coffee and discuss your wardrobe crisis."

Lily followed her into the tiny kitchen.

"Pull up a seat." Maxi indicated the kitchen chair in the corner. She rummaged in the cupboard for the container of coffee, then poured a carafe of water into the machine and flicked the switch. She yawned again and pulled two mugs from the cupboard. "So, did I hear you right? You need clothes to wear to church?"

Lily nodded, relishing the aroma of the fresh coffee filling the air. "I promised Nick I'd go hear him preach today."

Maxi raised an eyebrow. "I need to talk to that boy about his dating techniques. They need serious help."

"This isn't a date. It's a . . . favor."

"A favor?"

Lily twisted the end of her ponytail around one finger. "It's the least I can do after all he's done for me."

Maxi snorted. "So it's a guilt date."

Lily threw out her hands. "I don't know what it is, or how I got roped into going to the last place on earth I want to be." *My brain must've been addled from those kisses.*

"And now you regret it."

"Big time. My palms are sweaty, I can't think straight, and I have nothing 'churchy' to wear." She dropped her hands onto her knees, rubbing her palms on the denim.

"That's one mighty big problem." Maxi's lips quirked. "But I'm guessing the bigger issue here is your feelings for Nick."

"This isn't funny, Maxi. What if I throw up right in the middle of the service?" The way she felt right now, it was a distinct possibility. "Everyone's going to be staring at me, judging my every move." Lily groaned. "Maybe I won't have to fake being sick. I'm already nauseous."

Maxi poured the fresh brew into two mugs, added milk and sugar, and handed one to Lily. "Seeing I'm up so early this fine Sunday morning, why don't I join you?"

"You go to church?" Lily couldn't hide her surprise.

"I've been known to go on occasion. Besides I'd love to hear Nick's sermon."

The knots of tension in Lily's shoulders loosened a notch. Maybe with Maxi beside her, facing the churchgoers wouldn't be quite so daunting. "That would be great."

"Good." Maxi set her cup on the counter. "Now let's find you something to wear."

Even with Maxi beside her, Lily's anxiety level rose with each step she climbed up to the white clapboard church. Old memories of her father's brand of "fire and brimstone" rolled over her, and when they entered the foyer, the familiar smell of candlewax and flowers hit her hard.

Why did every church smell the same?

Her knees trembled as she looked through the open double doors into the packed interior. Sarah Jane, almost hidden behind a ridiculous hat, was seated front and center.

Peg and Jason Hanley sat a few rows behind. Even the sight of Chloe up front with her mother didn't help. The organist played a background hymn that didn't quite drown out the murmur of the people chatting. Lily could picture every head turning to stare at her as she entered, piercing her with their censured glances, whispering to each other about her. Would they see right through her and realize how much of a hypocrite she was coming to a place like this?

Oh, no, she really might throw up.

Lily's face must have given away her terror, because Maxi marched back and slipped her arm through hers.

"Come on. We'll sneak into the back pew. No one will even notice," she whispered.

Lily gripped Maxi's arm with steely fingers, sagging with relief when they took a seat in the last row, and not one person turned around. She ran a finger under the collar of the frilly white blouse she'd borrowed from Maxi. She couldn't believe this modest top actually belonged to her friend until Maxi explained her mother had given it to her for Christmas, and she'd never worn it. Not one for protocol, Maxi wore a denim mini skirt and wild floral shirt with a plunging neckline. Lily felt positively nun-like beside her.

The congregation surged to its feet when Reverend Baker, a gray-haired man in a white robe, entered through a side door and greeted them from the podium. Similarly dressed, Nick followed him in and took a seat on the altar. Images of her father at the pulpit intruded on Lily's thoughts. She pictured Tobias yelling at the parishioners, waving an accusatory finger, calling for sinners to repent.

But Reverend Baker spoke in a much softer manner, not threatening at all, and gradually Lily's tense muscles began to relax. At last, Nick took his place at the pulpit, and she sat up straighter to focus, knowing he would expect an honest opinion afterward.

"My dear brothers and sisters," he began, his voice firm, yet soothing. "What does God expect from us as followers of Christ?"

As Nick spoke, he looked out over his audience with quiet confidence, until his gaze met hers. A slight upturn of his lips made Lily catch her breath.

Throughout his sermon, Lily was amazed at how easy his words flowed and how different he was from her father. He was warm and engaging, including several personal anecdotes that made the congregation laugh.

"This is what God asks of us," he said near the end of his talk. "To learn from our errors and to strive to be perfect as our Heavenly Father is perfect. With His grace and sacrifice, His love and guidance, we can achieve this. Every one of us can be made worthy through Christ, every one of us is redeemable and precious in His eyes, regardless of how far we've fallen. I'd like to close with a verse from Ephesians: 'In Him we have redemption through His blood, the forgiveness of sins, in accordance with the riches of God's grace.' God bless you all."

Silence enveloped the church like a shroud. Lily clutched the hymnbook in her hands until her fingers ached. She blinked away moisture from her eyes. This was why Nick wanted her to come today. Not only to see that religion wasn't all bad, but to see that despite her mistakes, she was redeemable in the sight of God. His words touched a chord deep inside her that released a flood of longing. With everything in her, she yearned to believe it was true but sadly feared it was not.

Yet how would she ever know for sure?

At the end of the service, Nick hung up his robe and made his way out through the church, hoping to catch sight of Lily. He had to make sure she was all right, that being in church again hadn't spooked her. He prayed that his rather obvious attempt to expose her to God's loving message hadn't driven her away for good.

Outside on the lawn, Maxi's colorful outfit caught his attention, and he headed to where she stood chatting with Lily. Shadows from the branches of an elm flitted over Lily, caressing her delicate features. In a frilly white blouse and slim skirt, her hair pulled up in an elegant do, she looked as regal as the stately tree beside her. A tentative smile lit her face as she spotted him.

Nick stuffed damp hands into his pockets. "Hey, you two. Thanks for coming."

Maxi grinned. "Great talk, Nick. You're going to make an awesome preacher."

"Thanks. Glad you liked it."

He couldn't keep his gaze from swinging to Lily.

Maxi patted Lily's arm. "I'll leave you two alone. I need to talk to Jason anyway." She hiked her purse onto her shoulder and set off across the lawn.

"So, what did you think of the service?" Nick asked, surprised at his nerves.

"I know what you were trying to do, Nick."

"You do?"

"Yes." Lily paused. "I understand now what you meant when you said not all preachers are the same. This time . . . well, let's just say, I didn't throw up."

Nick burst out laughing. If he'd been hoping for praise, this was the best he was going to get. "I'm sorry. I'm not laughing at you. It's just not what I expected you to say."

A bemused frown creased her forehead. "I'm serious. I thought I was going to lose it there for a while."

He sobered, realizing how difficult it had been for her to come back inside a church. And she'd done it for him. He wanted to kiss her, right then and there. However, he didn't think it would go over too well with the parishioners, so he restrained himself. "I'm really glad you came. Can I ask what you thought about my sermon in particular?"

"It was very . . . nice."

"Nice?" Not exactly the glowing review he'd hoped for.

"Yes."

"I sense a 'but' coming."

She clutched her purse like a life preserver. "I only wish I could believe it."

Nick took one of her hands in his. "One day, Lily Draper, you'll believe how precious you are to God . . . and to me. No matter how long it takes."

She didn't say a word, just stared at him with huge, sad eyes — until Chloe arrived and broke the spell.

"Hey, cuz. That was an awesome sermon." She reached up and kissed his cheek.

"Thanks. I hope the professors thought so, too."

Chloe eyes went wide, and Nick noticed their similarity to Lily's.

"Your professors were here?"

"Second row on the left."

"Wow. I would've been so nervous. How'd you do it?"

Nick winked at Lily. "I think the Holy Spirit had more to do with it than I did. I was thinking about something else."

Chloe shot a grin in Lily's direction. "I'll bet you were. You look gorgeous today, as usual, Lily. Come and say hi to my mom." Chloe grabbed Lily's arm and pulled her in the direction of the church stairs.

Lily shot a panicked glance over her shoulder, but there was nothing Nick could do.

Lily had no choice but to follow Chloe over to where a group of gray-haired women stood on the sidewalk near the church steps.

Mrs. Martin moved forward as they approached. Though frail, she carried herself well. Even with the oxygen pack and the slender tube running to her nostrils, Sonia looked elegant in her navy blue suit and pearls, her graying curls held in place, no doubt, by a large quantity of hairspray.

"Mom, you remember Lily," Chloe said. "The friend who's been tutoring me."

"It's nice to see you again, Mrs. Martin." Lily pushed her apprehension aside, determined to get to know the woman who'd raised her sister.

Sonia Martin's blue eyes narrowed as she shook Lily's hand. "It's good to see you, too, Lily. I want to thank you for what you're doing for my daughter."

Lily smiled. "I'm glad I could help. I know how tough high school can be."

Mrs. Martin continued to regard her. "I appreciate your offer to help with the birthday party as well. Though I do find it odd for a newcomer to become so involved in my daughter's affairs. Especially given the difference in your ages."

Tension swirled through the small group as they waited in silence for her response. Lily felt the heat of Nick's gaze on her face. She swallowed before answering. "Maxi, Nick, and Chloe were the first people to make me feel welcome here. How could I not want to repay them in some small way?" She gave a slight shrug. "I have a bit of an artistic side, so decorating for a party should be fun."

Mrs. Martin's features softened. "Well, thank you. Chloe, we'd best be getting home. I have Sunday dinner to fix." She raised her gaze to Nick, and the love that shone there hit Lily like a fist. "You will be joining us, won't you, dear?"

"Of course, Aunt Sonia. When have I ever missed a Sunday?"

She smiled at him, her whole face brightening. "Good. We'll see you later."

Lily realized then that Sonia Martin's fierce overprotectiveness extended to her nephew as well. Once Chloe and her mother left, Lily blew out a long breath. She turned to talk to Nick and found him surrounded by about twenty parishioners, all congratulating him on his wonderful sermon. She scanned the crowd for Maxi but couldn't see her.

She was about to start walking home when Sarah Jane came marching up the path toward her, an unpleasant expression pinching her features.

Lily looked around for an escape route, but finding herself boxed in by the crowd on one side and a row of hedges on the other, braced herself for the inevitable confrontation. "Hello, Sarah Jane."

The woman walked right up to her, the brim of her hat almost knocking Lily in the eye. "You can save the pretense, Miss Draper. I know all about you and what you're up to here."

She kept her voice low enough that no one else could hear what she'd said. The hardness of her expression sent alarm bells off in Lily's head. What did she mean by that cryptic comment?

"I'm not up to anything." Lily managed to keep her voice steady.

Sarah Jane flashed a cold smile at odds with the warmth of the day. "Well, then you have nothing to worry about, do you? In the meantime, stay away from *my* boyfriend." She shook her finger at her, barely missing Lily's nose.

In that instant, the frightening similarity between Sarah Jane and Lily's father became clear. Both wore a virtuous mask to hide a darker nature beneath.

Lily held her temper in check.

"Sarah Jane, you're not causing trouble are you?" Maxi appeared at her elbow.

"Of course not. Just welcoming Lily to our church." She lifted her nose higher into the air as though daring Lily to contradict her. "Excuse me, I have to speak with Nick."

"What was that about?" Maxi asked as Sarah Jane stalked off across the lawn.

"I have no idea."

Maxi shook her head, her thin eyebrows coming together in a frown. "I don't want to worry you, Lily, but you better watch yourself. There's no telling what Sarah Jane will do to get Nick back."

17

On Thursday afternoon, Nick opened his door and greeted Lily with a huge grin. "Come on in. Doc should be here any minute."

Lily stepped inside Nick's house, very similar to the one she and Maxi shared. Twenty minutes ago, Nick had called and asked her to meet him here because he'd arranged for Doc Anderson to come over. Luckily she had the afternoon off so the timing was perfect.

He dropped a quick kiss on her cheek, and she smiled at him. "Thanks for setting this up. Do you think he'll help us?"

"We'll find out soon enough." He took her hand and led her down the hall into the living room where the high ceilings and wide crown moldings indicated the age of the structure.

Unlike Nick's rental house, this home hadn't been modernized at all. The faded wallpaper in the living room and old-fashioned furnishings likely meant Nick hadn't changed anything since his mother passed away. Maybe the familiarity was comforting.

"It's a bit outdated in here," Nick said in an apologetic tone. "I haven't had time to redecorate."

"I like it. It's homey." She walked toward the fireplace. Not a trace of dust anywhere, only the faint odor of lemon furniture polish.

"Can I get you some coffee? There's a fresh pot in the kitchen."

"Yes, please." It would give her something to do with her hands.

While he was gone, she wandered around the room, looking at pictures on the mantel, enjoying the cozy feel of the space. A small, framed photo of Nick as a boy caught her eye. She smiled at the familiar mischievous grin. Even at that age he was a charmer.

"Here you go. Milk and sugar, right?"

"Yes, thanks." As she took the cup from him, the doorbell rang. She took a quick sip and set down the coffee, smoothing her skirt with damp palms.

A minute later, Doc Anderson's wide frame filled the living room doorway.

"Hello, Lily." His greeting held a hint of

puzzlement.

"Hi, Doc. Thanks for coming." She gave him a nervous smile. What would Doc think of her story? More importantly, would he be willing to help?

He moved into the room. "I must admit I'm curious about the nature of this meeting." Doc raised his eyebrows in a gentle question.

"Have a seat, Percy." Nick followed in behind him, a hand on his shoulder. "Can I get you some coffee?"

"No, thanks, son. Caffeine keeps me up at night."

"Fine, we'll get right to the point then." Nick offered Doc a chair, sat beside Lily on the couch, and nodded at her to proceed.

She moistened her dry lips. "Remember I asked you about the Strickland case?"

His brow creased into a frown. "Yes, and I believe I was quite clear about the outcome. Adelaide Strickland succumbed to her injuries."

Lily leaned forward on the sofa. "I'd like to know who informed you of her death. Was it someone from the hospital?"

Doc's gaze darted from Lily to Nick.

"Was it the attending doctor?" she persisted, "or maybe one of the hospital officials?"

He shifted his bulk on the chair. "It was the hospital chaplain — I remember that much. Why is this so important?"

She straightened her spine. The time had come for full disclosure. She needed the truth.

"Since I'm your patient," she said slowly, "you're bound by patient confidentiality, correct?"

"That's right."

"Then what I'm about to tell you must remain between the three of us for now."

The doctor nodded.

She took a deep breath. "I am Adelaide Strickland. Lily Adelaide Strickland, to be exact."

His mouth dropped open. The whites around his pale eyes stood out under his wire-rimmed glasses. "But how is that possible?" he finally sputtered, looking to Nick for confirmation.

Nick nodded. "It's possible because Lily didn't die in that hospital. Although someone wanted you to think she had."

Lily pulled the birth certificate from her bag and handed it to him. He scanned it and gave it back. "Well, if that don't beat all. Why on earth would the chaplain lie about such a thing?"

"That's what I'm trying to find out. Is

there anything else you can tell me? Like why no one asked to see the body?"

Doc pulled out a white handkerchief and dabbed it to his forehead. "When the chaplain informed me of Addie's death, I told him we'd have someone from the funeral home come for the body. The man seemed surprised — said the body had already been cremated. Apparently, there'd been some kind of mix-up because there was no next of kin. When I told Sonia Martin, she got very upset. Insisted I file a complaint with the hospital, which I intended to do. But once we received the ashes, Sonia had calmed down. Said not to bother. What was done was done. She didn't want some poor person to lose their job over an honest mistake. We had Addie's funeral, and that's the last I ever thought about it."

Lily let out a slow breath. "That explains the lack of a body. But not why someone would go to all that trouble." She looked Doc in the eye. "Would you be willing to help me get my medical records from the Kingsville hospital? I need to see if I was pronounced dead there, and by whom."

Nick moved closer to her on the sofa, as if to protect her. "Could you get your hands on those, Percy?"

Doc rubbed his chin. "Shouldn't be a

problem. I believe they keep records back at least twenty years." His jaw tightened. "I'd like to clear up this mystery as much as you. Someone lied to me, and I want to know why."

Doc's eyes narrowed suddenly. He gave Nick a sharp look. "Does your aunt know about this?"

"No, sir. And don't worry. Lily's not planning on saying anything yet."

Doc speared her with a stern look. "Sonia Martin is not a well woman and a shock like this could prove detrimental to her health."

Guilt twisted Lily's insides. The time was coming when she would have to tell Chloe the truth, and Nick wouldn't be happy about that at all. No use worrying about it now. "I don't want to endanger Mrs. Martin."

"Good." He put both hands on his pudgy knees and pushed stiffly to his feet. "I'll be in touch when I have some news."

Nick and Lily rose as well.

"Thanks, Doc." Nick shook the older man's hand. "We appreciate your help."

In the hall, Doc paused to peer over his spectacles at Lily. "I am curious about one thing. What took you so long to come back, young lady?"

She shrugged. "I didn't know my real name until I found my birth certificate a few weeks back."

"I see." He smiled, his eyes warm. "Well, Missy, I never thought I'd say this, but . . . welcome home."

Lily jumped down from the ladder in the middle of the community center and stood back to survey her handiwork. The blue and yellow streamers spiraling out from the center point in the ceiling all seemed perfectly spaced. Bunches of gaily-colored balloons cooperated by remaining adhered to the walls. She blew out a satisfied breath. Step by step, the room was coming together for Chloe's big birthday party that evening.

"Looks great," Maxi said from behind her.

"So far so good. Can you help me put on the tablecloths?"

With the addition of royal blue coverings, white napkins, and flowered centerpieces, the hall began to look as elegant as Lily had pictured in her mind. She'd incorporated Chloe's favorite colors and flowers into the decorating scheme. Mrs. Martin had given Maxi a group of photos from Chloe's childhood, which they had used to create a fabulous collage mounted on an easel in the corner by the head table. Lily loved getting a glimpse into her sister's life.

Maxi looked at her watch. "We'd better get home to change. I don't know about you, but I could use a shower." She blew her bangs off her face.

Lily wiped dusty hands on her pants. "Me, too. Let me grab the trash, and I think we're done."

She turned to pick up the tape, scissors, and leftover ribbon. Just as she stashed it all in a tote bag, the door to the party room opened, and Mrs. Martin walked in. She stood surveying the room, her hand on a wooden cane. Her gray curls had not even budged in the breeze from outside.

"Hey, Mrs. M.," Maxi called. "We just finished. What do you think?"

"It's beautiful. Chloe will love it."

She hobbled forward with her cane, coming to stand near Lily, who found herself at a loss for words. The woman's pale eyes held no warmth. Why did this frail, yet formidable, woman make her so nervous?

"Is Chloe excited?" Lily finally asked.

Mrs. Martin smiled. "Oh, yes. She's flitting around the house like a nervous bird, fiddling with her dress and hair." Her gaze turned solemn. "This is the first big birthday party Chloe's ever had. I wanted to do this for her, before . . . before she leaves for college."

Lily felt sympathy for the woman who might not live to see her daughter start a career or marry. Despite the oxygen pumping through Sonia's pack, the blue tinges around her lips told Lily the severity of Sonia Martin's illness. According to Nick, Sonia would soon be on oxygen permanently.

"I'm sure Chloe will have a great time," Lily said.

"I hope so. Maxi dear, could you do me a favor? The birthday cake is in my car. Would you bring it in for me, please?"

A hint of panic rose in Lily's chest as Maxi left the building.

Mrs. Martin's shrewd blue eyes bore right into Lily's. "You and I need to talk. Alone."

Panic erased every coherent thought from Lily's mind.

"On Wednesday, Chloe will be staying late after school. Could you come to the house then?"

Lily clutched the strap of her tote bag. "I'll have to check my schedule, but I think my shift ends at three."

Mrs. Martin nodded. "Good. That will give us enough time."

"Can I ask what this is about?" Trepidation knocked at Lily's ribs.

The door swung open, and Maxi breezed in carrying a large box.

"Put it in the fridge for me, will you, dear?" Mrs. Martin motioned to the door that led into the small kitchenette.

"Sure thing." Maxi used her hip to push through the swinging door and disappeared inside.

Lily almost jumped when Sonia reached out to touch the necklace around Lily's neck.

Sonia fingered the locket thoughtfully and then looked up. "Yes, we most definitely need to talk."

18

Nick looked around the community center and grinned. Almost everyone in town had turned out to celebrate Chloe's birthday. The church ladies had cooked up a feast of chili and lasagna, salads and desserts. Aunt Sonia had even hired a local band to play country and western tunes after the meal, giving the guests a chance to try out their dancing shoes.

Nick's gaze fell on Lily, standing on the sidelines watching the dancers, and his grin widened. She looked especially lovely tonight in a gauzy green dress, her hair a cascade of curls down her back. With the stealth of a cat, he sneaked up behind her. "I hope you saved a dance for me."

She turned and rewarded him with a warm smile. "Of course. But are you sure you want to be seen dancing with me?" She glanced across the hall.

Nick followed her line of vision to Ted and

his perpetual scowl. "I'm sure. Ted doesn't get to control my life."

He reached for her hand and pulled her onto the dance floor where several couples swayed to a slow song. Lily held herself as stiff as a starched shirt within the circle of his arms.

"Relax. I don't bite," he whispered in her ear.

She pulled back to look at him. "Everyone's watching us. I feel like a bug under a microscope."

He scanned the crowd surrounding them. "You're right. Guess we'll have to do something about that." With a flourish, he led her off the dance floor, out into the hallway.

"Where are we going?" Her cheeks flushed pink, most likely from embarrassment.

"You'll see." He grinned and kept walking, his hand firm around hers. A red exit sign glowed at the end of the corridor. He pushed through the door and out into a private back courtyard, where a group of benches and flowering shrubs surrounded a stone water fountain. Pink and green lights illuminated the water as it sprayed upward.

"This is incredible," she said, eyes aglow like an enchanted child.

The cool breeze lifted her hair and blew it around her face. Nick resisted the urge to touch the silky tresses.

"Now we can finish our dance in private." He smiled, pulling her close to him.

She laughed as he waltzed her around the courtyard, humming a tune. This time she relaxed into his arms, warm and inviting.

"Have I told you how beautiful you look tonight?"

She smiled up at him. "Yes, but I don't mind hearing it again."

"That dress is fabulous. Green is definitely your color."

She swished the full hem of her skirt around her knees. "Why, thank you, sir."

They danced around in dizzying circles a few more times, until he slowed her to a stop. Under the glow of the moon, the world narrowed to include only the amazing woman before him.

"I've been waiting all night to do this." He lowered his lips to hers, drinking in the sweet taste of her. When she melted into him, he relished the feel of her arms around him, grateful she now welcomed his affections.

The sudden clearing of a throat startled him. Lily all but vaulted out of his arms. Nick turned to see Ted standing just outside the door, a scowl contorting his face.

"Nicholas, your aunt sent me to tell you

Chloe is about to cut the cake."

Nick wrapped a firm arm around Lily's waist as he regarded the older man. "Thank you, Ted. We'll be right there."

The two men locked stares for a moment, like a pair of dueler's facing each other before a battle. Nick held his ground until Ted finally turned and went inside. Nick's shoulders sagged in relief.

"He really doesn't like me," Lily said. "This won't jeopardize your position, will it?"

"Don't worry. I can handle Ted." Nick hoped his confidence wasn't misplaced. Knowing the good reverend, this wouldn't be the end of the matter. Brushing his concerns aside for the moment, Nick lowered his head for another quick kiss. "Come on. Let's go help Chloe blow out those candles."

After being caught with Nick in the courtyard, bad vibes followed Lily like a cloud for the rest of the evening. Thank goodness Chloe and her mother seemed oblivious to the heightened tension as the party continued to flow around them. Chloe sliced her cake and opened her presents, beaming the whole time. Lily had given Chloe her gift earlier in the day, not wanting it to be a public affair, and was pleased she'd loved the painting.

After the few speeches concluded, Lily moved off to one side of the room to get another glass of punch, content to watch her sister from the sidelines. The school year would soon be over, leaving about six weeks before Chloe would start college. Lily gave an inward sigh. Even though Nick wouldn't like it, she couldn't let Chloe go without telling her the truth about their family connection. But she wanted all the details about her family tied up before she told Chloe anything. Hopefully, Doc Anderson had been able to find some new information for her.

She sipped her drink, lost in thought until she felt a presence beside her. Mike Hillier stood ladling punch into his cup.

"Hello, Lily. How have you been?"

She tensed and focused on keeping her breathing steady. At least he wasn't in uniform today. "Very well, thanks."

He turned toward her and took a sip of punch. "Funny thing," he said, studying her. "Turns out my family knows some Drapers up near Bismarck. Any chance they're relatives of yours?"

Lily's fingers tightened on her glass. No need to panic. Mike wouldn't be able to connect her father to Draper, her mother's maiden name. She gave thanks once again for changing her name when she moved to Bismarck. Still, she couldn't shake the anxiety clawing at her. "It's possible. Although my father's side of the family isn't very big."

"What's your father's name?" The sharpness of his gaze belied the casual tone of his question.

Her body froze — her mind as blank as an erased whiteboard. "Tobias," she said at last, unable to come up with a quick alternative. She bit back a groan. Why couldn't she have said Tom or Timothy? Lying to protect herself had been natural before moving to Rainbow Falls. Now, she couldn't do it to save herself.

"Hmm, Tobias Draper. Doesn't ring a bell."

She inhaled through her nose. Mike would never find a Tobias Draper in North Dakota. Still Tobias was an unusual enough name to be worrisome. "Not the same family, I guess." Her damp palms slid on the glass in her hand. She darted a desperate glance over the crowd to see if perhaps Nick would save her. Unfortunately Reverend Baker had him cornered on the far side of the room, and Maxi was off somewhere with Jason.

With no one around to intervene, Lily needed a distraction — in a hurry.

"Could you do me a favor?" She turned the full force of her smile on Mike and nodded in Nick's direction. "Would you go over and save Nick from Reverend Baker?"

Mike's features didn't soften as she hoped. He leaned closer, eyes narrowed. "You're not fooling anyone, Miss Draper. I recognize an evasion tactic when I see it."

Lily swallowed hard. "I don't know what you mean."

He took one step back, never blinking. "I'll let it go for now, but I know you're hiding something. And I intend to find out what it is."

In direct contrast to their carefree dance in the courtyard, the atmosphere on the drive home was somber and dark. From the corner of her eye, Lily watched Nick as he drove. A nerve ticked in the hard line of his jaw. Since she'd seen him with Reverend Baker, his mood had changed for the worse. He'd hardly said a word to her the rest of the evening, and now his death grip on the steering wheel had turned his knuckles white.

"What did Ted say to you?" Lily asked when the silence in the truck became unbearable.

Nick's nostrils flared as he stared out at the road. "Nothing worth repeating."

Lily crossed her arms and frowned. "Someone upset you, and I don't think it was Mike." Mike had, in fact, broken up the Reverend's talk with Nick quite quickly.

Nick glanced over at her. The ridges on his forehead relaxed a little, and he blew out a weary sigh. "Ted raked me over the coals for kissing you. He wants to meet with me tomorrow to lecture me about the responsibilities of being a pastor."

Nick cracked the window, allowing a burst of fresh air into the cab, which did nothing to cool Lily's outrage.

"That's so unfair. Why do religious people always try to control your every thought and action?"

"Not all pastors are so judgmental."

Lily shook her head. "I'm sure *you* won't be like that, but you seem to be the exception to the rule."

They sat in silence for the last few minutes of the drive. Lily hated seeing her worst fears come true — that Nick's career would suffer because of his involvement with her. As much as she enjoyed being with him, Lily would not allow him to throw away his life, or his career, for her. She couldn't, in good conscience, put her own happiness above his.

When Nick pulled into Lily's driveway, she waited while he shifted into park to gather her courage. She twisted her hands together, fighting the depression that threatened to engulf her like the low lying fog now creeping over the lawn. When she spoke, her voice was barely a whisper. "Nick, I know how important becoming a minister is to you. If our being together is going to jeopardize that" — she took a breath — "maybe we should stop seeing each other."

She stared at her lap, not daring to look at him. Tension crackled in the air.

Nick shifted in his seat to face her. "Is that what you want, Lily?"

When she looked up, his face was cloaked in sadness, and she just couldn't lie to him. "No, it's not. But I won't let you —"

He silenced her with a lingering kiss that stole the air from her lungs. When he pulled back, a determined gleam shone in his eyes. "I will not let Ted Baker, or anyone else, dictate who I can care about."

Wisps of doubt continued to cloud Lily's brain, but another kiss from Nick made them evaporate . . . for the moment.

19

Nick parked his truck in front of Good Shepherd Church and turned off the engine. Despite his apprehension over the upcoming confrontation with Ted, Nick allowed himself a brief moment of happiness. Lily had come to church again this morning, without him even asking. Could this mean she was beginning to feel a tiny spark of faith? He hoped so — with everything in him.

Because although he loved Lily just as she was, he couldn't marry her unless she allowed God to be an integral part of their marriage — of their lives. Even if they weren't meant to be together, if God had other plans for their lives, it would be a comfort to know Lily had come to develop a trust in God which would sustain her in the future. At least the seeds had been planted. Now they needed time to grow.

Nick kept this idea in the forefront of his

thoughts as he approached the church office. He stood for a moment in the silent hallway, inhaling the familiar scents of pine soap and candle wax that drifted as far back as the office area. Once he felt focused, he knocked on the door.

"Come in."

Ted stood with his back to the door, staring out the large picture window. "Sit down, Nicholas."

The familiar dread returned. Nick had prayed long and hard that morning for God's help with his constant battle to control his temper. Now he took a seat, determined to keep calm.

Ted turned and sat down in his chair across the desk from Nick. Shadows underlined his faded blue eyes. The hollows in his cheeks seemed more pronounced today. A pang of guilt spiked through Nick at his less-than-charitable thoughts of late. Did Ted suffer from ill health? Could that be the real reason for his retirement? Nick straightened on his chair, vowing to keep an open mind to whatever Ted was about to say.

The older man removed his glasses, set them on the desk, rubbed a hand over his eyes, and then looked at Nick. "Thank you for coming. I'm sorry if I've come down rather hard on you lately, son, but believe me; it's for your own good."

"I understand. You only want the best for the parish you're leaving behind."

Ted gave a wan smile. "Exactly. Which is why I want to talk to you in more detail about the realities of being a minister."

He spent the next ten minutes describing the pitfalls of life as a clergy member, focusing on the importance of a spotless reputation, to be above reproach in every area of his life. Ted stressed the need for a supportive wife and helpmate, one who understood the rigorous demands of a pastor's career and who could, in a best case scenario, contribute her own gifts to the ministry.

Nick congratulated himself on his patience as he listened.

"The reality is that as pastor you are under a constant microscope by your parishioners. You cannot afford one misstep or you will lose their trust and respect. This goes for any potential spouse as well."

Nick squirmed on the hard chair and pulled his tie loose an inch. "I agree. As ministers we are role models of Christian behavior."

Ted hooked his glasses over his ears. "I'm glad you see the gravity of the position. It will make it easier to understand what I'm about to say, and why I feel it necessary to do so."

The uncomfortable sensation returned to Nick's stomach. "What is it, Ted?"

"The board of church elders have met with me to discuss your situation, and we are unanimous in our decision. I'm afraid if you continue to see this Draper woman, I cannot, in good conscience, recommend you, nor will the elders accept you, as my replacement."

Nick sat in stunned silence for a moment, reeling with the implications. Resentment settled in his chest like a stone, lodging his reply in his throat.

"If you truly believe God is calling you to this vocation as pastor of Good Shepherd Church, you must stop seeing Miss Draper. Immediately."

Nick clenched his jaw together so hard his back molars ached and counted to ten to keep his anger in check. His immediate reaction was to tell Ted exactly what he could do with his job. Yet he wasn't ready to throw away his career on a whim of temper. He needed time. Time to discern God's will for his life, to make sure his powerful feelings for Lily fit with God's plan.

When Nick felt he could speak in a civil

manner, he released a slow breath. "This isn't a decision I can make on the spot. I'll need time for serious consideration and prayer.

Ted stared at him for a good thirty seconds before responding. "Fair enough. But I'd like your answer as soon as possible. If God is leading you elsewhere, the parishioners need to know so they can seek the person God has in mind for them."

Nick got to his feet. "I understand."

Ted stood as well. "I hope you know this isn't personal, Nicholas. I have the larger picture to consider."

Not personal? How could it not be personal when the man he'd looked up to for years now seemed more adversary than friend? Any type of acceptable response escaped him. Nick gave a curt nod and left the room in silence.

When he reached his truck, the fury he'd pushed back now coursed its way through him until he thought he'd explode. He slammed his fist onto the hood of his truck. Pain radiated up his arm and into his shoulder.

How could his mentor, a man he admired and trusted, issue such a harsh ultimatum? Ask him to make this type of sacrifice?

Nick got in the truck and bowed his head

over the steering wheel, recalling the day he'd made the decision to become a minister. All the pieces of the puzzle had clicked into place, filling his soul with joy and contentment. At last he was on the right path, the path God wanted him to follow.

Then why had Lily come into his life? To test the strength of his commitment? Did God really want him to sacrifice his relationship with her in order to prove his worth? Or was that only Ted's doing?

Nick rubbed his chest, trying to loosen the pressure building there to the point of pain. The thought of having to choose between two of the things he cared most about in his life proved unbearable.

How would he — how *could* he — ever make that choice?

On Wednesday afternoon, Lily approached the Martin residence with nervous perspiration dampening her palms. She did *not* have a good feeling about this meeting, and Nick's odd behavior of late only made matters worse. He'd barely spoken to her since she saw him at church on Sunday. Nothing had seemed amiss then. In fact, he'd been pleased to see her. She'd gone, not only because it would make Nick happy, but because she sincerely wished to share that part of his life with him. Once again she'd been surprised to find comfort in the scripture readings.

One particular verse had stayed with her. "If we confess our sins, He is faithful and righteous to forgive us the sins, and to cleanse us from all unrighteousness." Could it really be that easy? Just confess your evil deeds and be made clean in God's eyes?

She'd wanted to discuss it with Nick, but he'd been busy all afternoon, which was understandable. She hoped he would call or come by after dinner at his aunt's, but he never did. By Monday afternoon, she broke down and called him. He'd been abrupt on the phone, given her a lame excuse why he couldn't talk, and hadn't called since.

Now, two days later, Nick's silence was deafening. Was he angry with her for some reason? Worse yet, had Mike dug up some dirt on her, and now Nick wanted nothing to do with her?

As she mounted the steps to the Martin house, she shook her head to clear the negative thoughts. Taking a deep breath, she knocked on the front door. Mrs. Martin pulled it open almost immediately, as though she'd been waiting in the entrance for her. Dressed in a loose dress and slippers, and wearing the ever-present oxygen tube, Mrs. Martin bade her enter.

"I hope I'm not late," Lily said.

"Not at all. Let's sit in the parlor."

She followed the frail woman into a sparsely furnished living room. Though the furnishings were worn, the room itself was spotless. Lily took a seat on the sofa and waited while Mrs. Martin settled into a brown velvet armchair.

"Can I get you a drink?"

"No, thank you." Lily would've loved a glass of cold water to ease her parched throat, but didn't want her to have to get up again.

Mrs. Martin continued to study her, and Lily grew more self-conscious by the moment.

"If this is about Chloe's grades . . ."

"This has nothing to do with school," Mrs. Martin said. "I want to know where you got that necklace."

Lily's mouth fell open. She searched for an acceptable reply, but nothing but the truth came to mind. She swallowed. "From my mother."

Sonia Martin's eyes narrowed. She thumped her cane on the hardwood floor. "That is a lie."

Lily pressed her lips together to hold back a denial. What could she say, other than admit Margaret Strickland was her mother? Lily clutched her hands together on her lap, wishing she could rush out of the house before the proverbial mouse trap snapped around her neck.

Sonia perched on the edge of the chair and pointed a bony finger at Lily. "I've seen that necklace before. It belonged to my good friend, Margaret Strickland."

Lily held her breath, paralyzed. She bit her bottom lip and said nothing.

"I'm going to ask you a question straight out, young lady, and I'll know if you're lying. Are you Adelaide Strickland?"

Lily gasped. How had Mrs. Martin figured that out unless she knew Adelaide hadn't died? She twisted her fingers around her purse strap, torn between keeping her promise to Nick and wanting desperately to confide in this woman. When she finally looked into Sonia Martin's eyes, she just couldn't lie to her.

"Yes," she whispered at last. "I am."

20

Lily looked on, horrified, as Sonia Martin buried her face in her hands and burst into tears. Lily had expected anger, disbelief, but never tears. With shaking fingers, she pulled a tissue from her bag and handed it to the distraught woman.

Sonia took the offering and blew her nose and then crumpled it into a ball. "All these years I've wondered if you were really dead." Her face softened as she looked at Lily with something close to affection. "I haven't seen you since you were a little child." She reached out a thin hand to touch Lily's cheek. "You're the spitting image of your mother. That's how I knew it was you. The necklace only confirmed it."

A ball of emotion lodged in Lily's throat, welling up inside until tears slid down her cheeks. "Will you tell me about her?" she whispered. "I only have a few memories of her. And no pictures except this." She clicked open the locket with her thumbnail. Inside, the tiny black and white photo had seen better days.

Sonia leaned closer to see the picture. She smiled sadly. "Yes, Margaret was only twenty-two when it was taken. It was her engagement photo. There used to be a picture of your father on the other side."

Lily closed the locket and wiped her face. "What was she like?"

A light glowed in Sonia's pale eyes. "Margaret was a wonderful person, a good wife, a dedicated mother, and a dear friend. She adored you children. You were her whole world."

Sorrow banded Lily's heart. With everything in her, she wished she could remember her brief time with her mother. "What about my father?" She clutched her hands in her lap, half-dreading the answer.

Sonia's expression hardened. "David was a good man, but circumstances intervened to change that."

"What sort of circumstances?"

With difficulty, Sonia rose from her seat and limped to the fireplace. "You know the old saying 'doctors make the worst patients'? Well, it was true of David. He was ill but ignored his symptoms until it was much too late." She turned back to look at Lily. "He had a brain tumor which affected his personality. Made him anxious, paranoid, and totally unreasonable. Every time Margaret begged him to go for tests, he refused."

The ball of tension in the pit of Lily's stomach began to loosen. "Why would he refuse?"

"Margaret thought it was because he knew something was seriously wrong. None of us ever suspected what it would lead to. That he would destroy his own family." Tears gathered in Sonia's eyes. She moved over to the sofa beside Lily. "I still can't believe you're alive. We were told you'd died in the hospital. We even buried your ashes." She pressed the tissue to her mouth.

Lily took a shaky breath. "I know it's hard to believe." She didn't want to upset the woman any more than she already had. Certain details, like Doc's quest for the truth, could be kept quiet for now.

"May I ask what took you so long to come back?"

"I only found out the truth a few weeks ago. My adoptive parents kept the story from me — most likely to protect me."

"Please, tell me about your family. I hope they were good to you."

Lily forced away the negative feelings about her father and concentrated instead on the woman who'd raised her. "I had a wonderful mother. She was everything a little girl could want. Kind, gentle, and loving. I was very happy for a while . . . until she died when I was ten."

The lines around Sonia's mouth deepened. "I'm so sorry. My husband, Leonard, died when Chloe was twelve. I've tried to make it up to her as best I can." She closed her eyes. "Only now my own health is failing."

Lily reached out to grasp Sonia's frail hand, aching for the grief Chloe would soon endure. A type of grief Lily understood all too well. "Is there nothing that can be done?"

Sonia sighed. "Unfortunately, no. It's a degenerative condition with no cure. My sister died not long ago from the same thing."

"I'm so sorry." Lily's thoughts turned to Nick having to bear the loss of his aunt so soon after he'd lost his mother. How did he stay so strong? Was it his faith that gave him such courage?

The two women sat together, hands gripped, bonded by shared sorrow.

"I'll be here for Chloe," Lily whispered through her own tears. "I love her so much already."

"Lily, I must ask you a huge favor." Sonia's voice quivered. "Please don't tell Chloe about this until after I'm gone."

Lily stilled. "I would prefer if you told her the truth yourself."

Sonia shook her gray head. "I couldn't bear for her to know her own father killed her family. It's better she thinks her mother was an unwed teen who gave her up. Besides, if she finds out I've lied to her all these years, she'll never forgive me." A sob escaped her thin lips.

"Chloe might be upset at first —"

"Please. You'll have her for the rest of your life. I may only have months left." Her desperation bored into Lily.

The cuckoo clock on the wall chimed the hour, and Sonia jerked in her seat.

"Oh, my stars. You have to go. Chloe will be back any minute." She gripped Lily's arm with steely fingers. "Promise me you won't say anything."

Lily hesitated, recalling Nick's concern for his aunt's health. For the time being at least, she could ease Sonia's mind.

"I promise."

Nick rubbed his hands over the three days growth of beard as he waited for the coffeepot to finish brewing. He'd barely eaten,

272

showered, or slept since receiving Ted's ultimatum, ignoring the phone and his e-mail — basically shutting out the entire world. He needed time to think and pray. To sort out his life's purpose and discern God's true plan for his future.

And he needed to do it alone.

In particular, he'd avoided Lily for the simple reason that she clouded his judgment. Whenever she was near, he couldn't think straight, overwhelmed by the powerful feelings she evoked in him. Instead, he spent a lot of time out by the falls, and in church, praying and thinking.

What did God want him to do? Nick knew what *he* wanted. To marry Lily and spend the rest of his life with her. But how did that fit with God's plan for him?

Lily had made her position on religion very clear. And even though she'd been coming to church, it didn't mean she was ready to commit to a life of faith, let alone become a minister's wife.

The coffeemaker sputtered out its last gasp. Nick grabbed a mug and poured a cup, inhaling the rich fragrance with an appreciative sigh. He swallowed the first sip, then startled when the doorbell rang.

Lily.

His heart percolating like the coffee in his

273

pot, he set the cup down and rushed to the door, realizing with a jolt how much he'd missed her.

But the woman on his doorstep wasn't Lily. Nick did his best to hide his disappointment. "Maxi. Come in."

Maxi pulled off her sunglasses to shoot him a disgusted look. "Aren't we a sight for sore eyes?" She sailed past him into the living room.

Perplexed, Nick followed her. "You want some coffee? It's fresh."

"No, thanks." She stood in the middle of the room, arms folded over her bright orange shirt. Her red hair stood up as if in preparation for battle.

"Have a seat." He gestured to the sofa.

"I'd rather stand."

He huffed out a weary breath. "What can I do for you then?"

She pinned him with a furious glare. "Do you know you're breaking Lily's heart? Making her think you care and then tossing her away like a rusty wrench."

"Who said I tossed her away? I just needed a little space."

"Space for what?"

"To sort out a few things."

She stomped across the carpet, her pointed boots stopping just short of his toes.

274

"Don't tell me you're trying to decide between Lily and Sarah Jane, because if you even have to think about it, you're an idiot."

Amusement quickly morphed into irritation. He took her gently but firmly by the arm and led her to the couch. "Sit down, please."

She scowled and plopped down on the sofa.

Nick joined her. "Now, tell me what's bothering you without aiming daggers at me."

When she raised her hazel eyes to his, he was surprised to see a film of tears.

"You know I don't have a lot of people in my life to count on." She paused. "Lily's become one of my best friends. She tries to pretend she's a hard city girl, but underneath she's as fragile as a piece of paper."

Where was she going with this? "Go on."

"She's been hurt a lot, and she's got a big wall around her. But you got through that. And now it's killing me to see her like this."

Alarm gripped his insides. "Like what?"

She shrugged. "All torn up. Crying and everything."

The air whooshed out of his lungs as though someone had sucker punched him. Lily was crying over him?

"I thought better of you, Nick Logan. But

you're just as bad as Jason." She jerked to her feet and crossed to the fireplace, her back stiff.

Sighing, Nick joined her, placing a hand on her shoulder. "He still hasn't noticed how you feel?" He could count the number of times they'd had this same conversation over the years, yet he would do his best to comfort her once again.

"No." She turned and sniffed into Nick's shoulder. "And I don't think he ever will. I'm just his best friend. Nothing more."

He patted her back, his big brother instincts taking over. "Maybe it's time you faced the truth . . . and let Jason go."

Two tears escaped to leak down her cheeks. "That's what I decided last night. After I'd finished with Lily."

Nick frowned. "What do you mean *finished* with Lily?"

"If you'd call her, you'd know."

Geesh, Maxi was as prickly as a pear. "Did something else upset her?"

"Maybe I will have that coffee after all."

Nick prayed for a truckload of patience and followed Maxi into the kitchen where he poured her a cup and topped off his own.

She took the mug and stared down into the dark brew. "Your aunt asked Lily to come over to talk."

Nick set his mug on the counter with a thud. "What did she want?"

"Lily wouldn't tell me. But I know it upset her, and she was already worried about you." She shot him a dark look. "It took me hours to calm her down."

Guilt tore at his gut to think about Lily being so distraught. And the fact that he'd contributed to it made it even worse.

"She thinks you're mad at her. That you've come to your senses and don't want anything more to do with her."

Exasperation wore through his patience. "Why would she think that?" Then, with a start, he remembered a brief telephone conversation from two nights ago. Lily had called to talk, and he'd been quick to end the call. Now that he thought about it, his tone might have been a bit harsh. He exhaled a loud gust of air and sank onto one of the kitchen chairs.

Maxi followed suit. "I think she's hiding things from her past. She won't talk about her family, but I know her father treated her bad. Maybe even beat her."

Nick's arm jerked, rattling the salt and pepper shakers on the table. "He beat her?"

"Didn't she tell you about her father? I'm pretty sure he hit her when she did something wrong. I think it made her feel unwor-

277

thy of anything good in her life."

Nick bent over the table, his eyes closed and his head in his hands. He knew all about feeling unworthy. About the effects of a father beating you. Why hadn't Lily told him the whole truth about her childhood? She must have known he'd sympathize with her.

Sudden clarity flooded his system as everything came into sharp focus. Lily needed him. That's why God had brought them together. It was up to Nick to help her feel worthy. To show her how much God loved her. "I need to see her and straighten out this mess."

Maxi smiled for the first time since she got there. "I was hoping you'd say that." She drained her cup and got to her feet, pausing to study him. "You're in love with her, aren't you?"

He glowered at her. "That, my friend, is between Lily and me."

She grinned. "You just gave me my answer. But I think Lily's the one who needs to hear it."

Lily followed Doc Anderson down the main corridor of his medical clinic and into his spacious office.

"Thanks for coming on such short notice."

Doc motioned for her to have a seat.

"I hope this means you have some news for me." Lily scanned the framed diplomas on the wall behind his large oak desk before perching on the edge of a guest chair. How she wished Nick were here with her.

"I do." Doc moved to the large credenza that sat along one wall. "Tried to get a hold of Nick, but couldn't reach him." He looked over his shoulder at Lily, a question in his eyes.

She shrugged. "He must be busy with work."

Doc stared at her for a moment. "Must be." He pulled out a drawer and removed a manila folder. "I went into Kingsville to the hospital yesterday," he said as he sank into the oversized leather chair.

Her pulse sprinted like a rabbit across a field. Maybe now she'd get some answers. "Any luck?"

He set the folder on the desk in front of her. "I think you'll find these quite interesting."

She opened the file and picked up the papers inside. The words danced on the page in front of her.

Lily Adelaide Strickland, age 5. Admitted on November 13th. Gunshot wound to the chest.

A bunch of medical jargon followed.

November 28th — Patient breathing on own. Still unconscious and unresponsive.

December 5th — Patient regained consciousness.

Lily skipped over more minutia about feeding tubes and bowel activity to the pages at the end. On the last sheet, the entry read: *December 19th. Patient recovered enough for release.*

December 22nd — Patient discharged. Released into adoptive parents' custody.

Dazed, she raised her eyes. "So the hospital never declared me dead."

"Apparently not. These were not the records I received. Looks like the hospital chaplain sent me a false report along with a fake death certificate." Doc's expression was grim.

"What possible motive could he have had to do such a thing?"

"I wish I knew."

"Were you able to learn the chaplain's name?" Her heart thudded against her ribs. She needed to know the name of the man who had changed her fate with the slash of a pen.

"As a matter of fact, I did."

"And?" Lily bit her bottom lip.

He steepled his fingers and looked past her. "I remember how upset Sonia was when they told us little Addie had been cremated." He gave a deep sigh. "If only we'd known you were still alive. You could've been raised with your sister."

Lily's hand stilled on the papers in her hand. She couldn't allow herself to think about that now. About how different her life could have been. "His name?" she prompted.

He focused his gaze back on her. "Ah, yes. The chaplain's name was Tobias Cunningham."

21

The night before Chloe's final exam, Lily finished her evening shift at the salon while Chloe worked on a mock test in the back room. As the last customer swung out the front door, Lily glanced at the clock on the wall. Half an hour more and she could go home.

Home to her empty apartment where she would nuke a frozen dinner and try not to think about Nick.

Peg sauntered up to the reception desk to mark an appointment in the book. She tossed down the pencil and stretched backward, hand at the small of her back.

"Well, I'm done for the day. You OK to lock up?"

"Sure." Lily smiled at her. "I appreciate you letting Chloe study here."

Peg patted Lily's shoulder. "Chloe's a good customer, and you're a good employee."

"Thanks. You're not so bad yourself." Lily winked.

Peg gave a rare laugh and then sobered. "Haven't seen that young man of yours around lately. Everything OK?"

"I'm not sure, Peg." Thinking of Nick made her heart hurt.

The larger woman shook her head. "Thank goodness I'm not young anymore. I go home to my cat, Tiger. He's good company and a whole lot simpler than a man."

Lily laughed out loud. "You have a point. Maybe I should get a furry friend instead."

Peg chuckled as she pushed out the door. "Don't stay too late now."

"I won't. Good night."

Lily watched Peg stroll down the sidewalk and let out a deep sigh. Even Peg had noticed a change in Nick's behavior. Lily wished she didn't care so much. The truth was she cared a lot more than she should.

Lily's mind wandered back to her visit with Doc Anderson and the shock of discovering her own father had been the chaplain at Kingsville Memorial Hospital. Why had he lied and told everyone she was dead? Was that before or after they decided to adopt her? She wished she could discuss it with Nick, but she couldn't afford to let him know her adopted last name. Much too complicated. Much too dangerous. Her deception had begun to grow like a bunch of bad weeds to choke her.

She looked up when Chloe appeared beside her, paper in hand.

"There, it's done." She slapped it down on Lily's desk. "Once I graduate, I'll never have to do math again. At least not without a calculator."

Lily smiled at Chloe's dramatic flair. "What about college?"

Chloe pulled a chair beside Lily. "I won't need math for what I'm taking."

Lily blinked. In all the conversations they'd had, she'd never once asked Chloe what she wanted to do after high school. "What are you planning to study?"

Chloe gave a tentative shrug. "I want to be a chef."

"That's great. Have you applied to any schools?"

"Two. One in New York and one in Boston." A wave of sadness swept over Chloe's features. "But I don't know if I'm going to go." She lifted sorrowful eyes to Lily. "When I applied last fall, I had no idea how sick my mom was. Now I don't know if I can leave her."

"Oh, Chloe." Lily put her arm around Chloe's shoulder. "Did the doctor say how long she has?"

Chloe blinked back tears. "Six months to a year, if we're lucky."

The selfish part of Lily wanted to tell Chloe she should stay in Rainbow Falls, but that wouldn't be fair. "What does your mom say?"

"She wants me to go. Says it's silly to put my life on hold indefinitely."

"She has a point. What if the doctors are wrong and she lives two or three more years? You could have your degree by then." Lily squeezed her arm. "Besides, she has Nick to watch over her."

"That's the only reason I'm even considering going. Nick promised to take real good care of her."

Lily set her jaw, inwardly vowing to do everything in her power to help Chloe realize her dreams so she wouldn't have to hustle drinks in a smelly tavern or sling hamburgers in some fast food joint.

Chloe seemed to make a deliberate effort to lighten the mood. "Hey, you'll come to my graduation, won't you? After all, I wouldn't be graduating if it weren't for you."

Lily sucked in a breath, picturing Chloe in her cap and gown. "Of course, if you want me to. When is it?"

"A week from this Saturday at my school."

"I'd be proud to come."

"Great. It'll be you, mom, Nick, and Maxi. My four favorite people." Chloe beamed at her.

A worrisome thought formed. What if Nick still wasn't speaking to her by then? It could prove very awkward. Lily bit her lip. She'd have to make the best of it for Chloe's sake.

The bell jangled a few minutes later while Lily corrected Chloe's mock test. Lily's gaze flew to the door, hoping it might be Nick. Instead, Maxi sailed into the shop and threw her purse down with a flourish.

Lily did her best to summon a smile for her friend. "Hey, where have you been all day?"

"Getting on with my life." Maxi did a pirouette around the front of the shop. Light bounced off her sparkly earrings as she twirled.

Chloe joined them at the reception desk, a soda in hand. "What's all the excitement about?"

"I've decided to quit mooning over Jason Hanley and go after my dreams." Maxi threw out her arms in a dramatic gesture, as if she were a performer on stage.

Lily shared a questioning look with Chloe. "What did you do?"

"Applied online to a dozen of the top salons in New York City." Maxi's smile could have rivaled the neon lights on Broadway. But Lily's mood plummeted at the possibility of losing both her friends to the big city.

Chloe whooped and rushed over to embrace Maxi. "Maybe we'll both be in New York together. You at the salon and me at the finest dining establishments in the country."

The two girls laughed and carried on with their outrageous imaginings. Lily tried to get into the spirit with them, but inside her soul cried out. Not only was she losing Nick, but her two best friends would be leaving as well. Why would God give her a taste of happiness, only to rip it away with the cruelty of a dictator?

"What's wrong, Lil?" Maxi watched her with a slight frown.

Lily shrugged and attempted a laugh. "What am I going to do without you guys?"

Maxi shoved her hands on her hips. "You'll come with us. Especially if Mr. Logan doesn't get his act together. You can be my personal assistant, and I'll pay you a fortune."

Chloe joined the fantasy. "The three of us will share a penthouse apartment overlooking Central Park and be sought after by all the rich bachelors in town."

There was something infectious about their joy, about the vastness of their dreams. Just being around them made Lily want to believe everything would work out for the best.

Even if her heart had to break in the process.

With a sigh, Lily focused on marking Chloe's paper. After she tallied the results and congratulated Chloe on her excellent score, Maxi offered to drive Chloe home.

On the way out, Maxi threw Lily a sly glance. "Had an interesting chat with Nick today. You might want to give him a call." She winked and let the door swing shut behind her.

Lily's pulse raced. Had Nick said something to Maxi about her?

She crossed the room to turn off the lights, and a fierce determination rose up inside her, overriding her paralyzing fear. She would not wait one more minute to find out what was going on with Mr. Logan. She grabbed her keys and her purse and locked the door behind her.

For better or worse, she would confront Nick and find out the truth.

22

Nick packed up his toolbox and tossed it with a bit more force than necessary into the back of his pickup. He'd wanted to talk to Lily before this, but Mrs. Winters had called with an unexpected repair job, and Nick couldn't refuse the elderly woman's request.

He jumped into the cab and started the engine. The clock on the dashboard read nine o'clock. He'd go home, take a quick shower, and head to Lily's. There were a few things they needed to settle between them, and he wasn't going to put it off any longer.

On the way through his front door, he grabbed the mail from the box. The return address on the first envelope slowed him. His exam results. The screen door slammed behind him as he walked into the kitchen, his mouth as dry as the dust he'd just cleaned up.

He laid the envelope on the kitchen table while he reached in the fridge for a bottle of water. After a long swig, he wiped his mouth on the back of his hand and picked up the envelope. The news inside could either make or break his decision about the future.

In one swift movement, he ripped it open and shook out the paper containing his final marks. A relieved sigh escaped him. *Thank you, Lord.* He'd passed all his courses, which meant the degree was his. He'd earned the right to those letters after his name. Surely this was a sign from God that he was on the right track with his career.

A sudden crash from the front of the house drew his attention. Loud footsteps clattered down the hallway. He let out a low groan. One dose of Maxi a day was enough.

Nick poked his head out of the kitchen, startled to see Lily storming toward him. The red of her shirt blazed as fiery as her eyes. Her dark hair streamed out behind her in a mass of unruly curls. Despite the fact that she looked less than pleased to see him, pure pleasure flooded his system.

She marched up and poked a finger in his chest. "I want to know what's going on with you, Nick Logan."

Instead of answering, he followed his instincts and pulled her against him, claiming her mouth in a sweet kiss. The moment she melted against him, his heart soared. He deepened the kiss, relishing the heady scent of her perfume, until she suddenly stiffened. With a jerk, she ripped out of his arms and pushed him back.

"Don't think a kiss will make everything better, because it won't."

The hard edge of the table pressed into his thigh, and he shot out a hand to steady himself. The vibration of her anger pulsed between them. "I'm sorry. That's not what I intended."

She crossed her arms in front of her, cheeks flushed. "I think I deserve an explanation."

He reached down to rub his leg. "Yes, you do. Can I get you something to drink first?"

"No, thank you." She scowled at him, her expression thunderous.

He longed to reach out and smooth away the lines creasing her brow but knew his touch would not be welcome yet. His aching thigh attested to that fact. "I was about to come and see you. After I showered, that is." He looked down at his dirty jeans and shrugged. "So much for good impressions."

"I don't care about that," she snapped. "I want to know why you've been avoiding me."

He pulled out a chair. "Why don't we sit down?"

"I prefer to stand."

"Then I'll sit." Bone tired after ten hours of physical labor, he sank onto the chair, moving the paper with his marks discreetly under a magazine.

He raised weary eyes to hers and took a moment to form his thoughts. "I'm sorry I've been so distant lately. I needed time to do some serious thinking, and I couldn't afford any distractions."

The drip of his kitchen tap matched the beat of her toe tapping against the linoleum. "Thinking about what?"

He couldn't tell her about Ted's ultimatum. Too much pressure on both of them. "About my priorities. About where my life is headed and where you fit in. A few minor things like that."

A flicker of emotion passed over her face. She moved to lean against the kitchen counter, arms folded in front of her like a shield. "Come to any conclusions?"

Her flippant tone didn't match the nervous gestures he'd come to know — fingering her necklace, licking her lips, the tiny nerve dancing in her jaw.

He pushed up from the table and walked over to place gentle hands on her shoulders.

Apprehension appeared in the depths of her brown eyes. A man could happily drown in those depths. He stifled an inward sigh. This wasn't how he'd planned to tell her, but fate had forced his hand.

Her nerves kept his own steady as he looked deep into her eyes. "I came to the conclusion," he said, "that for better or worse, I am hopelessly in love with you and want you in my life on a permanent basis."

Both pleasure and fear skittered across her features in equal measure. Then her bottom lip began to quiver. She bit down on it, but the tremors didn't stop. He felt the vibrations all the way down his own arms.

The sight of tears welling in her eyes undid him. He pulled her against his chest and held her tight, relieved when her arms came around him to clutch the back of his shirt. Great sobs racked her slim frame. Nick's gut clenched at the sound. "Don't cry, Lily. Please."

He murmured soothing words and pressed light kisses to the top of her head. Her hair teased his nose with the scent of ripe strawberries. "I didn't mean to upset you," he whispered.

She sniffed, swiped a hand over her cheeks, and stepped away from him. A moment of sheer panic hit as he looked into her solemn face. What if she didn't return his feelings?

"You shouldn't love me," she said at last. "I don't deserve it."

He brushed a knuckle down her cheek. "One of these days, you're going to believe that you're not a terrible person. That you're actually very lovable, and even if you can't accept it yet, that God loves you, no matter how unworthy you think you are."

She didn't smile like he'd hoped. "No one except my mother has ever loved me," she whispered.

Compassion overwhelmed him at the misery in her eyes. "My beautiful Lily." He reached out to cup her face in his hands. "It may not make up for the past, but I do love you. So much so, you've got me tied up in knots." In more ways than she knew.

Tears hovered on the brink of her lower lashes. "The problem is . . . I think I love you, too."

His heart somersaulted in his chest as joy warred with confusion. "Why is that a problem?"

She shook her head. "Because it won't work. I'm not cut out to be a minister's wife. I'll just ruin your life."

"No, you won't." He drew her closer and kissed her again, pouring all his love into the joining of their lips. Before things got out of control, he took a reluctant step back, and brushed a curl off her cheek. "Does this mean I'm forgiven?"

A slight smile hovered on her lips. "For now."

"So generous of you."

Her soft laugh filled his soul with joy. Maybe, with God's divine guidance and the hope that Lily's heart would warm toward God again, they could make this relationship work after all.

23

Seated beside Nick, Maxi, and Sonia Martin in Chloe's high school auditorium, Lily waited for the graduation ceremony to begin. As nervous and proud as a parent, she crossed her knees and jiggled on the uncomfortable folding chair.

Nick reached over to still her fingers tapping a frantic beat on her purse. "Would you stop moving for two seconds? You're making *me* nervous."

"Sorry." She entwined her fingers through his, relishing the roughness of his skin, as well as the warmth that radiated from him. He looked so handsome in his dark suit and tie, with his blond locks combed back from his forehead, showcasing the blueness of his eyes.

She still couldn't believe he loved her. In the week since his admission, the panicky feeling had lessened, and now when she thought about his declaration, a glow of happiness warmed her.

Nick Logan, a thoughtful, kind, caring man, loved her.

She'd even told Nick about her conversation with his aunt. He'd been worried, but relieved, that his aunt now knew Lily's true identity and that Lily had promised Sonia not to tell Chloe.

Lily glanced at Nick and smiled, her stomach doing a slow flip at the love shining in his eyes. She wasn't sure how it had come about or how long it would last, but she was in love, and she planned to drink in each precious moment.

Maybe God wasn't out to punish her after all. Maybe He figured it was time she got a break in life. Gratitude filled her at the thought, and she whispered an inner prayer of thanks.

The music started, forcing everyone to their feet as the graduates began their procession. A lump rose in Lily's throat at all the fresh faces in their blue caps and gowns. These kids had their whole futures ahead of them.

Unable to bear her father's hypocritical face pretending to be proud of her, she hadn't even attended her own high school graduation. Instead she'd gone carousing with a group of wild friends and come home in the wee hours of the morning. Firmly, she pushed those dark memories back into storage and watched for Chloe.

Lily caught sight of her sister walking in proud procession with her classmates and snapped precious memories with her cell phone camera. Nick placed a reassuring hand on her shoulder, and she reached up to squeeze it, grateful to be able to share this special moment with him.

The ceremony, though tedious in parts, ended quickly. After many hugs and pictures, Nick, Lily, and Maxi accompanied the Martins back to the house, where a small reception awaited. Sonia's friends had come over to put out the sandwiches, punch, and the huge cake Sonia had ordered.

Without the daunting presence of Reverend Baker, Sarah Jane, or Mike Hillier, Lily actually managed to relax and enjoy herself.

Until Chloe called the guests together in the living room for an announcement.

Lily looked at Nick. "Any idea what this is about?"

He shook his head. "None."

Lily rolled her shoulders to dispel her sudden anxiety and concentrated on Chloe. She looked so pretty in her pink dress and matching shoes — like a fairy princess come to life.

"I want to thank everyone for coming," Chloe said when they'd gathered, "and for all the cards, gifts, and good wishes. It means a lot to have you all here to share this wonderful occasion with me."

A murmur of appreciation went through the group.

"I especially want to thank my mother for everything. She's always been there for me, no matter what."

Beside her, Sonia raised a tissue to her eyes, blushing under the praise.

"And my cousin, Nick, who's been like a big brother to me. Thank you for all your support."

A film of tears shone in Nick's eyes, and his Adam's apple bobbed. Lily squeezed his hand.

"I also want to give special thanks to my friend, Lily."

When all heads turned toward her, Lily gulped. Nick tightened his arm around her shoulder.

"Without her, I would never have passed my math course and wouldn't have been able to graduate. I owe my success to her."

Lily's face burned as everyone clapped and whistled, until Chloe motioned for silence. "Which brings me to my announce-ment."

Judging by her beaming face, it couldn't be anything bad. Yet Lily rubbed her neck to ease the cord of tension, coiled and ready to spring.

"Not many people know that I applied to two culinary schools last winter. Yesterday in the mail, I received a full scholarship to the best school in New York City."

Everyone cheered. Nick hugged Lily hard. Relief swept over her, weakening her knees. This was good news for Chloe. She'd got-ten into the school of her dreams.

"The other surprise is that I received early acceptance, which means I'm entered in the summer program." Chloe took a deep breath. "So I'll be leaving for New York on Monday."

The air whooshed out of Lily's lungs. She froze amid the chorus of congratulations. Chloe was leaving on Monday? Only two days away.

Panic snaked through her system like an insidious vine. Her carefully laid plan was crumbling before her eyes. She needed time to think. She needed oxygen.

"Excuse me," she whispered to Nick, and turned to push her way through the group of people and out the front door. She stumbled down the stairs on shaky legs, gulping in the fresh air.

Get it together, Lily. You can't fall apart now. She paced up and down the lawn, waiting for a measure of calm to return.

"Hey, you OK?" Nick's face mirrored concern as he came down the steps.

She pushed the hair off her forehead. "Yeah. Just a bit of a shock."

He joined her on the lawn, still looking puzzled. "But it's great news. A full scholarship is nothing to sneeze at."

"Of course, and I'm happy for her." She paused. "I just thought I'd have more time."

The evening air held a chill. Lily rubbed her hands up and down the satiny sleeves of her blouse for warmth. Her mind raced with a million thoughts. She had no choice now. She'd have to tell Chloe the truth before she left on Monday.

Nick studied her, a strange expression on his face. "You're not thinking what I think you're thinking, are you?"

Lily couldn't quite meet his eyes. "What do you mean?"

"You're not thinking of telling her about your connection?" His voice rumbled with a hint of warning.

She opened her mouth to deny it, but the lie stuck in her throat. She owed him honesty, even at the risk of his displeasure. "I can't let her go without knowing, Nick. I just can't."

He stared at her, open-mouthed. "I don't believe this. You promised me, Lily. That day at Rainbow Falls."

The pain and fear in his eyes tore at her soul. "I promised not to say anything *yet*. I always planned to tell her before she left for college. I just didn't expect it to be this soon."

Nick's expression darkened. "So my aunt's health means nothing to you. You don't care that this will probably kill her."

Lily squeezed her shaking hands together. "You're exaggerating."

"Are you willing to take that chance? Because I'm not." Nick stepped forward and gripped Lily's arms. "You don't have to do this. Chloe cares about you. She'll keep in touch. And you can visit her in New York."

Lily shook her head sadly. "Friendships don't last when people move away. Especially one so new. If Chloe knows I'm her sister, it will change everything."

Nick dropped his hands as if he couldn't bear to touch her. "Did you ever stop to consider what this revelation will do to her? You'll turn her world upside down."

She lifted her chin. "Chloe deserves to know the truth. Trust me, it's no fun finding out you've been living a lie your whole life, no matter how well-intentioned the deception."

Nick threw out his arms. "This is coming seventeen years too late. We can't change what my aunt and uncle decided back then. Chloe will be furious at her mother for keeping this from her. Aunt Sonia will never survive that."

With nothing to offer that would help the situation, Lily remained silent.

Nick raked his hands through his hair as he paced. At last he stopped and faced her again. "When you really love someone, their happiness becomes more important than your own. You put *their* best interests first. This is your chance to do the right thing, Lily. Think of Chloe and Aunt Sonia. Put them first."

His eyes beseeched her, tearing the scabs off her scarred heart, re-opening old wounds.

Guilt. Always more guilt. She'd had enough from her father to last a lifetime. Her conflicted emotions beat a painful pulse at her temples. "No one has ever put *my* needs first, Nick. Now, I'm going to do what I have to do. For me."

He stared at her, disappointment etched in the lines on his face. She turned away as the energy drained out of her like a leaky tire gone flat. She couldn't face going back inside but didn't want to ruin the rest of her sister's big night. "Tell Chloe I had a headache. I'll call her tomorrow."

When he didn't answer, she headed to her car without looking back, unwilling to watch Nick's love die before her very eyes.

24

The next morning, Lily picked at her piece of toast and barely sipped her coffee. She should be at church, but in light of her falling out with Nick, and her confusion over the situation with Chloe, she couldn't face it. She needed the next twenty-four hours to make up her mind.

Never had she felt so tormented by a decision. Her strong feelings for Nick, as well as her concern for Sonia Martin's health, urged her to remain silent, but she could not give up her goal of claiming her sister. The past thirteen years since her mother's death had been a living nightmare. Yet she'd survived it all — every painful incident.

And over these past few months, she'd found a shred of hope to cling to at last. But now her one living blood relative was about to walk out of her life. Didn't she deserve this small piece of happiness?

She sighed, thinking longingly of Nick. If

he loved her so much, why couldn't he put *her* happiness ahead of his aunt's and cousin's? Chloe would get used to the reality of her true identity soon enough. She might be upset with Sonia for a short time, but Chloe had much too generous of a nature to hold a grudge for long. In the meantime, she and Chloe could bond as sisters. If only Nick could understand how much she needed this.

Nevertheless, Lily could understand Nick's point of view. Why couldn't she wait until a better time to tell Chloe? But who knew how long that would take? By then, Chloe might have forgotten all about her. Found new friends, a boyfriend, a whole new life that Lily might not fit into.

No, she couldn't risk it.

Lily got up, threw her toast in the trash, and sought solace in her artwork, hoping the answer to her dilemma would become clear. This time, however, dabbing colors on a blank canvas did little to quiet her mind. Her thoughts returned over and over again to Nick and Chloe. Frustrated, she cleaned her brushes and packed away her supplies.

With nothing left to lose, Lily turned to the only source of comfort she hadn't tried. She sat in the middle of her bed, closed her eyes and began to pray.

Lord, I haven't done this in a very long time, but I'm asking for Your help now. I'm trying to understand why You would let me find Chloe only to have her slip out of my life so soon. Is it wrong to want to acknowledge her as my sister? Am I being totally selfish? Please help me make the right decision. Amen.

When Lily opened her eyes, the room appeared the same. No magic solution came to mind. Still, it felt good to be able to pray again. To believe someone or something could be on her side.

A loud rapping on her front door startled Lily from her thoughts. Her heart picked up speed as hope poured through her. Was Nick here to work things out? When she looked at her watch, hope turned to disappointment. No, Nick would still be in church.

The knocking became louder, more insistent. Dread slid through her veins as she shot off the bed. Who could that possibly be?

"I'm coming. I'm coming." She hurried down the hall, pausing to smooth back her hair before opening the door.

Sarah Jane stood on the landing, hand poised to knock again.

Lily frowned. How had she gotten in the front door? Had Maxi let her in?

Sarah Jane lowered her hand and lifted her chin. "I need to speak with you."

Without waiting, the woman pushed past her into the apartment. Lily huffed out an annoyed breath and closed the door. Today of all days, she did not need Sarah Jane's hostility.

"Have a seat." Lily pointed to the living room on her right.

Once inside, Sarah Jane perched stiffly on the high back chair, while Lily took the sofa. The hard gleam in Sarah Jane's eyes did nothing to ease her anxiety.

"What are you doing here, Sarah Jane? Shouldn't you be in church?"

The girl patted her skirt into place. "I left the service early to find you. We have important issues to discuss."

Not again. Sarah Jane just couldn't let go of her fantasy relationship with Nick, no matter how many times Nick told her it was over.

Sarah Jane leaned forward in her chair, an unpleasant smile stretching her thin lips. "I want you to leave Rainbow Falls for good. And when you hear what I have to say, I'm sure you'll agree."

Nick walked into the kitchen, his shoulders sagging to match his mood. He tossed his keys onto the table with a loud sigh. Lily hadn't shown up at church this morning — which meant she'd only been going to please him, and because of their argument last night, didn't feel she had to keep up the pretense. Or maybe it was her way of punishing him. Either way, God wasn't in the equation, and Nick needed to keep that in mind.

He rubbed a hand over his chest where a dull ache had settled. There had to be a way to fix this mess, but the answer escaped him. Even prayer this morning had failed to ease his anxiety.

Somehow he'd have to pull himself together before tonight's dinner with his aunt and cousin. For their sakes, he'd pretend nothing was wrong. That his life wasn't falling apart around him. He slapped his palm on the kitchen counter. The dirty cups jumped and clattered like his unsettled nerves.

Lord, please show me a way out of this dilemma. Help me find a solution that will keep everyone happy. And Lord . . . draw Lily to You and guide her to make the best decision for everyone involved. Amen.

The shrill ring of the phone pulled him upright. Maybe after a night of reflection,

Lily had come around to his way of thinking.

Instead, the gruff voice of Ted Baker boomed through the line. "Nicholas, you left before I could speak with you."

Nick stifled a groan. He could not deal with Ted right now. "Sorry, sir. I have a lot on my mind today."

"I've set aside an hour for us to meet tomorrow. I can't wait any longer for your decision."

Nick's mind whirled with uncertainty. His answer, once so irrevocable, now wavered. "Tomorrow's not the best time for me. I have to see Chloe off at the bus depot."

He was stalling, but hoped to gain a few more days. He needed time to settle things with Lily first.

"I've already spoken with Sonia. The bus doesn't leave until four o'clock. We'll have plenty of time before then. Meet me in my office at two-thirty."

Nick closed his eyes, a feeling of doom washing over him. "I'll be there."

Tension coiled in Lily's torso like the old springs in her couch, making it impossible to remain seated. She sprang to her feet and stood, arms crossed. "Why would you think I'd ever leave Rainbow Falls?"

310

Sarah Jane stared at her, unblinking, like a cat waiting to pounce. "I had an interesting visit with your father the other day."

The blood drained from Lily's head and pooled into the soles of her feet. She grasped the back of one of the wingback chairs with shaking hands. "You have no idea who my father is."

"On the contrary. I know exactly who he is. Reverend Tobias Cunningham of Fielding, North Dakota. A charming little town just east of Bismarck."

Lily's body went numb. She counted to ten, trying not to panic. Losing control was not an option. "How did you find him?"

"With help from Mike Hillier. It wasn't too difficult. Oh, don't worry. Mike doesn't know what I've found, but he will — if you decide to stay."

Lily swallowed hard. She knew Mike was suspicious of her, but never thought he'd take it this far. "I see. And why do you think finding my father would make me leave here?" Sweat trickled down her ramrod spine as she waited for the woman's response. Each second seemed like an eternity as Lily focused on the ticking of the mantel clock.

Sarah Jane picked some lint off her brown tweed skirt. "Call me crazy, but I don't think you'd want Nick to know you're a fugitive from the law." She paused and shot Lily a look of pure venom. "Wouldn't do for a minister to be associated with a wanted criminal, now would it?"

Lily's hand flew to her throat.

"That's right. I know all your dirty little secrets." She let the insinuation hover in the air for a moment, seeming to relish the effect of her words.

The room made a slow spin around as Lily clutched the chair to keep from falling. Her legs, as limp as noodles, barely held her up.

God help me. What do I do now?

Sarah Jane rose in an unhurried fashion and fixed Lily with a hard stare. "Unless you want Nick and the rest of this town to find out all the sordid details of your past, I'd suggest you start packing. Immediately."

Something in the woman's smug, self-righteous smirk snapped the thin thread of Lily's control. She flew forward, rage shooting adrenaline through her body. She itched to enjoy the satisfaction of physical release and to see the fear in her opponent's eyes . . .

With a jolt, Lily pulled herself up short. Though every impulse begged for vengeance, Lily would not stoop to violence.

She'd be no better than her father.

She lowered her clenched fist to her side. "Get out of here. Now!"

Sarah Jane did not seem fazed as she strolled into the hallway. With a hand on the door handle, she turned to shoot one more dagger at Lily. "You have until tomorrow night to be gone — or I tell Nick everything."

The door slammed shut seconds before Lily gave a guttural scream and hurled a vase across the room, where it shattered into a thousand pieces.

Lily hobbled down the hall to her bedroom, her spirit as broken as the shards of glass littering the floor. She'd made the fatal mistake of underestimating her enemy, and now it would cost her everything. Stifling a sob, she pulled the shabby suitcases out of her closet and threw them on the bed. Tears coursed unchecked down her cheeks, dripping onto her T-shirt. She no longer had a choice — she had to leave this town she'd come to love. If she didn't, Nick, Chloe, and Maxi would learn all her sins, and she'd no longer be welcome. Worse yet, she'd be arrested. The fact that Mike Hillier had not beaten Sarah Jane to the punch surprised Lily. He seemed so dogged about finding out about her past.

If she cooperated with Sarah Jane, her secrets would remain buried. Maybe Lily would move to New York, too. And in time, when the dust settled, she could reach out to Chloe again.

As Lily grabbed handfuls of clothing from her drawers and crammed them into the cases, she determinedly banished all thoughts of Nick to the far recesses of her mind. She could not think about him right now, or she'd break into so many pieces, she'd never be whole again.

"Lily?"

Footsteps tapping on the hardwood floor jerked Lily to attention. Panic seized her insides, solidifying them into one gelled mass. She swiped her sleeve across her damp cheeks and buried her face in the closet.

"That must've been some fight, judging by the wreckage out there."

Maxi's amused voice caused twin pangs of regret and guilt to rise in Lily's throat. For her friend's sake, Lily needed to hold herself together.

"You going somewhere?" Suspicion entered Maxi's voice.

Lily dared not look up as she hauled out an armful of clothes and stuffed them inside the cases. "I don't know."

"Then why are you packing?" Maxi strode into the room and stopped beside the bed.

Lily's brain whirled to find a plausible explanation. "Actually, I'm going home. I need to see my father." Not a total lie. She needed to find him before he arrived to stir up trouble in Rainbow Falls.

"Must be something bad. You look upset."

Lily pressed her lips into a grim line to keep them from quivering. "It is." She banged the lid shut, then turned to look at Maxi fully for the first time. "Please don't ask me to talk about it. I can't."

Without a word, Maxi stepped forward and enveloped Lily in a fierce hug. "I hope you know you can tell me anything. I'm your friend no matter what."

Lily's body shook from the pent-up emotions warring for release. If only she could believe that. She squeezed Maxi hard, then moved away. "Maybe one day when we're living in New York, I'll tell you the whole sordid thing." Lily attempted a smile, praying Maxi would leave so she could curl up in a ball until morning.

Maxi pushed her hands into the pockets of her pants. "What about tomorrow? Aren't you going to see Chloe off?"

"I'll be there," Lily said grimly. "I'm leaving right after." She set her bulging suitcases on the floor beside the bed.

"Did Peg give you time off work?" Lines of concern furrowed Maxi's forehead.

She was fishing, hoping for a clue to Lily's odd behavior, but Lily would give her none.

She walked past Maxi into the hallway. "Not yet. I'll talk to her tomorrow."

Maxi followed her out to the kitchen where Lily pulled two bottles of water out of the fridge. With unsteady hands, she handed one to Maxi.

Maxi took the bottle, silent concern flooding her face. "You sure you're OK?"

Lily looked away as she twisted off the cap. "Not really . . . but I will be."

"If you need anything . . . money, a ride . . ."

"Thanks, but no." Lily cringed at the hurt that shone in her friend's eyes. One of the only true friends she'd ever had. She stiffened her posture to help her get through the next few minutes without collapsing.

Maxi shrugged. "Then I guess I'll see you tomorrow at the bus depot. Nick has an appointment, so I'm picking up Chloe and her mom. Bus leaves at four o'clock."

"I'll be there."

Maxi picked her way over the shards of glass in the hallway and opened the door. She looked back over one shoulder, worry creating furrows above her nose. "Call me if you want to talk. Or just come downstairs. I'll be there."

More tears burned at the back of Lily's throat. How she wished she could do just that — tell her the whole sad tale, and have Maxi wave her magic pixie wand to make everything turn out fine. But those were fairytales. Hadn't Lily always known her story would have no happy ending?

She swallowed hard and blinked to clear her vision. "Thank you, Maxi. You've been a great friend to me. The best I've ever had."

With a final nod, Maxi turned and walked out, but not before Lily saw the tears glistening in her friend's eyes.

25

Monday dawned gray and gloomy, much like Nick's mood. Threatening clouds hung over the town ready to unleash their torrents.

Not a good start to such a momentous day. A day when he would say good-bye to the girl who'd been like a sister to him all these years. How was he supposed to let her go off to the big city all by herself? A naïve little thing like Chloe?

Nick tore a long piece of wallpaper from the main wall in his living room and crumpled it into a ball. He'd spent the good part of the morning stripping wallpaper, a job that could have waited. But he needed something physical to do to keep from climbing the walls. Tearing paper off them instead gave him some relief for his frustration.

He stretched out his back muscles, then checked the time. Soon he'd have to change for his meeting with Ted. Another momentous occasion.

But worst of all — the thing that made his insides churn all night until he couldn't stand to stay in bed — was the deafening silence from Lily. Would she tell Chloe the truth before she left town? Or would she come to her senses and realize what a mistake that would be?

A loud, insistent rapping on his front door broke the silence. Hope flared like a beacon of light in the gloom. Had Lily come to make peace? To tell him he was right after all?

Nick raced to open the door. Hope slid from his soul at the sight of Maxi on his porch.

She pushed past him into the hallway. "Something's wrong with Lily."

The air leaked out of Nick's lungs like a balloon deflating. Reality hit him hard. Lily would not change her mind, not even for him. He'd trusted that her love would win out in the end.

He'd been deluding himself.

"She was packing her things yesterday," Maxi continued. "Says she's going home to see her father."

Nick's head jerked up. "What?"

"I don't believe it either. She didn't seem

319

herself at all. And there was broken glass all over her apartment."

Nick wiped his hands on a towel hanging from the pocket of his jeans and motioned her to follow him into the living room. He raked a hand through his already messy hair. "We had a big argument on Saturday night at the party," he admitted. "She could be upset over that. But I can't see her leaving town because of it."

Maxi stared at him as if he'd sprouted antennas. "You haven't talked to her since then?"

"No."

Maxi groaned, shaking her head until her earrings jingled. "Don't you know after a fight you need to go over with flowers and apologize?"

He picked up a trowel, his jaw as rigid as the metal tool. "She's the one who needs to come to me. This is one argument I'm not backing down on."

He attacked a new section of the wall. The loud scraping sound made further conversation almost impossible. He hoped Maxi would get the hint and leave. He'd had all the advice he could take for the present.

A few moments passed before Maxi sighed. "I hope you know what you're doing, Logan, because I'm afraid Lily might be leaving town for good."

An hour later, Nick stood in the hallway outside Ted Baker's office and took a minute to collect himself. Despite every effort to remain calm, his heart thumped out a staccato rhythm. He couldn't help it. This was one of those pivotal moments — the proverbial crossroads — where the direction of his life would change forever.

After much prayer and soul searching, he'd made his decision. All he needed now was the courage to go through with it. Taking a deep breath, he knocked on the door.

"Come in," Ted called.

When Nick stepped through the doorway, his gaze skimmed past Ted's gray head and slammed right into Bishop Brian Langford. Ted's superior leaned forward in his seat, a smile of greeting on his face.

Other than stalling his entry for a split second, Nick fought not to show any outward evidence of the shock he felt at this ambush. Since when had Ted invited the bishop to be part of this meeting?

Ted rose from his chair behind the worn wooden desk. "Hello, Nicholas. You remember Bishop Langford?"

Nick noted the hint of doubt under Ted's self-possessed demeanor and felt his own confidence slip. In this moment of truth, he tried to forget all Ted's recent manipulations and ultimatums. Instead, he remembered how the gentle pastor had taken a lost, rebellious youth and gently guided him to become the man Nick was today. He couldn't bear to disappoint the man who had helped mold his faith. So now he pushed back his resentment of Ted's high-handed tactics and stepped forward to shake the bishop's hand. "Of course. Nice to see you again, Bishop."

Brian Langford, a tall, lean man in his early sixties smiled warmly at Nick. "Same here. And please call me Brian. I hope you don't mind me sitting in on this little get-together."

"Of course not." *What choice did he have?*

The room seemed suffocating as Nick took a seat across from the two men. Obviously Ted had invited the bishop as a power play, to raise the stakes and make it harder for Nick to refuse the job. Guess he couldn't blame Ted for playing every trump card he had up his sleeve.

"We don't want to waste the bishop's time so let's get right down to the business at hand. Have you come to a decision about your future, Nicholas?"

Nick wished he could open the large

picture window and get some air moving in the stuffy space. He ran a finger around his collar. "Yes, sir, I have."

"Good. Well, please don't keep us in suspense."

Nick looked from one clergy member to the other. Now that the moment was upon him, giving Ted his decision was proving harder than he thought.

"Let me start by saying what a great honor it is to be considered as a possible replacement for you, Reverend Ted. Your devotion to the people of Rainbow Falls has been inspiring to say the least. On a personal note, your mentorship in my spiritual journey has meant the world to me." He paused to let his emotions settle. "To that end, I must admit I'm still interested in taking this position . . ." He noted the smug expression on Ted's face. "However, the unusual stipulation placed upon the acceptance of this post has proven unacceptable to me."

Bishop Brian's smile slid into a frown. "Am I missing something here?"

Ted's pale eyes darted between the two men. Nick pressed his lips together and waited for Ted to explain the situation, since he was the one who'd created it.

The older man folded his hands together

on top of the desk. "Unfortunately, Nicholas has been seeing a rather . . . unsuitable young woman. Someone who would not make a proper minister's wife. I suggested that if Nick truly felt God's calling to serve in this parish, then his relationship with this woman would have to end."

"In other words, if I want this position, I have to sever all ties with the woman I love." Nick didn't bother to hide his displeasure.

Bishop Langford pursed his lips, leaned back in his chair, and looked from one man to the other. "Not knowing the young woman in question, I will have to decline comment and defer to Reverend Ted's wise opinion. So tell me then, Mr. Logan, what is your final decision?"

Both men looked at him expectantly. Disappointment weighed heavy on Nick's shoulders. He'd hoped the bishop would side with him on this issue. He realized, however, that even if Bishop Langford disagreed with Ted, professional courtesy demanded he side with his colleague. Sweat dampened Nick's collar, but he raised his chin and looked Ted in the eye. "With all due respect, sir, I must decline the position."

Ted's mouth gaped open and Bishop Langford's eyebrows rose.

"You can't be serious," Ted said. "You'd throw away all those years of studying and your calling from God . . . for that woman?" His face had turned ashen.

Nick rose slowly from his chair and pushed his hands deep into his pockets. Out of respect for the bishop more than anything, he clamped his emotions down with an iron vice. "I am in love with Lily and plan to marry her one day. If God is calling me *and Lily* to serve Him, as I believe He is, then He'll show me another way." Of course, the "and Lily" part was still unknown. Before he proposed marriage, he'd have to know of her desire to serve God. He suspected she was moving back toward her heavenly Father, which gave him great hope, but she needed more time. *Please, Lord, show her the way to You.*

Ted's face grew even paler, but he remained silent.

"Thank you for your time, gentlemen. I wish you the best in finding the right person for this ministry." He sucked in air as the pain of realizing that he would not be that man radiated across his chest. With a nod in the bishop's direction, he turned and strode out the door.

He didn't take another breath until he reached his truck. Once inside, he gulped in a lungful of air. Lowering his head to the steering wheel, he concentrated on the simple task of breathing.

When at last Nick turned the key in the ignition, a new sense of calm descended. He'd been seeing the situation through an underwater blur, and now that he'd resurfaced, the world had become clear. With God's guidance, he'd made his decision, and there was no turning back now.

Only one further hurdle remained.

As he sped toward the bus depot to see Chloe off, he prayed Lily wouldn't let him down.

26

Time had run out.

Lily had delayed the inevitable as long as possible, but the sands of the proverbial hourglass had sifted to the bottom. With all her possessions packed into the back of her battered Toyota, Lily watched Chloe through the window of the bus depot as she waited in line at the ticket counter. In a few minutes, Chloe would board that bus and leave Rainbow Falls, possibly for good.

In some ways, Sarah Jane's timing had been fortuitous. With nothing left to lose, Lily had no reason not to tell her sister the truth. And if everyone hated her for doing so, well, no one could hate her more than she hated herself. She counted on family ties to win out in the end, and that once Chloe got over the initial shock, she'd want a connection with her only sibling.

Her resolve set, Lily stepped out of her car. The wind whipped about her, tearing at her hair and jacket as she walked across the street to the bus station, where Sonia, Maxi, and probably Nick would all be waiting to see Chloe off.

Her stomach dipped, imagining how upset Nick and Sonia would be when she told Chloe. She forced her thoughts from that painful scenario as her sister emerged from the depot, ticket in hand. Clad in denim shirt and jeans, and her brown hair pulled back with a blue-checkered kerchief, Chloe looked every part the student. Her face lit up when she spotted Lily.

"Oh, thank goodness. I thought you weren't going to make it."

"Of course I made it." Lily hoped her bright smile hid her anxiety. "I wouldn't let you leave without saying good-bye."

She looked around, relieved to discover Nick wasn't there. Only Sonia and Maxi waited on the bright yellow bench under the bus sign. They stood as Lily and Chloe approached.

Lily greeted them both and then stood silent, hands stuffed in the pockets of her jeans. Tension hung in the air between them. Even the unflappable Maxi jiggled nervously from one foot to the other. Sonia watched Lily with an uneasy stare, her eyes red-rimmed from crying.

"Cheer up." Chloe put her arm around her frail mother. "You're all acting like this is a funeral. Be happy for me. I'm going to do something I love."

Sonia sniffed into her hankie. "We are happy for you, dear. We're just going to miss you terribly, that's all."

"Ditto." Maxi squeezed Chloe's hand.

Despite the cool wind, Lily's damp shirt clung to her back. How was she going to drop this bombshell of hers?

"Chloe," she began, stepping closer. "There's something I need to tell you before you go." She forced herself to ignore the terror that leapt into Sonia Martin's eyes. The strong coffee she'd had this morning curdled in her stomach.

Chloe's smile faded. "What is it? You look serious."

Sonia Martin moved between the girls, her cane tapping the sidewalk. "The bus will be here any minute. Surely this can wait for another time."

Chloe frowned. "Mom, let Lily speak. I'm sure it won't take long."

Lord, please give me the right words. Lily ran her tongue over her dry lips, stalling. Even Maxi stared at her with open curiosity.

Just tell her.

At that moment, the Greyhound bus pulled up beside them and ground to a halt in a cloud of exhaust. Chloe's attention flew to the vehicle, a smile lighting her features. She bent down to pick up her bag.

"Wait, Chloe. Please." Lily reached out to grasp her arm.

The sound of footsteps approaching turned their attention to Nick walking toward them. Lily stared, unable to look away from the man she loved, knowing this could be the last time she saw him. Her vision blurred as she drank in the sight of his windblown hair and blue eyes shrouded with pain. Her shoulders sagged. His presence made everything she was about to say that much harder.

He stopped beside his aunt and placed his arm around her as if to shield her from what was to come. Lily couldn't bear the tortured expression on his face.

Chloe flew over to give Nick a huge hug. "You almost missed me. I'm glad you made it."

He kissed her forehead. "Me, too. You take care of yourself, kiddo. If you ever need anything, call me, day or night." The sadness in his voice brought a lump to Lily's throat.

With Chloe gone, the only one he'd have

330

around was his ailing aunt. Thank goodness he'd have his position as minister to keep him busy and help him forget once Lily left.

"I will. I promise." Chloe hugged him again then spun around. "Oh, Lily. I'm sorry. What did you want to say?"

Lily wavered. Her heart pounded louder than the bus's engine. With shaky fingers, she toyed with the locket around her neck, running it back and forth along the chain, as her thoughts whirled in rapid succession. Could she bear to see Nick's disappointment, his silent accusation of betrayal? Did she have the right to rip Chloe and Sonia's world apart?

She looked into Chloe's expectant face, a face so full of excitement for the future that she literally shone from the inside out. How could Lily take that away from her?

"I want you to know how much your friendship has meant to me . . ." The lump in her throat swelled, making it impossible to continue.

Tears appeared in Chloe's eyes. She closed the gap between them and engulfed Lily in a tight embrace. "I'm the one who should be thanking you after all you've done for me. I'm going to miss you so much."

Chloe pulled back and wiped her face.

Lily was astonished to find her own cheeks wet.

Chloe squeezed her hand. "Was that all?"

"No. There's more."

She heard Sonia's sharp intake of breath, sensed Nick's unspoken plea.

You're my sister. You're my sister, and I love you.

At that moment, Nick's words echoed inside her. *"When you really love someone, their happiness becomes more important than your own. You put their best interests first."*

The truth slammed through her, shaking her. Revealing her secret right now was *not* in Chloe's best interest. All the pent-up energy drained from Lily, leaving her limp. She couldn't do it — couldn't ruin Chloe's happiness.

As if in slow motion, Lily reached up to pull the gold chain over her head. For a brief moment, she held the locket in her palm, rubbed her thumb in a last caress over the engraved casing, then held it out to Chloe. "I want you to have this . . . to remember me by."

Chloe gasped and shook her head. "No, I couldn't. I know how much that necklace means to you."

Lily took Chloe's hand and placed the locket in her palm, curling her fingers closed. "Take it. Please."

Chloe waited a beat and then finally nodded. With silent tears dripping down her face, she unfolded the chain and slipped it over her head.

"Be happy," Lily whispered. "I love you."

"I love you, too." Chloe hugged her hard. "You're like the sister I never had."

Pain seared through Lily, as sharp and searing as the blade of a knife. She bit her lip to keep from blurting out the truth. Instead, she hung on for dear life, memorizing the smell of Chloe's citrus shampoo.

The waiting bus driver blared the horn.

"I have to go." Chloe grabbed her tote bag, hugged Nick, Maxi, and her mother one more time and then leapt onto the bus.

Lily's bones solidified into one brittle mass. Feeling as though she'd crack if she moved a hair, she prayed for the strength to hold herself together until the bus moved away. Long enough to get away from Nick and Maxi. She was about to fall apart, and she would do it in private.

She raised her hand in one last wave as the bus rumbled off. Aware of the eyes on her, she made an abrupt turn toward her car and stumbled ahead a few feet until the sight before her stopped her cold. Her heart — the one that had pounded only seconds ago — now stilled in horror.

A police car pulled up to the curb beside her. From behind the wheel, Mike Hillier's mouth formed a grim line. She looked past him into the passenger seat where the burning gaze of her father stared back at her.

Mike unfolded himself from the driver's door. Adjusting his belt and holster, he stepped toward her, a hint of sympathy in his eyes.

"Hello, Lily. I'm afraid I have to inform you that you're under arrest."

27

Nick gaped in disbelief, his feet rooted to the cement. The wind picked up, blowing some discarded candy wrappers and leaves along the sidewalk. The remaining foul stench of the bus fumes filled his nostrils. This had to be one of Mike's practical jokes. What other explanation could there be?

But when Mike took out a pair of hand-cuffs and clipped them on Lily's wrist, reality exploded like a starburst in Nick's brain, propelling him forward. "What do you think you're doing?"

Mike shook his head. "I'm sorry, pal. Lily's father is pressing charges."

"What sort of charges?" Nick struggled to wrap his mind around what was happening.

"Breaking and entering. And theft under a thousand dollars."

Theft? Nick shifted his focus to Lily. She held her pale face averted, her eyes cast down at the sidewalk. Why wasn't she saying anything to defend herself?

The man Nick assumed to be her father stepped out of the cruiser and came forward. He wore his untidy gray hair swept over a thinning hairline. Small, beady eyes sunk into a wrinkled face. A sharp nose and thin lips reminded Nick of a rat.

"Took me a while to track you down," the man said, glaring at Lily, "but you're finally going to pay for your sins." He fingered his clerical collar as though it were a badge of honor.

The shame fled from Lily's demeanor. Her head snapped up and anger sparked from her eyes. "You owe me a lot more than a few hundred dollars." Lily spat the words at him.

The effect hit Nick like a blow to the solar plexus. Had she really stolen that money from her father?

He'd just thrown his career away for this woman.

While he grappled with the revelation, Mike placed Lily in the backseat of the police car. Lily's father climbed into the passenger seat. A group of curious onlookers had begun to gather at the curb beside the cruiser, their murmurs buzzing like busy insects around him.

Mike walked back to where Nick stood on

the sidewalk and leaned his head toward him. "I'm taking her down to the station until we can sort this mess out," he said quietly. "Why don't you take your aunt home and meet us down there."

Unable to find his voice, Nick could only nod.

Lord, what sort of test are You putting me through now?

As he watched Mike drive away, Nick's mind swirled like the tumultuous clouds in the gloomy sky overhead. How had Lily's father ended up here in Rainbow Falls right when, according to Maxi, Lily was supposed to be going home to see him?

And this arrest? The charges had to be false, fabricated by an embittered father.

"What are you going to do about this?" Maxi appeared on the sidewalk beside him, flags of red staining her cheeks.

Nick offered up a quick prayer for patience. "As soon as I drive Aunt Sonia home, I'll head over to the station."

"I can't believe this. That man must be lying."

"It won't do any good to speculate. Just wait until I go down there and get the facts."

Maxi tapped a foot on the sidewalk. The wind tousled her spiky hair. "I don't understand anything going on here lately."

"That makes two of us."

She thrust her hands on her hips. "I'm coming with you to the station."

Nick drew in a deep breath and kept his voice low to avoid the attention of the now dispersing group of onlookers. "Not a good idea. Too many people will only complicate the situation."

He thought Maxi would argue with him, but her slim frame slumped, as if the fight had drained out of her, and a sheen of tears moistened her eyes. Weariness trickled through his veins. He placed a comforting arm around her shoulders. "Would you do me a favor and take Aunt Sonia home? Then I can head over there right away."

Maxi glared at him with suspicion, but at least the tears disappeared. "Fine. But call me the minute you know anything."

"I will."

Ten minutes later, Nick pushed through the door of the police station. Instead of the chaos he expected, an eerie quiet filled the building. The ever-present smell of stale cigarette smoke hung in the air. He scanned the main room, noting the empty reception desk. Where was everyone?

Without knocking, he strode into the chief's office and found Mike hunched over a stack of paperwork. Nick's presence cast a shadow on the desk. "Tell me this is a bad joke, Mike."

His friend looked up, an expression of guilt and sorrow shadowing his eyes. "I'm sorry, pal. I wish it *were* a joke. I've had my suspicions all along something wasn't right, but I never expected this."

Nick clenched his back molars together. "How did all this happen?"

Mike's gaze slid away to the desktop. "I found Lily's father, a minister up in Fielding, and realized she'd been using a different last name. Probably because there was a warrant out under her real name."

Nick scrubbed a hand over his face, as though he could wipe away the confusion clouding his brain. "I don't understand. Why were you looking for her father?"

"Just following my gut. Something about her didn't add up. Next thing I know, Reverend Cunningham arrived here declaring that an arrest warrant had been issued and demanding I arrest his daughter." Mike shrugged one shoulder. "I had no choice."

Nick paced to the other side of the office and back. For the moment, he pushed aside the churning resentment. He'd deal with Mike later. Right now, only Lily could give him the answers he needed. He stopped in front of the desk. "I have to see her, Mike."

The officer shook his head. "Sorry, pal. I have to transfer her to the Bismarck station. The car will be here any minute."

The last thread of Nick's patience snapped. He pounded his fist on Mike's desk and pinned him with a furious stare. "As your friend, I'm asking you to cut me a break. I think you owe me that much." He clamped his mouth shut to avoid saying something he'd regret. Like how friends didn't betray friends.

Mike closed his eyes, lines of weariness etching his skin. He looked as miserable as Nick felt. "Three minutes. That's it."

Relief eased the pressure off Nick's chest, and he let out a huge breath. "Thank you."

He followed Mike into the outer office, which remained empty. The bitter scent of burned coffee assaulted him. "Where's her father?"

"I sent him home. He'd only make matters worse."

Nick unclenched his fists. "Good. I won't be tempted to throttle him."

Mike stopped and shook his head. "You're so convinced she's innocent, you're not even willing to hear his side of the story?"

Nick shoved his hands in his pockets and ignored the question. "Can I see her now?"

Mike sighed, then continued on to the

small, enclosed room and took out a key. "Wait here." He entered, but emerged a minute later, a defeated expression on his face. "Sorry, pal. She doesn't want to see you."

The words hit him like a punch to the gut. He'd pictured Lily, scared and anxious, waiting for him to come to her . . . To do what? Rescue her? Comfort her? Now she wouldn't even talk to him. Nick's anger bubbled to the surface. He pushed past Mike through the still open door. "Lily, I need to —"

What he saw halted him in his tracks. His heart constricted, creating a slow ache that radiated outward from his chest. Lily lay curled in a ball on the stark metal cot against the wall, her hair in disarray, her back to the door. "Go away."

The terse words shook him. "Lily, please. Talk to me."

She turned over to pierce him with an angry stare. "If you're here to find out whether I'm guilty or not, the answer is yes. I took the money. So you might as well leave." She flipped back to face the wall.

It couldn't be. There had to be some other explanation. "Why?" he whispered.

"Does it matter? Just go, Nick. I told you I'd ruin your life."

The disgust in her tone tore through him like the slash of a knife. He stood still for a moment, trying to absorb the pain. Who was this harsh woman? What had become of the laughing, tender Lily he'd come to love? She was in there somewhere. He was sure.

He had to try one more time to get through to her. "There's no crime so terrible that God won't forgive. That *I* won't forgive. We can sort this out together — if you'll just talk to me."

Her back muscles visibly stiffened. "Leave. Me. Alone."

The loathing in her voice sapped the last of his strength from him, rooting him to the spot, in a nightmare he couldn't wake up from.

"Let's go, Nick." Mike's firm hand on his shoulder broke Nick from his immobility.

He stumbled backward, made an abrupt turn, and strode straight out through the station, not stopping until he reached the street. The first drops of rain hit his face as he jumped into his truck and laid his forehead on the steering wheel. Harsh gasps wheezed from his lungs.

Why had Lily kept this secret? He thought they'd moved past the stage of distrust to something deeper. Thought his love would be enough to conquer her inner demons.

He pounded his fist on the dashboard until pain shot up his arm. This would not be the end of their story. No matter what it took, he'd get to the bottom of this mess and figure out a solution. He sagged back in his seat and closed his eyes to pray.

Lord, I need your help. Send your healing grace to all of us involved in this unfortunate situation. Show us a way out of this abyss we've fallen into. If there is any way out . . .

With God all things are possible. His favorite verse from Matthew crept into his mind. As he recited the rest of the passage, a calming sense of peace invaded his muscles. He was not alone. God would be with him through this whole ordeal.

He had no idea how long he'd been sitting there when the door to the police station opened and Mike led Lily out in handcuffs. Nick straightened in his seat, noticing through the rain-splattered window the Bismarck police car now parked in front. For one brief moment, Lily glanced his way, their eyes locking. The stark sorrow on her face mirrored his own misery.

She ducked her head when Mike handed her into the waiting car. As Nick leapt out of his truck, the sky opened up. A solid sheet of rain pelted him, soaking him to the skin within seconds. Alone in the middle of the road, he watched the squad car pull away, taking the woman he loved off to jail.

28

Following an almost sleepless night, Nick rose early with a plan of action in mind. Somewhere in the pre-dawn darkness, he decided to pay Tobias Cunningham a visit. If Lily wouldn't answer his questions, maybe her father would. And maybe, just maybe, he could persuade the man to see reason.

After a hot shower and a quick cup of coffee, Nick grabbed his keys from the hook in the front entrance and jogged down the steps to his truck.

His hand froze on the door handle at the sight of Sarah Jane standing in the driveway, hands clasped in front of her. Nick swallowed a groan. This was the last thing he needed right now.

"Hello, Nick. Can I speak with you for a minute?" The wind blew strands of hair around her serious face.

He pulled his keys from the lock. "Actually, I was just heading out."

"It's important."

The beginning of a headache pulsed across Nick's forehead. "Fine, but I am in a hurry."

Sarah Jane seemed to make an effort to soften her demeanor, relaxing the pinched lines around her mouth. "I hear Lily was arrested yesterday. You must be upset."

Nick folded his arms and leaned a hip against the vehicle, tamping down his impatience. "Of course, I'm upset."

"I also heard you turned down Uncle Ted's position."

Wisps of temper wound through his system. Sometimes the gossip mill of a small town frayed his last nerve. "That's right."

"All because of Lily Draper?" Her voice rose a notch, competing with the sound of a car whizzing by.

"Right again."

Her brows crashed together in a scowl, her disapproval no longer hidden behind a mask of politeness. She stepped forward, her eyes hard. "Now that you know her true nature, I'm sure you'd like to reconsider your decision."

The hint of challenge in her voice raised the hairs on the back of Nick's neck. He straightened, moving away from the truck.

"Sorry to disappoint you, but my decision stands."

Sarah Jane's mouth fell open. "You'd give up your vocation for a — a convicted criminal?"

The teeth of Nick's temper took hold, and he yanked the driver's door open. "She's not convicted yet, and I am not discussing this with you."

Sarah Jane's footsteps skittered across the pavement. "You're not the man I thought you were, Nick Logan. I guess God isn't important enough to you after all."

Nick froze, his insides solidifying to stone, as he made a slow turn to face her. "What did you say?"

"If you can choose a woman like that over God's calling . . ." Her nose wrinkled in disgust as though she'd just smelled something rotten.

Blind fury raced unchecked through Nick's veins. "My relationship with the Lord is none of yours — or anyone else's — business."

"I can't believe Mike and I went to all that trouble for nothing." Her eyes widened and a hint of fear crossed her features. She took a step back, pulling her cardigan tighter around her.

"You had no right to go digging around in

Lily's life." Betrayal stung like an angry wasp at the idea of Mike conspiring with Sarah Jane behind his back.

Her cheeks reddened. "We were just looking out for you. Because we care about you."

Nick didn't believe for one minute that Sarah Jane had any true feelings for him.

She stuck out her chin. "I thought you'd be glad to know the truth. A future minister can't afford to associate with the likes of her."

A core of hot anger burned up his spine. "Who are you to judge? You know nothing of the circumstances surrounding Lily's actions."

Hard lines bracketed her mouth. "What does it matter? Sin is still sin, no matter what the circumstance."

Nick leveled a steely gaze at her. "You're right. It doesn't matter." That much had become crystal clear to him. "I love Lily — no matter what she may have done in the past."

Sarah Jane's smile of triumph slipped, and she clamped her thin lips together.

Nick leaned closer to make his point. "This conversation is over, and I don't ever want to hear of you bothering Lily again. Is that clear?"

He glared at her until she nodded. Then

he pulled his keys out of his pocket. "Now if you'll excuse me, I have somewhere to be."

29

Lily woke in the Bismarck jail with no conception of what time it was. Dread saturated her spirit as she stared at the bleak cement walls. With a groan, she rolled over on her lumpy cot, the one she'd lived on for twenty-four hours now. The springs squeaked out a noisy protest at her movement. Silent tears leaked onto the scratchy wool blanket beneath her. She tried not to think about Nick and the look of shock on his face the last time she'd seen him. How he must despise her after everything that happened, not to mention the cruel way she'd treated him. She would rather have walked over hot coals than hurt him like that, but it was the only way to make him see that she was no good for him — that they could never share a future together.

By now Sarah Jane would be gloating over Lily's downfall. She'd probably go to offer Nick comfort. Maybe even convince him *she* was the right woman for him after all, now that he realized how much of a sinner Lily was. A sob escaped to echo in the sterile room.

Everyone else must hate her, too. She'd left Peg high and dry. Left Maxi with no explanation. Lily pulled herself upright on the rickety bed, clutching her knees to her chest. How she missed them all. In a short amount of time, they'd become her family.

One thing she didn't regret was her last minute decision not to tell Chloe she was her sister. God had guided her to that truth, she was sure of it. He must have known she was about to become an incarcerated criminal. Not exactly the type of person Chloe would want for a relative.

She sighed and brushed away useless tears. This kind of thinking was pointless.

What was done, was done — nothing could change that. She needed to focus on the present, get through the next few days and accept the consequences of her actions. Once she atoned for her sins in the eyes of God and the law, she could move on with her life. Get a job. Maybe try to reconnect with Chloe at some point in the future.

Lily swung her legs over the side of the cot. Cold cement shocked the soles of her bare feet. She searched for her socks and pulled them on. The dank air in the jail cell crept into her body, chilling her insides.

Her dark thoughts turned to her father and how smug he'd looked when Mike dragged her into the police station. He'd waited all these years for a way to get back at her for the trouble she'd caused him. In his mind, she could never pay a high enough price for her supposed crimes. He would never be proud of her or happy for her, no matter what she accomplished. She was a noose around his neck — an inconvenient responsibility — nothing more. She realized now that even though she hadn't lived under his roof for nearly seven years, his destructive influence still haunted her.

She pushed to the floor and paced the small area. Her body shook with a combination of toxic emotions. She'd been running from this man for years now. It had to stop before she let his poison destroy the rest of her life. Avoiding Tobias hadn't seemed to work. Perhaps she needed to confront him. Get the answers she needed about the past and break her ties to him. She would get the closure she needed to move on — once and for all.

Lily moved to the bars of her cell and looked down the corridor. The glimpse of a uniform confirmed the guard's presence.

"Guard," she called out. "I'd like my one phone call now please."

Of course Tobias had agreed to come. He couldn't resist gloating at seeing her locked up like an animal. Lily lay on the bed and counted the minutes until he arrived, planning the things she would tell the man she no longer considered a father. At last, the click of the cell door roused her from her lethargy.

A burly guard stood in the frame of the door. "You have a visitor."

Lily pushed up from the cot. Instant nerves jumped in her stomach.

"Says he's your father. Do you want to see him?"

Lily pressed her lips together then released a shaky breath. "Yes. Thank you."

She followed the guard down a narrow corridor to a waiting room equipped with a metal table and two folding chairs. Tobias sat at the table, hands clasped on top.

She halted partway through the door, peering closer to make sure it was her father. He'd lost so much weight, she hardly recognized him. His shirt hung on his thin frame. A growth of stubble hugged his ragged face. The door clicked closed behind her, jarring her into action. She stepped further into the room. "Hello, Tobias."

He grunted. "If you think you can get me to drop the charges, you're wasting your time."

"That's not why I asked you here." She took a careful seat across the table from him.

"Why then?"

She held her hands in her lap so he wouldn't see them tremble, unwilling to give him the satisfaction of seeing her rattled. "I found the newspaper clipping in your lockbox. I know all about my past. About my real family."

He winced at her words. "Figured as much, since the papers were gone."

She kept her gaze steady. "I need you to answer some questions." At his lack of response, she licked her dry lips and forged on. "When you and Mama adopted me, why did you tell the doctor in Rainbow Falls that I had died?"

An expression close to fear passed over his face before he dropped his gaze. "I don't know what you're talking about."

For a supposedly pious man, he lied easily. She inhaled and counted to ten before speaking. "Doctor Anderson told me the hospital chaplain, a Tobias Cunningham, called to inform him of my death. You also sent him falsified medical records and a fake death certificate."

The only change in his demeanor was a tick in his jaw.

"What made you do something like that?"

For a minute, she thought he'd refuse to answer. Then his demeanor changed. His hunched shoulders seemed to deflate, air whooshing out of him like a punctured tire.

He shook his head, eyes fixed on the tabletop. "All your mama ever wanted was a child. For some reason, God saw fit to deny us that gift." He lifted his bloodshot gaze to her. "When you came into the hospital, orphaned and so near death, Laura insisted on coming to see you. Fell in love with you right away. I didn't want her getting attached, figuring you would likely die. But you didn't." Bitterness laced his words.

"No, I didn't." Lily bit her lip, thinking of her beloved mother who always made her feel adored and wanted.

"Despite my reservations, Laura insisted on adopting you. I would've done anything to make her happy." He paused, a faraway look in his eyes, obviously lost in his memories. "I had to make sure no one would come back to claim you. Some distant relative or another. I couldn't bear that for

Laura. I figured if everyone thought you were dead, there'd never be a problem." His mouth twisted into a grimace.

So he'd done it for her mother. A woman he loved to the point of obsession. "Why didn't you tell me the truth after she died?"

His gaze narrowed. "My Laura was gone. Nothing else mattered." His tone turned accusatory.

Lily lifted her chin and confronted his resentment head on. "You always blamed me for her death. I want to know why."

Tobias shifted on his chair. Color returned to his ashen cheeks. "You came home with the chicken pox. She caught it from you and died because of it. I couldn't forgive you for that."

Lily gasped as memories swamped her. Mama dabbing calamine lotion on itchy scabs. Bathing Lily's fevered brow. Reading her stories, singing her songs. Had her mother nursed her back to health only to contract the disease herself? "I'm sorry. I never knew it was the chicken pox." She swallowed a ball of guilt, finally understanding why her father had blamed her. Grief, especially one as deep-seated as her father's, was never rational. Nevertheless, it didn't excuse the years of neglect that followed.

She pulled herself upright on her chair. "I

have some things I need to say to you." Sweat dampened her palms. "I know my behavior as a teenager was far from ideal, but the way you treated me was reprehensible." She stopped to compose herself but refused to look away. "I needed a father after Mama died. Instead you acted like you . . . hated me."

Tobias shuddered. "You have no idea what losing Laura cost me." His voice wavered. "She took everything when she went. I had nothing left to give."

A trickle of compassion wormed its way into her heart but not enough to excuse his actions. "Face it, Tobias," she said sadly. "You never wanted me. From the moment I came to live with you, you resented me taking Mama's attention away from you."

He hung his head, picking at a spot of dirt on the table, his silence confirming her claim.

"The neglect, the beatings, the emotional abuse . . . they all scarred me in ways you'll never know." She took a breath, willing herself to get through this last speech without breaking down. "Since I've been in Rainbow Falls, I've learned the truth about the God you worship. He isn't harsh and vindictive, as you wanted me to believe. He is loving and patient, compassionate and forgiving." She took a deep breath and exhaled. "And because of that, I am going to try very hard to forgive you — more for my sake than yours — so I can move on with my life."

He remained stone-faced, avoiding her eyes.

"For what it's worth, I am sorry about the money, and I did intend to pay you back one day."

His head shot up at last, eyes blazing. "I don't believe that for one minute, and neither will the judge."

Of course he didn't believe her. Tobias had never given her the benefit of the doubt, not once. The stale air in the enclosed room became heavier, blanketing her in regret. "I want you to know no matter what happens in court tomorrow, our relationship is over. I'm no longer your responsibility or your family. I plan to officially change my name back to Strickland, or maybe I'll keep Draper. Mama would've liked that."

He gripped the edge of the table until his knuckles turned white.

She rose, her chair scraping against the cement floor, and studied him with objective eyes. For once, the usual hatred didn't stir in her chest. She was able to view him as a man to be pitied. A man who, though he claimed to love God, had no real concept of what the word meant. His love was not God's love. Of that she was certain. In a moment of clarity, she understood that no matter what she'd done in her life, her Heavenly Father had never stopped loving her. Warmth filled her soul with the knowledge she was not alone and never would be again. "Good-bye, Tobias."

She crossed the room, knocked on the door for the guard, and waited.

"I'm dying."

She barely heard the soft-spoken words. They hung in the air between them.

"I've got terminal cancer. Only a few months to live."

Heart thrumming, she turned to face him. No wonder he looked so thin and sunken. A brief surge of compassion enveloped her, but she refused to allow the smallest hint of guilt or responsibility to surface. "I'm very sorry," she said, and meant it, but she could not let herself be roped back into his life now. She'd finally made peace and gotten closure. Most likely she'd be in jail anyway. "Good-bye," she said quietly. "I hope your parishioners will be a comfort to you."

The door clicked open behind her. She gave him one last look and then turned and left.

■ ■ ■ ■

After an eternity of waiting across the street from the rectory in the tiny town of Fielding, Nick straightened in the cab of his truck. A dark sedan slid past him and pulled into the driveway.

He inhaled deeply and scrubbed a hand over his face. *Lord, You know how I struggle with my temper. Help me get through this without losing control. Help me to leave this man's punishment up to Your infinite wisdom.*

He gave Tobias time to get inside then walked up to the run-down looking home and knocked. Tobias Cunningham came to the door, frowning. His small eyes narrowed even more when he saw Nick.

"What do you want?" His haggard face was wreathed in weariness.

"I'm Nick Logan from Rainbow Falls. I'd like to talk to you about your daughter."

Tobias peered at Nick. His black clerical shirt and suspenders hung loosely on his thin frame. Graying hair, that had appeared wild yesterday, had been tamed into submission. "You from the police?"

"No. I'm a friend who wants some answers."

His expression hardened. "I've answered

enough questions for one day."

Tobias started to shut the door, but Nick jammed his foot in the opening, barring the door from closing. "I won't take up much of your time." He stepped inside before the man could object and found himself in the living room.

The interior of the house was as decrepit as the exterior. The furniture looked to be from three decades earlier. Books, newspapers, and other clutter crowded the tables. A thick coating of dust cloaked the mantel, and cobwebs clung to the drapery at the windows.

Tobias scowled. "You might as well sit since you're here."

Nick waited until Tobias sat down before he perched on the edge of the worn sofa, hands clasped loosely over his knees. "I'd like to know exactly why you had Lily arrested."

The man grunted. "Why should I tell you anything?"

Nick hesitated. "I'm in love with Lily and plan to marry her one day. Before I do, I'd like to know what possible sentence she might be facing."

Tobias snickered, folding his arms across his chest. "Finally got a man to propose. That's a first."

Nick shifted on the lumpy couch. "What did Lily do?" he repeated.

Tobias raked a gaze over Nick from head to toe. "You're a far cry from my daughter's usual type. Guess you have a right to know the truth." He paused as if relishing the moment. "She broke into my house and stole my emergency cash fund. And it wasn't the first time she's stolen from me."

Nick absorbed the information without changing expression. "When did this take place?"

"Couple of months ago. Had the police looking for her ever since."

A thread of irritation crept up Nick's spine. "Did it ever occur to you that Lily might have been desperate and in need of help?"

The man only snorted. "She's been in trouble since she was fifteen years old. A parent can't keep bailing a child out forever."

Obviously appealing to the man's compassion wasn't going to work. "How much did she take?"

Tobias's eyes narrowed. "Eight-hundred-and-sixty dollars — give or take a few."

Nick reached into his pocket for his wallet. "I'd like to pay you back for the amount she . . . borrowed." He took out a wad of bills totaling over twelve hundred dollars. Almost his entire savings account. "If you'd be willing to drop the charges, that is." The musty smell of the room irritated his nose as he waited.

Tobias sneered. "Why would I drop the charges? That girl needs to learn a lesson, once and for all. Face the consequences of her actions." He banged a fist on the rickety wooden table beside him. A small lamp shuddered but didn't topple.

The anger Nick had been holding back since he arrived sprang to life. "Don't you think Lily has already served a life sentence . . . for a crime she didn't commit?"

Tobias stared at him open-mouthed.

"First losing her real family in a tragedy, followed by her adoptive mother's death at such a young age, and then having to live with . . . never mind." Nick clenched his fist around the money in his hand. His pulse hammered a loud refrain in his temple. "Why don't you take the cash, and we'll call it even. You'll never have to see Lily again."

Tobias looked at the stack of bills in Nick's hand and seemed to waver for a moment. Instead his eyes hardened. "No. That girl *will* pay for the humiliation she's caused me all these years."

Nick shook with suppressed rage. In a

deliberate move, he rose from the couch and slid the money into his pocket. "I guess we'll leave the matter up to God and the judge. I pray they can see through your bitterness and need for revenge."

Nick stalked to the front door, the thud of his steps echoing across the space.

"Wait."

The anguish in the man's voice stilled Nick's movements. With his hand on the doorknob, he hesitated, his scruples screaming at him. Before he could decide whether to hear him out, a loud thud sounded behind him. Tobias had collapsed on the floor, his body shaking.

Nick's anger vanished as he rushed to his side and pulled him onto the sofa. He slid a cushion under his head, scrutinizing the man's ashen complexion and sunken cheeks. How had he not noticed that Tobias was a very sick man?

"I'll get you some water."

Nick strode to the kitchen, pulled a plastic cup from one of the cupboards and filled it with cold water. Back in the living room, he helped Tobias sit up to take a sip of the liquid, after which Tobias sank back onto the pillow.

"Are you ill?" Nick asked quietly, pulling a chair closer to the sofa.

The man closed his eyes for a brief moment. "Pancreatic cancer. It's terminal."

Compassion edged into Nick's heart. "I'm sorry. How long have you known?"

"Found out after I filed charges against Lily. You think God's trying to tell me something?" He gave a harsh chuckle that turned into a fit of coughing.

Nick scrubbed a hand over the back of his neck. What did he do with this information? He drew in a deep breath, his nose wrinkling at the smell of rotting garbage coming from the now open kitchen door, and asked God for guidance. As a future minister, Nick would have to deal with many such situations with his parishioners. Whether he liked them or not, it would be his duty to minister to the sick and dying. Maybe God was asking him to do the same now.

He leaned forward, hands clasped over his knees. "Is there anything I can do for you?"

Tobias threw him a sharp glance. "I thought you hated me."

Nick sighed. "I don't hate you. I'm just angry for everything Lily's gone through and how it's affected her. How she doesn't feel worthy of love or happiness in her life." He held the glass of water back out to Tobias who took a long drink. "She changed a lot since she came to Rainbow Falls and"

— he almost said "and fell in love with me," but that didn't sound right — "and found her sister. She even started coming to church."

Tobias's eyes widened as though he thought Nick were lying.

"Maybe it's because she has someone else to worry about, to set an example for. I only hope being sent to jail won't undo all the progress she's made."

Tobias scowled, creating more lines on his weathered face. "You blame me for all her problems. I can see it in your eyes."

"You're right. I do. When Lily's mother died, she needed support, guidance, and love, but all she got was anger. No wonder she acted out. She was crying for attention in any way she could."

Instead of arguing as Nick expected, Tobias grimaced and squeezed his eyes shut. "Lily said the same thing to me today. Said she was trying to forgive me." A silent tear escaped from the corner of his eye and rolled down into his sideburns.

"You saw her?" A thread of hope wound through Nick's system. Lily was trying to forgive her father. Maybe she hadn't returned to her former hardened self after all.

"She asked me to come to the station. Tore a strip off me about the way I treated her, but she didn't seem to hate me anymore. Just told me she was moving on and that our relationship was done."

Nick smiled sadly. "She was getting closure on her past. Making peace."

"I think so." Tobias wiped his face and struggled to sit upright on the sofa. "Maybe she has changed."

Nick met his eyes. "It's not too late for you, Tobias. You still have time to make amends. To do the right thing for your daughter."

A shadow of sorrow passed over the older man's face. "I'll think about it. That's all I can promise."

Nick nodded and rose slowly to his feet. His glance slid across the debris-filled room. He tried to picture Lily living here as a teenager, but pain held the image back. No point in holding a grudge. Tobias would be in God's hands soon enough.

Nick crossed the room and paused at the front door. "I'll be praying for you, Tobias. No matter what you decide."

30

Lily stared up at the cracks in the ceiling. At some point today she would go to court for her arraignment, where she would plead guilty. In a strange way, it would be a relief. No more hiding the truth. She'd face her actions, receive her punishment, and prepare to pay for her sins.

She tried to pray, tried to feel the presence of God there with her in the cell, but couldn't call it forth. The peace she'd found yesterday during her confrontation with her father eluded her today.

In a futile attempt to escape her thoughts, she pushed up from the cot, used the crude facilities and brushed her teeth with the toothbrush they had provided her. Using only her fingers and a bit of water from the tap, she twisted her hair into a long braid and sank back onto the bed to wait in desolate silence.

A few minutes later, an officer came to

unlock her cell door. "Your lawyer's here." He indicated with a flick of his head for her to come with him.

"I don't have a lawyer." She rose on unsteady legs.

"Court appointed."

"Oh."

She followed the man down the corridor to the same room she'd met Tobias in yesterday. A thin, balding man stood at the table, shuffling through papers in his brief-case.

He looked up as she came in. "I'm your attorney, Lionel Jones. We don't have much time, so I need to know how you're going to plead today."

She stood across the table from him in her orange jumpsuit. The bleakness of her soul matched the décor of the sterile room. "I'm pleading guilty."

His hands stopped moving for a split second. "Good. Makes my job a whole lot easier." He snapped his briefcase closed. "Let's be on our way."

The next few hours played out like a scene in a movie. Oddly removed from reality, Lily waited in an anteroom until her turn arrived. The guards ushered her into the courtroom through a side door and led her to a table where Mr. Jones sat scribbling on a notepad. As she took a seat beside him, she managed a glance at the room behind her. Only a handful of people filled the chairs, none of the faces at all familiar. She bit her quivering lip. At this point, she might even welcome the sight of her hostile father. Instead, she faced her fate alone.

No, not alone. She had to believe God was with her, whether she could feel His presence or not.

Moments later the bailiff announced, "All rise."

The judge swept up to his desk. He looked like a kind, grandfather type. Her hopes soared for a brief second. Maybe he would be lenient with her. Only give her a fine. But reality snuffed out the last shred of hope. It didn't matter. She wouldn't be able to pay a fine anyway. She'd still end up in jail.

The legal banter back and forth was a blur to her. The noise behind her of people coming and going from the spectator area served as background static, yet the tick, tick of the ceiling fan above her echoed loudly in her ears. Only when the judge requested that she rise, did she focus her attention back on the proceedings.

She stood beside Mr. Jones as the judge read the charges against her. Breaking and entering, as well as theft under a thousand dollars.

"How do you plead, Miss Cunningham?"

One irrational thought circled her brain — that technically speaking, she hadn't broken in — she'd used her old house key. But it wasn't worth the energy to argue the point. "Guilty, Your Honor."

The judge's bushy eyebrows rose a fraction of an inch above his wire glasses. Before he could utter his verdict, a loud clatter sounded behind her and a man crashed through the swinging gate.

"Your Honor, I want to drop the charges against Miss Cunningham."

Lily's mouth fell open. Tobias stood in the aisle beside Mr. Jones.

"And who are you, sir?" the judge bellowed, gavel in hand.

"I'm Reverend Tobias Cunningham, the defendant's father. I'm the one who brought the charges against her in the first place."

The stern man leaned forward on his desk to peer down at Tobias. "And why are you suddenly rescinding this action? Were the charges false?"

Tobias clasped his hands together in front of him. "No, sir. But I now realize my daughter only borrowed the money and intended to repay me in the future."

Silence covered the courtroom while the judge spent several moments in quiet regard of Tobias, as though trying to assess his sincerity. Lily thought everyone must be able to hear her pulse thundering in her ears.

"How did you come to that conclusion?" the judge asked.

Tobias shot a sideways glance at Lily, then returned his attention to the front. "I had a conversation with my daughter yesterday. And later, her friend came to see me and convinced me she was telling the truth."

In the audience behind them, someone coughed, another person scraped a chair back. A door creaked open. Lily held herself completely still as she awaited the judge's next words.

He turned stern eyes to her. "Miss Cunningham?"

"Yes, sir?"

"Do you have the money to repay your father?"

Her last hope floated away. "Not at the moment, sir."

Tobias took another step forward. "I'll accept installments, Your Honor."

The judge pressed his lips together in a firm line. "This is highly unusual." He paused, eyeing them both, then let out a weary breath. "Very well. Seeing this is more of a family dispute than anything, the charges are hereby withdrawn. Case dismissed." He banged the gavel.

Lily swayed on her feet and laid her palms flat on the table to steady herself. She lowered her head to make the dizziness subside.

Thank You, Lord. Thank You.

Mr. Jones stuffed his papers into the leather case and snapped it shut.

"What happens now?" she asked him.

"They'll take you back to the police station to have your release papers processed and get your personal items. You should be free in an hour or two." Mr. Jones rose. "Good luck to you, Miss Cunningham." He nodded and disappeared through the courtroom.

Tobias approached the table. For once the usual air of hostility didn't follow him. He fingered a battered hat and shuffled from one foot to the other. "I know this doesn't make up for the past, but I suppose it's the least I could do for you."

Lily could barely take in what he'd done for her. "Thank you. I'll start paying you back as soon as I get a new job." She pulled herself up to her full height. "Can I ask what made you change your mind?"

He shrugged. "Guess you could say I had a wake-up call." He shot a quick glance over her shoulder toward the back of the court-room. "Your friend, Nick, seems like a decent guy."

In slow motion, Lily turned to follow his gaze. A shock of blond hair caught her eye. Nick was here — in the courtroom. And not only Nick. Maxi, Sonia Martin, Chloe, and Peg stood beside him. She bit her lip to hold back the sting of tears.

As the guard came to lead her away, a mixture of emotions fought to gain a foot-hold. For a brief moment, her blurred gaze locked with Nick's. She stumbled, but the guard yanked her upright and pulled her out of the courtroom.

The single cell seemed much smaller as Lily paced on legs as unsteady as a new colt. She had no idea how long it would take to process the necessary paperwork to free her. Would Nick and the others wait for her, or would they leave now that they knew her fate?

At last the key clanged in the lock and the door swung open. The guard from earlier handed her the package containing her clothes and personal items.

"You can put these on. I'll be back in five

minutes to release you."

Her spirits lifted as she changed, thanking God for one small miracle. She wouldn't have to spend any more time in jail. Two days was more than enough.

Dressed in jeans and a wrinkled cotton top, Lily stepped out of the cell and once again followed the man down the hall. The murmur of voices grew louder as she entered the main area of the police station. The stale smell of coffee, cigarette smoke, and grease rose to greet her. Her legs shook with each step. Would anyone be waiting for her?

When she rounded the corner, tears of disbelief pricked her eyelids. They were all there, crowded together in the outer room — Nick included.

Her initial burst of happiness gave way to uncertainty, freezing her feet to the floor. What would they think of her now? A common thief — a criminal just released from jail. She swallowed her nerves and her pride. No matter what happened, she owed her friends a huge debt of gratitude for coming. She would thank them and say her good-byes. Wiping her damp palms on her jeans, she moved forward.

Chloe and Maxi, the first to spot her, let out a cry and darted forward to envelop her in a huge hug. Lily clung to her friends until she feared she would break down and sob. Then the sudden realization hit her that Chloe should be in New York.

She pulled away to gape at the face so similar to her own. "What are you doing here?"

The girl gave a watery smile. "I came as soon as I heard."

"But your studies —"

"They can wait." She paused, tears leaking from the corners of her amber eyes. "Do you think I'd let my sister face this kind of crisis alone?"

Lily gasped. Her gaze flew to Nick, then back to Chloe. "You know?"

Chloe nodded. "Mom called to tell me after you were arrested."

Lily struggled to comprehend how, after all the secrecy and the conflict, the decision had been taken out of her hands. Sonia Martin had decided to tell Chloe herself. A bubble of near hysteria rose in Lily's chest. She didn't know whether to laugh or cry. Instead she pulled Chloe into another fierce hug. Then she moved through the group to find Sonia who stood smiling through the tears on her wrinkled cheeks. Mere words could never express her gratitude to this woman. Lily simply stepped into her arms and embraced her.

"Thank you," she whispered. "Thank you so much."

Sonia hugged her hard before she pulled back and placed a hand on Lily's cheek. "I'm sorry it took me so long to overcome my fear. I finally realized that by telling the truth, I wouldn't be losing a thing. I'd be gaining another daughter."

Lily broke down and wept as the woman kissed her on both cheeks.

"I want you to come and live with me," Sonia told her. "Now that Chloe's away, I have lots of room."

"But how can you forgive me after everything I've done?" Lily sniffed and wiped her eyes on her sleeve.

"There's nothing to forgive, my dear. We've all made mistakes. Especially me, for not telling Chloe the truth from the beginning."

The simple generosity of these people humbled Lily — that they could overlook all her flaws, all her mistakes, and accept her anyway. For the first time in her life, she truly understood what it meant to be a Christian and to love as Christ loved. She vowed she would earn every ounce of their respect and trust from now on.

"Enough of this chit-chat," Peg piped up,

dabbing a tissue to her eyes. "When can I expect you at the shop?"

Lily turned, dumbfounded. "You mean I still have a job? You'd trust me after this?"

Peg waved a hand and snorted. "I've seen you pick up a penny and place it in the till. I've no worries about you."

Lily pressed her fingers to her mouth. Could she really return to her life in Rainbow Falls?

At last, she let her gaze fall on Nick. She drank in the sight of him in his suit jacket and jeans. Below a stray lock of hair waving over his forehead, his eyes were misty.

She took a step toward him, her heart knocking against her ribs. "Thank you." Her dry throat barely allowed the words out. "I assume it was you who got my father to change his mind."

His lips curved up. "It wasn't just me. I think God played a big part in it, too."

She smiled back. "You're right. Only a miracle could explain Tobias's change of attitude." She wished Nick would pull her close and hug her so she'd know how things stood between them. She searched his face for clues as to how he was feeling now that he knew all her secrets. Did he still care, or would he let her down gently? Tell her a minister couldn't afford to be involved with someone like her — a common criminal. She bit her trembling lip.

Nick's smile widened as he held out a hand to her. "You must be exhausted. Let's get you home."

She nodded through fresh tears and placed her hand in his.

Home. She liked the sound of that.

31

Nick's soul filled with quiet gratitude as he steered the truck down Elm Street, lifting a prayer of thanks heavenward that everything had worked out so well. Tobias Cunningham had come through at the last minute and dropped the charges, saving Nick the necessity of paying whatever fine the judge might have imposed. For now, his savings could go in the bank where it belonged.

His pulse sped up as his thoughts turned to Lily. Even dressed in wrinkled clothes, her hair in a messy braid, she looked amazing to him. He'd dropped her off at her apartment so she could shower and change before going over to see Chloe and Aunt Sonia. Although his pride stung that he wasn't at the top of her list, he understood Lily's need to connect with her sister now that she knew the truth. Besides, Chloe would be heading back to New York tomorrow, whereas he would have . . . forever . . .

to catch up with Lily.

He had so many things he needed to tell her — like how he'd turned down the minister position — but all that could wait. Right now Lily needed time to recover from her ordeal, and once things had settled back to normal, they would have a serious talk.

Nick slowed to a stop in front of the Strickland house. After two hours of stripping wallpaper, trying to curb the impulse to run over to his aunt's just to be near Lily, he'd received a call from Chloe asking him to meet Lily here. What he couldn't figure out was why? Maybe Lily needed this last piece of closure on her past before she could move forward to the future. A future he hoped would include him.

The reason didn't matter. He was just happy for the chance to see her again. He couldn't believe how much he'd missed her, how much he'd feared losing her to a jail sentence.

Thank you, God, for sparing Lily that terrible fate.

Nick shut off the engine and hopped down from the cab, anticipation spiking though his veins. He jogged up the walkway to the stairs and pushed through the front door. Following his instincts, he made his way back to the kitchen. He found Lily standing by the back door, sunlight streaming over freshly washed hair that surrounded her face like a cloud. Dressed in a simple white blouse and clean blue jeans, her beauty mesmerized him.

As if sensing his presence, she turned and caught sight of him. A huge smile bloomed, illuminating the brown depths of her eyes.

"Hey, gorgeous." A silly grin spread over his face at the blush that colored her cheeks. He crossed the room and, without actually intending to, pulled her into his arms. Pleasure and surprise lingered on her face, but it was the hint of insecurity that got to him. Slowly he lowered his mouth to hers, relishing her familiar taste — a sensation he thought he might never experience again. "I missed you," he whispered into her hair, when he'd pulled his lips from hers.

"Me, too." Her voice sounded husky. "I'm so sorry, Nick, for everything. Especially for the way I treated you at the police station."

"It's OK. I understand why you did it."

"You do?"

"You were trying to get rid of me — but it didn't work." He laughed and captured her lips for another lingering kiss.

Finally, she moved away from him. "Don't you want to know why I asked you here?"

"I'd rather kiss you instead."

She gave him a swat.

He laughed again. "OK, why are we here?"

"Let's go sit in the living room." She took his hand and pulled him along the hallway.

In the musty room, he removed the cover from one of the sofas and they sat side by side.

She seemed nervous suddenly, clasping and unclasping her hands. "I need to explain a few things to you."

He reached over to wrap his fingers around her icy ones. "You don't have to explain anything to me."

She held his gaze. "I want you to hear my side of the story and make sure there are no more secrets between us before you decide whether you want to continue our relationship . . . or not."

The vulnerable expression on her face tore at him. He wanted to tell her there was nothing to decide but sensed she needed this sharing of her heart with him. "Go ahead then."

She pulled away her hand to grip her fingers together on her lap. "I want you to know that I understand what I did — taking the money from my father without asking — was wrong. I told myself that since I intended to pay my father back, that made it OK, which of course it wasn't. That night

I was desperate. I had nowhere else to turn. If I'd asked my father for a loan, he would've turned me down flat, like he had many times before."

He kept his eyes steady on hers. "I believe you."

"Thank you." Her gaze faltered, and she lowered her eyes to her lap. "Before I met you, I lived a life I'm not proud of. When my father kicked me out of the house, I did some horrible things."

"Everyone makes mistakes, Lily."

She shook her head. "Not you."

He smiled sadly. "Yes, even me. When I was a teen, I was angry all the time, and I made some bad choices. Almost ended up in jail myself. If it hadn't been for Mike and Ted mentoring me, my life might have taken a very different turn."

The corner of her lips tugged up in a smile. "That helps. I've secretly thought of you as "Saint Nick."

He rolled his eyes on a groan. "Please. I still struggle with my temper and trying to do the right thing. The main difference is I trust God to help me." He paused. "I know your heart, Lily. Whatever you've done in the past, you based your decisions upon the life you knew. You saw God through your father's skewed view. But now you know better."

She shook her head. "It would be so easy to blame all my problems on Tobias, but I have to take responsibility for my part." She hesitated, lifting troubled eyes to him. "Do you think God will forgive me for everything I've done?"

The hopeful note in her voice brought out all his protective instincts. "Of course. God forgives everything if you ask Him to. And I do, too." Nick put his arm around her, drawing her close. He held her in silence for several minutes while she sat in the cocoon of his embrace. He hoped she could now accept this truth and believe in her worthiness as a child of God.

A few seconds later, she pulled back to look up at him. "I asked Tobias to come and see me in jail."

"I know. He told me. That was very brave of you."

Appreciation crept into her eyes. "I had to forgive him so I could move on with my life. The minute I did, Nick, I felt God there with me in the room. This incredible sense of peace came over me and I knew no matter what happened, I'd be OK."

The sting of tears hit the back of Nick's throat. At long last, Lily had started to trust in God's grace. *Thank you, Lord.* "That's the best news I could ever hear."

She sat up straighter, her expression serious. "This may sound crazy, but I feel the need to make up for my sins somehow. Do some sort of penance and pay my debt to society."

He squashed his initial urge to disagree with her. "I don't know about penance, but I have an idea how you can turn your past into something positive. You could mentor the teens in the youth group, share your experience with them and help them avoid your mistakes."

She swallowed. "Share my past?"

He raised a hand to brush her cheek. "You could start off slow, sharing what you're comfortable with."

She nodded. "I could probably do that — if it would help the kids."

"I'm sure it would." He studied her, praying his next words wouldn't upset her. "My other idea might be more difficult. It has to do with Tobias."

A wariness crept into her eyes. "What about him?"

"I think he may be open to a new kind of relationship with you — now that he's dying. Maybe we could visit him sometime?"

She bit her bottom lip. Turmoil swam in

her eyes. "I don't know. Maybe. You'd come with me, right?"

A surge of protectiveness rose in his chest. "Of course. I'd be there to make sure he never hurts you again. But nobody should die alone and with regrets."

She gave him a soft smile. "For you I could do just about anything."

He kissed her forehead, sure he never loved her more than at that moment.

Lily captured his hand in hers, a slight frown creasing her brow. "That reminds of something I need to ask you."

"Shoot."

Her eyes searched his face. "Why did you turn down the minister's job? I couldn't believe it when Chloe told me."

The hollow pit of disappointment still echoed inside him whenever he thought of relinquishing his position at the Good Shepherd Church. But in the deepest part of his being, he knew he'd made the right choice. Now he had to trust God to work the rest out in His own time.

He rubbed a thumb over her fingers. "Ted gave me an ultimatum. He made me choose between the job and you." He shrugged. "I chose you."

More tears bloomed. "But —"

He silenced her with a finger to her lips.

"No buts. If I'm meant to be a minister, God will find a way for it to happen . . . with you as part of the package."

Time to lay all his cards on the table. He took both her hands in his and looked deeply into her brown eyes. "I love you very much. Right now my future is up in the air, but no matter what happens, I can't picture my life without you in it." He smiled softly. "Will you marry me, Lily?"

Lily's thoughts swirled faster than the dust motes dancing in the air around them. He'd sacrificed his dream for her, and now he wanted to marry her? She shook her head, afraid to believe this was real. "Are you serious? After everything I've done?" Her pulse beat an erratic rhythm as she awaited his answer.

His gaze remained steadfast. "I'm very serious."

"But —"

"Do you love me, Lily?" His blue eyes held hers as gently as his hands.

"You know I do," she whispered.

"Do you love God?"

She blinked, thinking of the presence she'd felt with her in jail. "Yes, I do. And I know now that He loves me, too."

A slow smile dawned on his beloved face.

"That's all I need to know. Except to ask if you're willing to share my life with me — no matter what the future holds."

He still loved her and wanted to marry her. After everything he knew about her. A rush of emotion moved through her, blocking her throat. Fresh tears welled at the back of her eyes. She swallowed hard, and for once, let her heart answer for her. "Yes, Nick, I'll marry you. As long as you're sure."

A grin stretched across his face, creating brackets at the side of his mouth. "I've been sure for a long time now. Just waiting for you to catch up and to realize that God never left you."

With amazing tenderness, he lowered his mouth to hers. Her eyes closed on a sigh, relishing the warmth of his lips on hers, the strength of his arms surrounding her. Her heart swelled to the bursting point with joy.

"I love you, Nick Logan," she whispered, silently vowing to one day be worthy of him, of the sacrifice he'd made for her. But in the meantime, she had a gift of her own. "That brings me to the reason I asked you here."

One golden eyebrow rose in question. "It does?"

"Yes." She rose and pulled him to his feet, a cloud of dust rising with them. "Since I'm partly responsible for you being without a career at the moment, I want to do something to help." She pulled a folded paper from the pocket of her jeans. "So Chloe and I discussed it and we have something for you." Anticipation tingled through her at the thought of the surprise she and Chloe had concocted.

With a puzzled frown, he took the paper she handed him. She held her breath while he opened it and read the words. When he looked back at her, his expression was a mixture of stunned surprise and disbelief. "You're giving me this house?"

"Yes. To open your shelter."

She waited, her smile frozen in place. Outside, a car drove by, breaking the silence. He stood stock-still, staring down at the paper, his mouth a straight line. Slowly, he refolded the page and handed it back to her, a resigned expression shadowing his face. "I can't let you do that."

"I . . . I don't understand. Why not?" She thought he'd be overjoyed at the news — that one of his dreams could still come true.

"It's your inheritance. The only thing you have left from your parents. I can't take that away from either one of you."

She grasped his hand in hers and pressed the paper back with a smile. "That's not all our parents left us. Apparently they had a pretty sizeable nest egg, which has collected interest all these years. Chloe and I will each get a nice amount of money, so I can pay Tobias back and have more than enough to spare."

His mouth gaped open. "I had no idea . . ."

"Chloe and I want to do this. And I'd like to help you run the shelter. Think of it as a partnership."

He hesitated a moment more, raking one hand over his jaw. "You're sure?"

"Absolutely."

An enormous smile broke out over his face and he grabbed her, swinging her up off her feet. She laughed out loud and wound her arms around his neck, joy filling her soul. The old saying was true. Giving was so much better than receiving.

When he set her back on the ground, he kept his arms around her. "How can I ever thank you? Both of you."

The sight of tears in his eyes filled her with tenderness. She raised a hand to his cheek. "Just be happy."

He shook his head. "I can't believe this."

"You'd better believe it." She winked at him. "Now, how about we go share our news with the rest of the family?"

"I'd like that."

And a little while later, as they walked down the steps of the Strickland house, hand in hand, Lily gave silent thanks for Nick's persistence in loving her and for God's persistence in bringing her home.

The employees of Thorndike Press hope you have enjoyed this Large Print book. All our Thorndike, Wheeler, and Kennebec Large Print titles are designed for easy reading, and all our books are made to last. Other Thorndike Press Large Print books are available at your library, through selected bookstores, or directly from us.

For information about titles, please call:
    (800) 223-1244

or visit our Web site at:
    http://gale.cengage.com/thorndike

To share your comments, please write:
    Publisher
    Thorndike Press
    10 Water St., Suite 310
    Waterville, ME 04901